T0278912

A
CONSTELLATION
OF MINOR
BEARS

ALSO BY JEN FERGUSON

The Summer of Bitter and Sweet
Those Pink Mountain Nights

A CONSTELLATION OF MINOR BEARS

JEN FERGUSON

Heartdrum
An Imprint of HarperCollins Publishers

This is a work of fiction. Any references to real people, organizations, events, establishments, or locales are intended only to give the fiction a sense of authenticity and are used fictitiously. All other names, characters, and places, and all dialogue and incidents portrayed in this book are the product of the author's imagination and are not to be construed as real.

Heartdrum is an imprint of HarperCollins Publishers.

A Constellation of Minor Bears
Copyright © 2024 by Jen Ferguson
A Note from Cynthia Leitich Smith copyright © 2024 by Cynthia Leitich Smith
Interior art © Adobe Stock
All rights reserved. Printed in the United States of America. No part of this book may be used or reproduced in any manner whatsoever without written permission except in the case of brief quotations embodied in critical articles and reviews. For information address HarperCollins Children's Books, a division of HarperCollins Publishers, 195 Broadway, New York, NY 10007.
www.epicreads.com

Library of Congress Control Number: 2023948486
ISBN 978-0-06-333422-9

Typography by Laura Mock
24 25 26 27 28 LBC 5 4 3 2 1
First Edition

To the ones who have a need to look upon
new trees, pine cones. To those of us caught
under the swell of big change, struggling
to keep pace with the spinning world
whichever way we can. To the ones
who learn, who grow. To the ones who
name themselves *enough*. And to Faith.

A FEW THINGS ABOUT THIS BOOK

If you've been following along, if this isn't your first Jen Ferguson book, you know that I value you the reader and the safety of your heart foremost.

That's why I want to tell you that this book follows a character who can't quite figure out how to manage her emotions, and while she knows she shouldn't, she's still thinking ableist thoughts about her brother's accident and subsequent disability in the early pages. It's also important to say that this book is fat and body positive. But since the world is not built for fat bodies (or disabled bodies!), and since my characters are living in this kind of world, the story features instances of fat abuse and fat phobia from outside and from adults who should already know better, but never from inside the friend group. There are instances of anti-Indigenous racism, thought, and actions.

Take care of yourself while reading in the ways you know work for you. If you're not ready to read now, that's completely absolutely okay. Unlike foodstuffs, books don't have "best before" dates. Molly, Hank, Brynn, Tray, and the Pacific Crest Trail will be waiting when you're ready. <3 Jen

✦

THE INTRO STAR

This is the part of the song that invites you to listen, the first star in the sequence, the one that kicks off the design. Here, at the molten core, you meet the fiddle and the spoons.

More portable than a guitar, the fiddle is easily tuned by ear. There's a feel to the fiddle—it's ephemeral but also grounded, in the way of all good paradoxes. Styles vary depending on community, influences.

The spoons are cheap, easy, found in every kitchen. It's no coincidence the kitchen is where the heart lives on, where the music is born.

LATE JUNE
EDMONTON, ALBERTA
Molly

I drag my pack down the stairs, wondering if it really is too heavy, if I'm carrying too much baggage to pull off this freaking trip. Before I decide to empty the thing out and reweigh each item one by one, searching for what to leave behind, my brother, Hank, comes barreling into the kitchen. Loudly, the way he used to.

"Morning, Mols," he says, and grabs his favorite mug. It's all text, no images: *Well, the Dentist Is Afraid of You Too!*

Ignoring how my heartbeat pounds too fast, how the past week's arguments still thrum around inside my body, I put this first. "How are you? Today?"

Hank shrugs, which, lately, is his normal answer. Sips his coffee, changes the subject. "You look festive."

I'm already wearing my grad outfit, knee-length bright pink tulle paired with a plain white tank. I'd forgotten how the tulle itches, how in summer's heat skin against skin chafes. But I don't have time to switch it out and nothing else in my heavily merino-wool wardrobe fits the occasion.

Hank's wearing sweatpants. But since my brother's not

1

graduating, he doesn't have to be at the school as early as I do. "Thanks. You look half-asleep."

Hank laughs.

There's a fiddle, a few strings broken, on our kitchen table. While my dad was raised by a white family, and later married our white mom, these days, Dad works to keep the Métis Nation accountable, as they more often than not barrel over First Nations' rights while fighting the government to establish their own. And because my dad spent some time in prison when he was younger, years before he met our mom, my dad acts as a mentor for Indigenous peoples newly released from provincial and federal institutions when he isn't working on recording and arranging the old songs.

But let's be honest, the old songs, this fiddle, that's where his heart lives. This instrument and the seven or eight others just like it that he has, they mostly live in this kitchen. Or they do now.

"You ready?" Hank asks as he spreads homemade saskatoon berry jam on health-food bread without toasting it.

I look at my very bright hiking pack. "I'm pretty certain I'm leaving something important behind."

I'm not trying to start that up again. The fight. But I can't say it either.

Hank only nods, eats his breakfast.

My dad wasn't around for a lot of my childhood. Hank's dad, who's white, hasn't ever been around. And while Hank grew up with his grandparents for the first eight years of his life, he moved in with us after they passed. Years later, our mom and my dad got remarried.

I know, right? That hardly ever happens.

Across the kitchen along the long wall are my mom's pretty, mostly floral-themed political cross-stitch projects. *Keep Your Hands off My Uterus. Abortion Is Healthcare.*

Yes, my parents raised me up so that I don't believe in colonial borders or faux apologies made by the church for genocide or other violences. But I've always been a little angry, a little mad that the world around us seemed too large, too unwieldy. Until science camp, the summer before Grade 6, and suddenly everything made sense. With science there are answers.

Hank's still eating, still ignoring me.

Our mom comes into the kitchen to start on her boiled-egg breakfast, and a minute later, so does my dad. Even if Hank was going to tell me something important, he can't now. He spends the rest of breakfast typing on his phone, though after his accident, the doctors highly recommended he avoid too much screen time. It's not that our parents mean to do it, or maybe they do, but Mom and Dad seem to shut things down. When they're around, I never ask Hank how he's doing. Because they'll only redirect the conversation to something else, Mom's latest win in reshaping policy or my dad's epiphany over the arrangement he's been working on.

It's so frequent, it's like it's planned.

But they wouldn't do that to me, right?

Graduation looks nothing like how I imagined walking onto a stage to receive my high school diploma would. Unlike in middle school, there's no stage, no valedictorian, and the only person to make an unsettlingly awkward speech is the principal. We're all stuffed into the gym, standing on the too-shiny floors, in our out-door shoes, which on any other day is a crime, our families in the bleachers as we suffer the heat.

The doors leading to the north field are propped open.

It doesn't help any.

Traylor Lambert, my brother's best friend and the person I currently dislike most in the universe, holds my left arm. But since he's also my best friend, this is complicated, like explaining the atom, something that nobody can see but that affects everything. Tray's brown hair is braided, tied with a strip of leather. He's wearing the nice pants I helped him pick out for a funeral two years ago, a brand-spanking-new white button-down, and his Métis sash. It's similar, but not identical to the one my dad and uncle wear.

I don't know exactly how they're different. Only that they are. This is a question I've never asked, and that's on me.

From the front end of the procession, Shawn E. throws his voice: "Yeah, graduaaa-shawn!"

He's probably been waiting to do that for four long years.

Most snicker. But not me, or Tray.

The principal shushes the room. In the stands, my brother and cousin Lou hold up their pink glitter-glue *GO MOLLY* sign, and to follow the no-exuberant-outbursts rule outlined in the principal's welcome speech, they mime cheering. It's too, too much. When they fall into laughter, my cousin's beaded earrings catch the light and shimmer in the manner of stars.

This time, the principal taps the mic, clearing his throat dramatically. He's slightly above shushing spectators.

"I mean," Tray whispers, "if your name is Shawn, how could you not?"

I shrug, performing another turn in this overblown marching number. In the process, I lose sight of my family.

They've dressed up.

It bothers me that we graduates aren't wearing traditional gowns over our dresses and suits. The boys are in churchgoing clothes, the girls wrapped in shiny material, mostly Nordic colors, like they're presents in a holiday IKEA display.

I would have preferred the grad gown. In that billowy thing, we wouldn't be in competition, showing off our parents' wallets and our bodies. Nobody has a thigh gap in a grad gown. Some of us haven't ever had one, are thick-thigh girls.

When the final lap begins and I pivot in the wrong direction, Tray corrects me. "No, left."

I've been so torn up over my brother's last-minute decision to drop out of our grad trip, because he hasn't *actually graduated*, he says, as if that's a good enough reason not to go through with something we've been planning forever. So I skipped last week's not-so-voluntary choreography practice.

What are they going to do? Ungraduate me?

This is the major difference between myself and Traylor Lambert: I'm torn up Hank isn't coming on our trip, and Hank's best friend doesn't seem bothered.

"No, right this time," Tray says, and if I were wearing heels, I'd be eating dirt.

From the podium the principal glares at me. The couple behind us in the procession start whispering. I hear my name. But don't worry, I'm used to it.

The powers that be dropped me into the spotlight when they decided to skip me straight to Grade 10 after I finished middle school with perfect scores in every class. Teachers took it as a personal challenge. My new classmates weren't cruel, not by high school standards, just didn't like when anyone made themselves exceptional for the wrong reasons.

Let me say it so it's clear: knowing all the names of the bones in the human body is a wrong reason. I don't tell anyone I memorized this at six years old anymore.

So while skipping grades is frowned upon, something about social development, so is having a student who sleeps through the curriculum and still aces the tests.

Emma C. eventually gets brave. "It's like *she's* the one with the brain damage."

My fingers curl into fists.

Tray must know I'm thinking of the way he's tangled up in my brother's accident. But all he does is say my name in a tone that suggests I'm being unreasonable. My fingers tighten. While Emma C.'s inane comment is supposed to be a dig at me, it's also making fun of my brother's disability. Which fires me up.

But I can't turn around and deck the girl for insulting Hank. Not with my family watching. In the bleachers, Auntie Louisa is beading something gorgeous like she does. My uncle Dom sits beside her, texting, a smile all over his face. In the row above, my parents are holding hands like they're high school sweeties, their eyes trained on me as I turn, turn around out here. And in the top row my brother, our cousin, and our cousin's boyfriend are telling stories in modulated tones, catching up like they didn't see each other just last weekend for the Creamery's annual kickoff.

My nails bite into my palms.

Though I want to real bad, I for sure can't turn around and deck my classmate, not while wearing these bright yellow-and-pink beaded earrings, a gift my dad made me in celebration. Graduating from high school at seventeen, honor roll all six terms, even after the weeks when all I did was sit next to Hank's hospital bed making deals with every god whose name I've ever memorized if only they'd wake him up.

I'll become the best doctor anyone has ever seen. I'll fly through med school. I won't make a single mistake. I'll save so many kids, dedicate my life to this, if only you'll help Hank.

Gently, Tray straightens my fingers. "Don't let them bother you. We're almost done. And once we break bread, we're free of this place. Forever, yeah."

It came upon me slow and then all too fast. A sinking feeling, how I've imagined it's like being caught up in an avalanche. I've made countless promises to an absolute bevy of powerful beings, and I'm not sure I can keep any of them. The stack of mail, of emails, I've been ignoring is too heavy. My tulle skirt, like the complete dick it is, punctuates that thought with more unstoppable itch.

I force myself to use the voice I've been throwing Tray's way for months now. Something calm, something empty. "Sure thing. Good plan."

On the outside, I'm as chill as can be.

Inside, I seethe. I think of the one university I bothered to apply to. Of the May 1 deadline I let pass.

Next to me, Tray hums like he can get enjoyment out of even this tinny pomp-and-circumstance music. I want to hiss at him like a cat would.

I want to sharpen my nails.

We turn and turn on the gym floor, the music building to a peak, and I'm dizzied. When I don't go to university in September, what retribution will gods across cultures, across time, have for the girl who deceived them? Good science said the longer Hank was out, the less likely he'd recover. So, to me, it's obvious: my brother was helped by some entity.

Will you accept a leave of absence, a temporary stay? Stall the payback clock until I can figure out my future, this terrifying thing that's only sudden the way accidents are, time slowing, time crunching. Will you wait, will you bend until I can make everybody happy?

I complete the last turn, coming to a stop beside Tray, and the audience is finally allowed to clap.

On the north field, there's a lunch. Sandwiches on white bread that never expires, never molds, with barbecue chips, not ketchup, which are superior. For dessert, there's a cake done up in the school's colors. Vanilla slab cake is my favorite, even if it is basic. And I bet the school hasn't gone risky, opting for chocolate. I'm working my way through the crowd to the lunch table when my brother tracks me down.

He wrestles me into a rough hug. "Congrats, graduate!"

It's not that I want to untangle myself. I love Hank in a too-big way. But also, part of me wants to disengage. When we conceived this trip on winter break more than three years ago, we always planned to take a gap year. To bag our first through-hike together. And in all this time, we've never once talked about changing things up. Not even when Hank was in the hospital.

"How are you?" I ask because I can't not ask it. But in the same breath I also say, "I'm still pissed, in case you're wondering."

Hank's wearing his favorite T-shirt, a cartoon dinosaur holding a toothbrush, the dialogue bubble proclaiming *Brush Those Chompers*. A gift from Lou. It's not formal by any means, but the yellow shirt is one hundred percent Hank. Ever since he got braces and crushed tragically hard on his orthodontist, he's had a thing for teeth.

"Mols, summer school will get me back on track."

Reclaiming my personal space, I stare past my brother at the food. "I know."

And I do know this. But knowing and being okay with it are like that childhood experiment where you discover how at the molecular level oil and vinegar repel each other.

"Then get over it," Hank says. "So we can enjoy this sad party and our last hour together for the entire rest of summer."

Once I start walking, odds of running into a slab cake are not great. I want a piece bad. Still, this unwelcome, too-loud anger clings to me like a bur. "But it was our grad trip. Not mine, ours."

"And I don't know if you noticed, ye of the unusually strong observation skills, but I didn't graduate in there." Hank's got a straight face. He's not dicking around. "How can I go off on a grad trip when I haven't done the deed?"

My brother's hair has grown back in from the surgery the doctors performed to relieve pressure on his brain, but unlike his old look, which was shaggy and unkempt, now Hank keeps things buzzed military short. It's unsettling.

"That's not the point."

"It is," my brother says, rolling his shoulders.

Before the accident, Hank never got flustered, wasn't the grumpy-bear kind. Even if he couldn't get a climbing route, had been trying for days, he never quit, never let anyone run beta for him, just chalked up and went at it again, smiling to showcase his perfect teeth. On particularly rough days, I'd layer an impromptu dance party onto my good-luck run-and-jump hug.

But these days the run-and-jump hug has been retired from the rotation and nobody feels much like dancing. This one's on me. I didn't ask those gods to bring my brother back exactly like he was. I'm not greedy. I only asked for one of them to wake his ass up.

Squinting against the early afternoon sunshine, I exhale. My chest stays tight. "I don't want to argue."

"Then why you doing it, Mols?"

That's new too. That nickname.

I grumble under my breath. These days, we tiptoe around each other, caught in a boring stalemate. And I don't even have a slice of cake as consolation.

To make things just a little worse, this is when Tray approaches. I've been watching him say goodbye to his mom, who's a partner at an Indigenous-owned law firm downtown. They're working a case: local Native nations are joining a class-action lawsuit against the world's big polluters. It's really important.

My brother takes Tray's arrival as an opportunity to escape our mini fight. Maybe that makes me the winner. But it doesn't feel like I've won anything.

"Congrats, buddy. I'm chuffed for you!" Hank hugs his best friend, not the way guys normally do, slapping each other on the back like they're trying to make it hurt, but tightly, closely.

Hank after the accident gives better hugs than Hank before. I don't like thinking on that. But it's truth.

The three of us used to be fused together the way some bones are.

Now we're fractured.

And even if my brother has, I can't forgive Tray for what he let happen.

Arm in arm, my parents approach us. They forgave Tray too. Did it even before Hank woke. Over by the slab cake, where I really want to be, Auntie Louisa and Uncle Dom are teasing my cousin's boyfriend. Now that we're outside, everyone is gabbing and laughing, someone with a high-pitched voice recounts each turn in the march like it was interesting, and Shawn E. won't stop hollering, "Yeah, yeah, yeah, graduaaa-shawn!"

The anger inside me pulses like it has its own veins and arteries. The noise, the pressure, is overwhelming. A breeze brushes tulle against my heated skin. I want to crush something or run a 5K race or sit down in the grass and have a big cry, a full-fledged temper tantrum, and I have no idea which.

My mom hands me a bouquet of grocery-store daisies, dyed bright, bold colors. "I know it's been a hard year. That I haven't

11

been as attentive. That you're still bummed about your bad grade. But you did it, Molly."

Yes, I prefer daises toxic, a bit radioactive.

"When you graduate from Calgary in a few short years," my mom continues, smiling wide, "I'll triple the size of the bouquet. Or the blooms. Your choice."

I force myself to return the gesture. To act as if nothing is wrong. It's not like I'm lying to them, dear gods, goddesses, and goddi. Way back in the day when they laid down the rules for the through-hike, they freaking cosigned a gap year. The people in my life have assumed a lot. Even if they don't know it yet, they know how the saying goes. When you assume shit, we're all ass-holes in the end.

I comment on the flowers. "You do know I'm leaving as soon as this lunch is over. Or as soon as Lou's ready, whichever comes first. What exactly am I going to do with daisies on the trail?"

There's a pause, a moment of silence.

I taste old pennies and shame tightens my throat.

My mom asks her next question in a heated rush: "What if you didn't go?"

Not this again.

"Mom, we talked all week. My bags are literally packed, and my plane takes off in"—I check my phone—"three hours and fifteen minutes."

"Plans can change, ma fii." This, my dad's addition to the conversation. His hair is graying, and since Hank's accident, Dad looks not so much tired as worn.

"Well, this one isn't."

The crease between Mom's eyebrows deepens. "Traylor hasn't backed out now that Hank's staying behind, right?"

My mom loves Tray so much that he basically moved in after he befriended me and Hank, and now both my parents wonder where he is if he's at his own house for dinner. They miss him when he goes up north to see his dad. My mom, who often emphasized when I was growing up that I was half-white, she's Tray's biggest fan even though he fights her on the fraction thing every time she lets it slip.

"I do not need Tray to take care of me. I take care of myself."

My mom opens her mouth as if to speak. Eventually, she only nods.

"We know," Dad says. "We only worry, Molly Lee. It's a parents' prerogative, that."

The cake is disappearing slice by slice, and even though I'm standing perfectly still, the tulle scratches. I'll have a gross rash once I shed the skirt.

"You can stop," I say. "It's going to be fine. It's walking. How hard is walking, really?"

I speak the words and instantly regret them. My eyes burning, I blink hard to keep from embarrassing myself. Because it took months for Hank to walk well again. He still has balance issues, especially when he's overtired. But I can't retract the statement either. Can't show weakness.

Mom, ever the unbeatable activist, shifts tactics. She interrupts the boys, who are having a conversation about some gear that's just landed at Mountain Equipment Co-op. "You're still going, right, Traylor?"

Tray pivots, steps closer. "Wouldn't miss this for the world."

"That's a relief." Mom exhales. "And you promise to take care of my daughter? Not that she can't take care of herself. But . . . she's only seventeen."

Tray smiles at me weirdly.

I want to protest on multiple fronts.

My dad speaks before I can: "It's not about age. It's always helpful to have another person sharing in the labors."

Tray agrees fast, like he hasn't already stood by while one of the Norris-Norquays ended up hurt.

I scratch at my thigh with the daisy stems. "If that's sorted, I'm going to go get cake."

Nobody says a word.

It's impossible, this. I don't know how to navigate my parents' needs when they butt up against my own. Don't know how they've forgiven Traylor. In my heart, I know I never, ever will. And that sucks because, as messed up as this is, I miss my best friend. The problem, she whistles like a songbird. Shawn E. yells again, as if he's happier than he's ever been. I walk off, holding the tulle far from my legs, as if to stay pain that's already rooted deep.

I shouldn't do it. But after cake I sneak back into the building, climb to the second-floor biology/chemistry lab. The door is locked. I peer through the window. Lab benches and a few stray beakers. This room used to give me an under-the-skin buzz. A full-body thrill like when you spin in place against gravity, arms thrown wide. I got giddy the period before, the same low-down-in-the-stomach excitement that adventures with my brother and

Tray have always provoked.

We aren't supposed to be inside. But I wanted to see if a B in Grade 12 Biology would dull the roar. It hasn't. My heart thrums loudly. For the first time today, I'm excited about the trip.

Footsteps echo in the hallway behind me. It's Lou. "Traylor said he saw you head up here."

I thought he was watching.

"Is it time to go?"

Lou shakes her head, her earrings shimmering with movement. "No, actually, I wanted to talk with you. And I didn't want to do it in front of everybody else."

During lunch, I heard Lou's mom ask her to drive to Lloyd tonight instead of going back to Calgary.

"It's okay if you can't give us a ride." I want to make sure she doesn't feel guilty. At all. Things are going to go wrong on this trip.

"We're still going to take you. But then we'll go home for a few days. Dom could use some help and, well, King misses his dad." Lou smiles, but it's not a happy smile. "I came up here to check on you."

"I'm fine," I say. "A little tired."

"You're angry," Lou says.

My body freezes in place. "I'm not."

I meet her gaze.

"Anger's easy," Lou says slow. "And when have you ever gone for easy?"

I nod, the smallest of movements.

"I'll meet you outside, when you're ready."

I stand in the hallway for fifteen minutes before I can risk being around people again.

Now we're driving south toward the airport. I'm in the back seat of Lou's red Toyota Prius, trying to extract myself from this tulle monstrosity. Next to me, Traylor stares out his window. Lou grins in the rearview mirror. A beaded dinosaur charm dangles there. "Are you two excited? Wait, are you getting naked in my car?"

From the passenger seat, King laughs. It's deep, joyful. He places a hand on Lou's knee.

"Are you laughing at me?" she asks.

King nods. "You're so damn cute."

Lou isn't distracted by the compliment. "My cousin could have changed at the school. In the bathroom, like a regular person would. Traylor did."

I'm going to miss Lou and King. They're good fun. Don't treat me like I'm a kid, even though they're older, basically full-fledged adults at this point. Lou's in grad school, and King has a novel coming out next year. And yeah, Lou is right: anger is easy.

While they argue over what it means to be a regular person, I try again to get the skirt's zipper to release.

"Need help?" Tray interrupts, without turning from the window.

I have no idea what he's looking at. The view is uninspiring. "No," I say, even though I've been shaking my head already.

He waits a minute. "You sure?"

It slips out of me: "Also no."

At that, Tray laughs, starts humming like he has something to say but isn't going to risk saying it.

When I finally get the zipper to cooperate, I sigh. I wasn't trying to be funny. This is just what life is like now. Before Hank's accident, I was sure of everything. And now, well, now I'm not.

LATE JUNE
VANCOUVER INTERNATIONAL AIRPORT
Traylor

There's Coast Salish art all over the terminal, but we don't have time to admire things. Hiking pack chest straps bouncing about unsecured, we're running, counting down the gates. In my head, where the music always lives, we're doing this to that vintage anthem "Paper Planes." I match the beat to our footfalls, imagining this frantic run entirely slower than it is.

Now this song will be part of the soundtrack of my life.

The last time I was in this airport the song was "We Will Rock You" and I was taking what nobody but me knew was my last trip as a hockey player. My calf muscles tighten. It isn't a good memory, but it's all tied up in that Queen song. If I set a memory to a beat, it lives forever. Which is both an incredible gift and a curse. But I wouldn't give it up for all the moose-meat tacos in the world, for all the chances to break big, not even to set things right between Molly and me.

And that's saying everything.

Running slightly ahead of me, she grumbles: "This is on you."

"Probably so."

I don't deny it, expect a smile, something to say that exuberant but always plain-speaking Molly is still in there. What she gives me is more of the same flatness. As if she hadn't meant for the real Molly to sneak through.

The chorus hits. It's weirdly fitting for an airport, for running through an airport. These cash register sounds are out of time, absolutely anachronistic, but so is this run.

Customs held us up.

Because they could.

Maybe US Border Protection would've treated us better if I'd still been dressed in a button-down. This old T-shirt won't make it home, won't survive the trail, but it's not much different than what other guys my age are wearing. I can admit *You Are on Native Land* might be a loud choice. I do own other shirts. If I wore one of them, would shit have happened differently? Maybe it's that butterfly effect. One action somewhere changes everything, sends Molly and me into that particular agent's line . . .

Overhead, the speakers crackle. "Attention, passengers! This is the final call for Flight 555 to San Diego. If you don't get yourself to the gate in the next one hundred and eighty seconds, I'm closing the door. And a closed boarding door doesn't open again. That's the law of the skies, people!"

We dodge children whose parents aren't paying attention, those lawless carts with their tiny horns, driving anywhere they please. Though I can run faster, I don't need to be the leader. I'm the kind who can follow and not let it chew up my ego. Those hockey lessons about strong teams stuck.

And I could follow Molly Lee forever. Even when she's in a snit.

Between inhales, she admonishes me like this is my fault. "Hurry up, would you?"

T-shirt choice aside, it's really not. But she can't see that.

Not the way she's been thinking that I hooked her brother, my best friend, up with gear I knew would fail on purpose. I picked the gear, yeah. It was new and shiny. Pink, Molly's favorite color.

She's already going close to full out, but when I kick things up, Molly does too. It's not that she's short, because she isn't. The top of Molly's head hits my chest, and the rest of her is proportional. She hates her shoulders, the way they're wide set like her dad's. But I think everything about this girl—shoulders, hips, smile—every part of Molly is basically perfect.

Some might call her thick, fat.

Some have.

She's healthy, gorgeous in the body she has, even now, sweating in an air-conditioned terminal, loaded down by a summer's worth of gear.

We're nine gates away.

These days, Molly, she needs it bad. To be in charge. If she were one of those acts-first-thinks-later cis guys I played hockey with from the time I could walk, she'd have thrown a solid hit, broken my nose months ago. We'd have drunk pilfered beers, her hand smarting, my nose still bleeding some, and gotten over this. Instead, the night Hank was transferred to the rehab center, she found her dad's stash of rye and sobbed half-formed words in my direction. I tried to listen. Caught some of it. *Your . . . fucking . . . fault.* But mostly she'd been inconsolable.

The next afternoon, when she woke, rolled over on her side,

propped up by all the pillows I could find so she wouldn't do damage if she threw up in her sleep, she went right back to pretending we hadn't tried.

And she might not remember, the way getting that drunk can mimic some of the aftereffects of a head injury. I'm entirely too chickenshit to ask. To tear open the wounds. And I'm a little PO'd at both of us for . . . giving up.

Five gates now.

"Attention, passengers on the concourse. This is the final, final call for Flight 555. If you want to go to America's Finest City, the City in Motion, you need to report to gate 46, that is gate four-six, immediately. Ticktock, people! And not the social media app. This is a ticktock classic."

The gate agent is funny.

I want to laugh but don't have the breath. My stomach's knotted up with regret and frustration. The border guards kept us way longer than any other passenger. After fifteen minutes of random questioning, the younger guy called his superior over to examine the notarized letter Molly's parents signed so she could cross as a minor. After they returned the letter my mom drafted, they started up on the Jay Treaty, though it doesn't apply to the Métis. I said so twice. I was polite, yeah. But they wouldn't drop it, didn't seem to care there's a difference between First Nations and the Métis. The older one kept asking if we thought it was fair Natives could cross land borders without a passport, like it mattered to the situation at hand.

The song is cresting.

Molly scrambles for her phone, her hiking boots digging into the carpet so she won't run down the gate agent. "We're here!"

A few people cheer.

"They made it in the nick of time, friends and foes! I won't even call the refs to confirm." The gate agent tempers her voice. "So, what kept you two? And don't say Starbucks or I'll curl into a ball and basically die."

Molly and me, we're both breathless.

I recover first. "The line at customs was . . . long."

That part is true. The other, it won't garner us sympathy.

Never does.

Not with a racist coach or a classmate who can't stop making jokes about all Indians being alcoholics even after you tell them it's not even a little humorous, to check their vocabulary because it's way-the-fuck out of date.

The gate agent's still smiling, examining our passports. "Well, thanks for not breaking my heart. It's Starbies this, Starbies that around here most days. But you're supposed to be at the airport three hours early for international flights for exactly this reason."

"Oh, we were." Molly scans her boarding pass. "We connected in Vancouver with no issues. Then we had to pass through pre-clearance customs. Homeland Security kept us for, like, an hour and a half asking the same thing on repeat."

Molly's not bothered by all the BS. It comes across in how calm she is recounting what just happened to us. She doesn't get caught up when a person says what a person can't help but say when they find out they're talking to somebody Native.

"It's like that, is it?" The agent sighs loudly. But then she rolls her eyes, surprising me. "They can be overzealous. Now onto the plane, friends. Everyone is waiting."

As we shift through, our hiking packs held awkwardly, the folks in first class give us the eye. I crouch some. Molly's shoulders squeeze inward, like she's afraid to take up space inside this metal tube.

"Hold it!" a flight attendant hollers, closing baggage compartments in the main cabin. "We don't have any room. You better hope there's some in first or we're going to have to delay."

A few passengers groan.

"The plane is never going to leave if you two don't sit down," a woman with extra legroom privileges says as we pass her again like we don't know that fact.

"Sorry about this," I offer, and I do mean it.

But it's also peacekeeping. I wouldn't put it past Molly to do something to shut this lady up, something that would get us kicked off the plane entirely. Maybe even added to the No Fly List. She's got an anger problem these days.

It's quiet, just a stumbling note, something flat, but maybe I do too.

The note, it's not enough to knock my song off course. The fiddle trills in my heart, and the spoons keep the beat. If Molly jumps into the fray, I'll always jump in after her. The why doesn't matter to me. That's how we are, the three of us, intense, always there, while the adventure burns hot *and* after it's over.

My Molly-moo only blows air from between her lips and walks away, carrying her hiking pack, a mess of bold '80s colors, in front of her. "Do they really think we did this on purpose?" she mutters, and throws me an inscrutable look.

I used to know all her looks. That stumbling note rings again, louder before the fiddle can smooth things over. Molly hasn't asked me a direct question in months.

In first class, I check already-closed bins. I heft Molly's pack into a free compartment. "You know people suck at remembering the rest of us aren't out to maliciously hurt or inconvenience them."

She sighs. "True story."

Our gear tucked away, we push through to the rear of the plane. We've been assigned a middle and a window seat. The white gentleman finishing out our row gets up with a huff. He probably thought he had all this to himself. So, it has to burn.

"Sorry," I say again. It's going to be a long flight with a grumpy seat neighbor. And even though I'm about to sandwich myself between two of them, I do it. "You first, Molly."

"You sure?"

That's two questions.

I smile. "Yeah."

Once we're seated, the plane starts taxiing as the flight attendants do the safety brief. I drop my hands in my lap. Planes are too tight for most people, and I haven't flown since I was heading to that once-in-a-lifetime training camp in Boston with the U16 AA hockey team. But now I'm next to Molly and we're about to have an adventure. I stow my unkind feelings, refuse that stumbling note when it tries to lead me off into the bush, and remember my own good advice: it's not like Molly's out to maliciously hurt me; she's only reacting, only grieving.

She lifts the armrest that's cutting into her side and keeping me from taking a full breath. Her thigh presses against mine.

I grin. Flying was never this good with hockey.

I made the right choice.

My leg stretches into her zone, and when she doesn't complain, I think, this is just fine. It starts with questions. Soon we'll be back to how we were before that awful Saturday. Me teasing Molly, the way she's a serious science person one minute and all unbridled enthusiasm for bagging another Banff peak the next, Molly teasing me in her prickly way. The fiddle and spoons agree.

We've been in the air forty minutes. I'm trying to mix M.I.A. with John Denver's classic "Leaving on a Jet Plane," my waterproof notebook and tiny nub of pencil in hand. It's turning into an unexpected ballad. All soft and full up on longing. Funny how *lethal poison* in the right context becomes the refrain in a love song. I'm humming only when I need to hear the notes. Focusing on the lyrics, how meaning shifts when the beat around them changes, is amplified. It's always driven Molly to grind her teeth when I do this out loud. And Hank-the-Tank would hate it if I helped his sister wreck her teeth.

Shifting in her seat, scratching at her legs, pressing her thigh against mine, then moving away, Molly restlessly scrolls through her phone. It's distracting in the best worst way.

"Want to work on a new mix with me?" It's something we used to do together sometimes, after a long day hiking in the back-country, taking up new routes at the climbing gym, or racing to see who could sell the most, or the weirdest, gear during a shift at MEC. Molly mostly kept me company. She's not big into music.

Like she had to stake herself another ground, something entirely different than her dad, after he left.

"I'm kinda busy."

Her voice is clipped, draws out the flat note until the note turns sour.

"Doing what?"

"Organizing things."

"How fun."

Molly ignores me.

I like her sharp edges, like that her heart isn't earned easy. Taunting her always used to be a good time. Ever since I moved to Edmonton in Grade 6 and met Hank and Hank's little sister, I've been in love with the two of them, was welcomed into the Norris-Norquay household when my mom was too busy working her sixty-hour weeks to do much more than shuttle me from school to practice. I've always known that I can sleep on the futon mattress stored in Hank's closet and that the Norris-Norquay pantry is as much mine as theirs. That Hank and Molly's mom, Lisa, and their dad, Maurice, trust me completely. When I go hunting up north, where my dad lives, and we take a moose or a buck, I bring most of my share to their deep freeze. My mom thinks it more than a fair trade, a gift for the people who love her kid like he's their own. Not the way the white lady who took care of me after school in Lethbridge did. She tallied each granola bar.

"Want to watch something?" I close my notebook, stow the pencil. "Bet we can press start at the exact same time so there's no annoying lag."

"No, thank you."

She's so angry and it's breaking my heart.

"I'll let you pick the movie?"

Molly adjusts, then readjusts the window shade. "So you know," she says, looking anywhere but at me. "This trip is never going to work if you try to trade your codependency on Hank for one with me. You need to get that straight as a freaking art-room ruler before we land."

Ouch.

She can't say love, can't admit that we love each other, so she's found a therapy-level word to clobber me with. Even the fiddle retreats from this.

But I have a secret weapon. One that my Molly can't resist.

And her anger won't last. Not forever.

Neither will mine.

I learned that with my therapist.

This isn't how love works. And this isn't our story.

"What if I told you I have those premium movie snacks?" I offer, like I wasn't going to share them with her anyhow.

She softens. "Where?"

"In my pack. One of the outside pockets, yeah. Easily reached in case of a snack-mergency."

She raises an eyebrow, the way she does when she's asking a very important-to-her question. "Sour Skittles?"

"And white cheddar popcorn, not the health-food kind. Along with a family-size pack of peanut M&M's."

Her favorites.

"I still get to pick the movie?" she hedges.

This is good. I refuse to gloat. And, in truth, I'd rather watch whatever Molly wants. But I can't give up that secret, not when it would derail our tiny détente. "Why not."

She needs to win the hard way, always has.

No shortcuts for Molly Lee.

"Okay, I'll watch something," she offers, like she's not happy she's come out on top, in all the ways that count but the one: that she's agreeing to spend time with me.

"Be back in a jif."

I convince the man in the aisle seat to stand, then make my way up through the little curtain they use to separate first class from everyone else. Almost as soon as I step across that line, a youngish flight attendant with bright red lipstick speaks: "Sir, you can't be up here."

I point at the luggage bins. "I need a few things from my bag. I'll make it quick."

She nods, satisfied, and returns to serving dinner on real plates with glassware. One day, if I can convince people that covers are great, that mixes can be as exciting as original songs, and you know, do it without passing out and embarrassing everyone I know, my entire community and all the ancestors too, I'll fly first class, my guitar stored somewhere up here. If I'd continued with hockey, gone pro, I would have had a chance at this life too. But this way, I get to take Hank and Molly along for the ride.

Even if music makes me millions, I won't let it change me. I'll remember that nothing separates these people from the rest of the airplane except access to money. They aren't better, only luckier. I'll still be the guy who spends weeks out in the bush with his dad, tracking and hunting so that the people who attend the language camps can eat throughout the winter. Still be the guy who plans on building an ice rink in the backyard of his future home for his future kids, teaching the entire neighborhood to skate.

As I extract snacks from my bag, the man sitting below me cocks his head. "You Native?"

If it's not the T-shirt giving it away, it's my hair. It's important to me not to pass as a settler. "Métis, yeah."

The man's suit is gray, his tie a boring blue. This man wasn't held up by customs. He probably breezed on through.

He makes a noise in his throat. It's a sign of nothing good.

"Does that really count these days?" he asks offhand, like he's not trying to start shit while absolutely starting shit. It's in his smile. The way he holds his liquor, pinkie finger extended away from the glass.

"Listen, I'm not debating my Nation's existence with you."

"I do a lot of business up in Canada, sorting legal issues in the oil fields," the man says. "And it's always First Nations this, Métis that."

He leaves the Inuit out and that's telling as fuck.

The overhead bin closes a little too roughly. My bad. "Maybe it should be that way stateside too."

The man laughs. "Three words, kid: Doctrine of Discovery."

I'm holding Molly's treats in one arm and I'm reminding myself that most people are good, or at least have the capacity for good, when the flight attendant with the red lipstick approaches.

She steps between the man and me. "Sir, can I offer you the Mediterranean chicken or the panko-crusted lamb tonight?"

"The lamb," he says, waving his free hand dismissively. "Did you hear this kid?"

The flight attendant smiles but doesn't show her teeth. She's acting, placating him. "Oh, no, I wasn't listening in."

"Well, let me tell you . . ."

The flight attendant turns my way. "You ought to take your seat now. We could hit turbulence at any time."

"Yes, thank you," I say, and escape.

It doesn't matter where I go, someone has something they need to say about Indigenous peoples and they say it, even if I'm not open to listening. This man throws around the Doctrine of Discovery as if the concept of "uninhabited land" isn't a flawed one, one that we've taken apart over and over again as we fight colonialism. At school, on the ice, at the climbing gym, these people cannot stop themselves. The Safeway checkout line, when all I want to do is get the good movie snacks, is a special hell. It's exhausting. I'm hoping this summer, out on the trail, offers a break.

At the rear of the plane, Molly has the movie keyed up on both our screens. "What happened? Did you get lost up there?"

"Something like that."

I smile when I see her choice. She watches this movie when she's sad, when she's celebrating, and every year on her birthday. That she picked it simply means she still cares. As angry as she is, at the world, and even at me, she still gives a damn. It's a fiddle solo, no sour notes in sight.

This past year is the only one in memory where I haven't watched *Saved!*, Molly's non-ironic favorite, with the Norris-Norquays, in their living room, the three of us piled onto the same couch, fighting over who gets the good blanket, only to decide we'll share it in the end. Hank and I laugh at the movie, how it's dated but still subversive, yeah, while Molly shushes us.

She tears the tab on the Sour Skittles with her teeth.

Hank would call foul.

I'm only impressed she pulled off the move. "Oof," I say.

"Do not tell my brother."

The three of us, we don't keep secrets. Not real ones. This is Molly trusting me, in a real, small way. I've been burning sweetgrass, sending prayers up, gathering all my intent in all the ways I know how for Hank to keep healing. For his sake, yeah. So he can find his way back to his life, whatever he wants for himself. Even if it's different, if coming out the other side means things have to change. And I do it for Molly too.

Maybe it's selfish.

The plane shakes. I flinch, close my eyes.

Molly's hand lands on my arm, tentatively. "I've got you," she says.

I love them both completely. And I'll keep loving them until the end of all things, until my body returns to the land, until the land returns to the sun, until the sun returns as cosmic dust to the universe. Until the stars burn out. This love is at the core of everything.

When the plane climbs to find calmer air, Molly retracts her comfort.

I have seven weeks to make things right. Seven weeks to get a handle on my own feelings. I didn't cause Hank's accident. All I did was pick the shiny, new metallic-pink gear. But what watching my mom do her job has taught me, watching my dad too, is that it's impossible to change someone else's mind: the harder you try, the more they dig in. Even when it's against their best interests.

So Molly-moo will have to change her own damn mind. But I'll be there when it happens. And after, I'll get brave and my secret impossible crush on this girl won't stay secret any longer. I grab a handful of Sour Skittles, returning the red ones to the bag because they're her favorite. When I shift to watch Molly's screen instead of my own, she doesn't lean away or chastise me.

Another win, yeah.

And the unpleasant note that's been ringing in my ears on and off for months, it quiets too.

MILE 0.0

Molly

We're riding at dawn in the bed of an elderly couple's truck near the border. Across from me, Tray sits his back against the wheel well, singing, like he's been doing since we exited our motel room almost an hour ago. Our carefully loaded packs crowd the space between us. Mine is hot pink with orange, yellow, and purple accents done up in neon for the zipper pulls, his that boring nature green every outdoor manufacturer can't stop using. As we turn off Highway 94, the truck clunks over divots in the dirt road. If my brother were here, he'd berate me for clenching my jaw.

It's bad for your teeth, you know.

I still haven't answered my family's latest round of texts. I dial the screen brightness all the way down.

HankIsBack: Is T behaving? Need me to come down and set him on the straight and skinny? *skull emoji* *disco ball emoji* *tooth emoji*

Mom: This isn't set in stone. You can change your mind.

Mom: Andrew at MEC says he has shifts for you to pick up . . .

Mom: You could even spend the summer in Calgary
with your cousin prepping for classes . . . That
would be a kind of adventure, right?

I turn my phone off entirely, as if to save our solar charger the work. Yesterday, at the USPS, Tray and I mailed out bounce boxes, all the gear we'll need farther along the trail, like replacement hiking boots, fresh wool socks, and easy, carb-heavy, freeze-dried meals. He still believes I'm returning home with him, didn't notice my extra shipments. But I decided, when the thrill was dying out, that I'd finish the Pacific Crest Trail at the border of Washington State and E. C. Manning Provincial Park in BC instead of somewhere in Northern California like our revised plan says we will. And the longer it takes Tray to get wise, the better.

Paired with road dust, the questions come rapid fire. Do gods have a sense of humor? Will they maybe find all this a little funny? I know enough to know that tricksters will be into how I've tied myself up so that the only option is to flee. They like journeys. And when things don't go to plan. So here I am fleeing and I'm hoping, and I'm still stuck, still listening to the problem whistle.

Tray smiles, catching my eye, as his song ends.

"What?" I say, not thinking of the school hallway, of my last view of the lab, of Lou.

You're angry.

My brother's best friend, all he does is keep on smiling. He begins the song again. It's a threatening invocation: *Soon may the Wellerman come.*

"Seriously, stop looking at me like that," I say, all calm.

34

I'm not angry. I'm not.

Tray shrugs, shifts his gaze. But he never stops singing.

Yesterday, after the post office, because Hank insisted we still go, Tray and I spent the day at the zoo. Even the world-class San Diego Zoo didn't feel right without my brother. It's a fact: when a doctor amputates a limb, there's this sensation, like your brain thinks the limb is still present even after it's gone. That's how I feel. Like Hank used to be as much a part of me as my own arms and legs, and now he's not. That when he moved in with me and our mom, that when I was six years old I absorbed him into me.

Hank's gone, but then again he isn't.

It's a freaking magic trick and I've never liked the idea of magic. The way people lean on it when everything under the sun, under the wide sky, is science. Yes, I know I'm not supposed to feel this way about Hank. I'm the first to defend him when someone's cruel. Still, shame coating my throat, making it harder to swallow, to breathe, is familiar to me now.

I stash my phone in my pack, as if one of my mom's sayings, *out of sight, out of mind,* actually works.

Back at the motel, the pressure inside me worsened, grew its own teeth. It was the woman a few doors down yelling at her kid for jumping on the bed, the TV from a second-floor room blaring an advertisement for prescription meds, and it was Tray's camp sandals on the concrete walking away, texts buzzing against the bedside table, my heartbeat thumping, all those promises I made strung out like spider silk across every doorway.

Heavy like an old-school corset, tightening and tightening, it's with me even now. The way my body feels bloated, overfull with it. The tiny hopeful part of me can't compete, is statistically insignificant.

Out of the truck window, the driver hollers at us. "You two still all right back there?"

I offer thumbs up.

Tray smiles at me. Again.

The vintage truck continues along slowly. This couple likes to take part in the adventure of a lifetime by giving hikers a lift out to Mile 0.0. I'm thankful for the ride, but too wound up to relax. My grip tightens. The metal's already heating up.

In an hour, it will be unbearable to sit here.

Un-freaking-bearable.

I pull the red bandanna I got at a No More Stolen Sisters rally up over my mouth and nose. This boy thinks he can figure me so sharp, how he showed up earlier with coffee and a piece of leftover slab cake. As if he can barter sugar for my forgiveness. I worry that's what he's been doing: on the plane, that unasked-for, unexpected cherry pastry at the zoo, and this morning. Trying to sweeten me.

I ate the cake. Come on, you would too.

I won't let it temper me, I think, over and over, trying to tune out Tray's song, wondering how a person might go about praying to Lady Luck. Not that I believe in luck or prayer. If all that BS existed, Hank would be here, laughing, sharing terrifying facts about dentists and teeth. And I would be untangled, not thinking in easy ways about impossibly complicated shit.

The truck shifts into park, and Tray jumps the tailgate to open it like I couldn't do for myself. We drag our gear next to the trail monument and the big, ugly metal fence the US government hired some contractor to put up, like this does anything but mark out the flawed concept of land ownership. In front of that sits a smaller chain-link fence, topped with barbed wire strung in convex arcs the way fairy lights hang.

It's absurd, upsetting.

Outside the truck, the driver's gray-haired wife stretches. She offers us bottled water. And then she asks the question that's been on her mind: "Aren't you a little young?"

She peers at me pointedly. She's not asking this of Tray.

"Darlene, they all look young nowadays," her husband says, before lighting a big, fat cigar. He steps away, to keep the smoke out of our lungs but doesn't quit the conversation. "It's us . . . We're getting old."

"He's right." Darlene drinks for a long time. "Well, be safe, now. I worry when I see you young women going out these days. It's not the same as it was. It's not as safe. But the world isn't either. Now that's changed too."

I don't know what to say to her.

Of course the world isn't safe. It never was for some of us. I think of Auntie Louisa, my whole body tightening. Of those rallies, the ones we keep having to hold, and I think about mass graveyards out back of residential schools, all these places where the government and the Church took Native kids from their families, as if it was for their own good. As fucking if. And yes, I'm thinking of Hank, even though my brother is a white, cis man, even though what happened to my brother wasn't planned, wasn't intentional.

Traylor, who values keeping the peace, who hates getting dragged into these kinds of conversations but goes anyway if he's defending himself or the Métis and other kin, chimes in. "Thanks again for the ride, yeah."

Nostalgia butters Darlene's voice. "Oh, we love doing this. Brings back memories of when we got our own lift out here, weighted down with supplies. You going all the way back to Canada on foot?"

"They're late starting. Probably won't make it all the way to the end," Darlene's husband offers. "Not this season."

And I want to prove an old man wrong. If only to show myself that in a changed world I can still do this one thing. That my body, even if I'm not the type you'd imagine out on a long-distance hike, my body is strong enough to do this. It's more than adventure for adventure's sake.

Tray chats up the trail angels while the man finishes his cigar. But once they leave, that damn song starts from the top again. Yes, his voice is objectively pretty. Like he could out-sing Hozier. But if Tray sings this sea shanty once more in his too-pretty voice, I will end him.

"One day, when the tonguing is done / we'll take our leave and go . . ."

We're not carrying ice axes. Because by now most of the ice has melted. But we do have a tiny folding shovel to share between us.

Breaking from his song, in his raspy, pretty, criminally infuriating voice, he says, "Let's take pictures, yeah?"

The following two beats of silence bring immediate relief.

Finally, I can see past the fence, the barbed wire, as if Tray's noise was holding me up from taking this place in. The landscape is like the Alberta badlands, minus the hoodoos. Dry, mostly brown dotted with spots of sage-green brush. It's breathtaking. My head quiets. No questions. No deep need to hurt Tray.

Anger is easy.

I exhale for a three count, like I learned in the one yoga class I attended with the boys before we all learned we weren't yoga people. If my brother were here, this moment would be perfect. Standing a little after dawn, on the rise of a tiny hill, ready to begin. I try to let it be. To call forth the thrum of a new beginning.

I force myself to answer Tray's question. "Pictures? Sure thing."

"With our packs or without?"

My left eye twitches. Like it's been doing forever these days. Tray didn't understand months ago, when super drunk on my dad's rye, I tried to spell out every little thing. Each of my complaints. The very depths of this pain. He won't understand now. I swallow my ire, my stomach hardened into stone.

"Both?" I say, but phrase it like a question.

Yesterday, this boy wanted to move on, to hang out at the zoo like nothing happened. And for a few minutes in front of the ridiculous bonobos, I fell into it. Laughing in the easy way that used to exist between us, laughing until my muscles hurt, but in spite of the hurt, I wanted to keep going.

Now I feel like I've betrayed my brother. Who is at home, waiting for summer school to start. I pushed and pushed for this trip to happen, to not let Hank's accident change things, and Tray, he followed. In the end, we're doing this without my brother. My ears pound like one of my dad's drums echoes within me.

"You got it." Tray's been agreeing with me a lot lately when before he used to push. "As soon as we get signal, let's send them to Hank."

The pounding intensifies.

Breathe and let oxygen carry away the bad feeling. It's what my brother told me he's been doing. A very hot, very gay PT—Hank's words—at the rehab hospital taught him the trick during a grueling session where he'd wanted to throw in the towel, permanently. Hank claims it works wonders, like fluoride. Also, that the hotness of the PT had been motivational. *You just can't give up in front of a hot physical therapist, Mols.*

"He'd love that," I say.

"Yeah," Tray agrees, and both of us know we're lying.

We smile in the photos. Tray's arm is hitched around mine.

As soon as we're done, I heft my pack onto my shoulders, like I need something to ground me. We've planned for years. I have weighed and reweighed, sorted and reorganized my gear until I know exactly where everything is. I really can handle myself. It doesn't matter what my parents think. I need Tray like I need an 82 in biology on my transcript.

Placing one foot in front of the other, I walk away from the Southern Terminus without fanfare, walking away from the monument where we took photos we'd always planned to take as a trio. When we planned this trip, I hadn't ever kissed anyone, had always assumed that the way we didn't let anybody in, didn't need anyone else around us, that my first kiss would have been with Tray.

That my first kiss would have been nothing but an experiment with a friend.

Behind me, I hear him: "Wait up, eh?"

Instead, I kissed that sad, anonymous white boy in the hospital cafeteria. A week later, in the same cafeteria, I kissed that sad girl.

And both times, it wasn't anything like what I expected. Rush of adrenaline and crisp air and sore, screaming muscles, late-night card games. That's what I expected from a kiss. What it's like to make adventure plans, to execute them with my favorite people. Split across the three of us, we've collected only a handful of broken bones. My radius. Tray's ulna. Hank's hallux. That's the big toe, in case you're wondering. And against all odds, my brother's accident only added one break to the tally, his clavicle. That is, if we don't count the way surgeons drilled into his temporal bone.

Okay, two additional breaks.

But other parts of the body don't mend the same way bones do. After trauma, some never return to how they were before. The doctors call what happened to Hank a TBI, traumatic brain injury, with post-concussive syndrome. These injuries come with a load of symptoms. My brother's are related to mobility, balance, brain fog, and headaches, some minor memory loss.

Hank is lucky.

Behind me, the sea shanty starts from the top again: every note tightens the bind across my chest, the ghost fingers at my throat. People in my life, they call me smart. Teachers. My parents. Even Tray. *Listen to Molly-moo, she's the brilliant one here, yeah.* But I don't think I'm that smart. If I were, I wouldn't be in this mess.

I focus on what I can see in front of me, a dirt trail heading north. Day one, hour one, let's go.

* * *

Things warm fast.

I tie my red bandanna across my hairline. We pass through incredibly dry land, open and close half a dozen large metal gates along the trail meant to keep livestock we never see from wandering too far from water. Now my legs ache in a way that reminds me I'm real. When I drop my pack, my shoulders will burn. I'll sleep hard tonight.

The only thing that could make this better would be having Hank here.

I freeze, my face heats. It's only my limbic system flooding my body with signals, processing raw emotion. But I berate myself anyhow. It's not like my brother's dead. Instead of everything stopping, everything changed. Somehow that hurts as bad.

Traylor catches up, drops his pack, stretches his shoulders and his neck. "How are you feeling? We could do another few miles or we can stop here, where we planned."

It's the first time we've spoken in hours.

Hank has always been the one to reel us in. *Twenty and a half American miles is plenty for the first day. It's not a goddamned sprint, guys, gals, and nonbinary pals.*

And I like a good challenge. Like when my body screams at me. Still, I say, "We stick to the plan."

"All right, my Molly-moo. We set up camp, over there. There's a reliable water source nearby."

He points with one of his long arms toward Hauser Creek, and that only half distracts me from the way Tray called me *his.* As if humans can belong to each other. As if Tray isn't trad AF and knows that it's not belonging but reciprocal relations holding the world together. As if Tray shouldn't already know to keep my name, and the nickname he gifted me after that ridiculous incident with a mostly grown cow on my uncle's farm the summer I turned fourteen, out of his mouth. As if Tray should know, deep in his bone marrow, that when he let Hank get hurt, he tore whatever reciprocal relations that might have grown between us over the course of the last seven years to unfixable shreds.

I'm in pieces. There's no whole Molly, no Molly to be owned or held or—

"Okay, fine," I say, in that empty, calm voice. "But don't call me that."

"Shit, sorry, Molly. I'm trying."

"Please try harder."

We're alone on the trail, well behind the herd. Through the major passes in California, we'll see less snow. Probably none at all, all the way to the Oregon border. But by the time I make it to Washington, if I make it that far, I'll be mired in it. Being alone with Tray burns, so I remind myself we're not really alone. We're surrounded by living things. Plant life and animals, all the various lizards we spotted today, the land itself. Later, once it gets fully dark, the sky will turn to velvet and the stars will sparkle like . . . some thing or some other.

I'm not a freaking poet. I'm supposed to be a doctor. A Métis doctor, serving her community. The way my mom tells it, I wanted it from the first board book we read about the body, clapping when she asked if, when I grew all the way up, I wanted to be a doctor. Years later, I promised it to the gods, and now I'm truly dicked.

I sigh, loudly and dramatically, and I know Tray's hazel eyes will catch it. I used to love that. But these days, he sees much more than I want him to.

My brother calls what happened *an accident*. Everyone does. Even I can admit that Tray didn't intentionally hand Hank fucked-up gear, that the gear belonged to the climbing gym, that Tray didn't on purpose do a shit job spotting. Accident or no, the damage was horrific. Tray has zero right to look at me like that, like he understands.

Anger is easy.

It's Lou's voice, her intonation.

When Tray swings an arm around my shoulder to bear the weight of my pack, I try not to do the easy thing. I shrug out of the straps. What I'd give for a hot tub right about now. Of course, take away what my mom calls creature comforts and suddenly they're the most important thing. Not that I'm hot-tub people, normally. But Hank loves them and so I've spent many a winter night post-ski soaking.

While I set up my tent, which, yes, is obnoxious pink, Tray ignores his own, helps with poles and pegs.

"What do you miss most?" I ask in a daze, still thinking about that mythical hot tub. Like the one the three of us spent all night in, one-upping each other until we overheated with ideas for our next big plan. That was the weekend we decided we would hike the PCT and that it would be the hardest and best thing we'd ever do.

My parents were already fast asleep in the connecting room. I was a month and a half from fourteen. The boys a year older.

44

No wonder my brain is stuck on hot tubs.

When Tray crouches to unzip the bug screen, a weird look in his eyes, I say, "I'm not trying to bait you. It's only a question."

He responds immediately. "Hank-the-Tank."

"Jesus." I recoil. "I meant like a food or something."

"Oh. Um, pizza." Tray hopelessly brushes dirt from his dry-fast pants. "That place your parents took us on the way back from Banff that year. You know the one? I dream about that meal, like, once, twice a week."

It's the utter sincerity in his voice. I blow air out of my mouth, an almost laugh. My spine settles, my muscles unclench. "Oh, that pizza. I miss it too."

"It fucking haunts me, Molly." He shrugs. "The pizza, that is."

Hank-the-Tank.

We used to believe nicknames should be longer, not shorter than your name, that nicknames are about love, about that love overflowing and not about ease. They aren't a way to shorten, to simplify, but to expand, to take up space, to love on a person out loud.

My brother doesn't like his nickname anymore, not since he woke, three weeks and four days after the accident. But a lot changed once Hank woke up.

In the quiet, Traylor helps hammer my tent pegs into the dry ground and then we unpack rice, beans, freeze-dried moose meat, and fresh veg with sleeves of Pop-Tarts on the side. A high-cal, high-protein dinner. We won't see pizza or slab cake again until we hike into town, and even then, nothing is a guarantee.

And it will never be *that* pizza. And we'll never be like *that*

45

again. The three of us close, as if we could never hurt each other. That's what I have to spend my walking hours learning to become okay enough with. The bones, they remember. Because even once healed, the wound remains visible.

"Want help with your tent?" I offer, feeling full, magnanimous, my whole body tired but loose.

It's because of how he answered the question. That is, Tray's original answer.

My mom's first kid, the one she had too young, with her mean ex. He's been Hank-the-Tank since he came to live with us after his grandparents died, only a few months after my dad left. When Hank moved his Legos and his skateboard into the bedroom across from mine, things got steady. I didn't miss my dad because I had a brother. But now I feel the same riotous emotions as I did when Dad first left. Like my world's coming apart, cell by cell. It's only fact: my brother isn't missing, isn't gone. But he's different. He has to be. That's how survival works. We become new, changed, in order to keep going.

And here I am unchanged when everything around me, all the fixed points in my personal constellation, are becoming something othered.

"I didn't pack a tent." Tray holds his fold-flat bowl and shrugs. "The weight, it wasn't worth it once Hank decided not to come with."

It's settled. I am going to tiny-folding-shovel-murder this boy.

It must be all over my face.

Throwing his hands up in defense, Tray smiles that too-big smile of his. His shit-eating dimple emerges.

46

"You think I'm sharing? Think twice. Then twice more," I state, calm, collected. Like everything else, it gets easier with practice. "You can cowboy camp."

"Molly . . . ," he says in his perfectly devastating voice. "You wouldn't have me sleep out here? Where the bears could get at me, yeah?"

I don't think there are bears this close to the border. California did claim the bear for its flag. But settlers overharvested and stole the land for their cabins, their swimming pools down this way too. I might not be in my context, on the land I know, but some things are the same all over. Not that I can look up wildlife stats in the one guidebook I decided was worth carrying, at least in segments, not while Tray watches.

He knows this stuff. Loves this stuff.

If he says there are bears . . .

"Okay." I grind my teeth in a way that if Hank were here, he'd call me out on. "Until you buy your own tent. At the first opportunity. And you're dealing with our food. I'm not spending twenty minutes finding a suitable tree. You say there are bears—you do it."

I'm calling his bluff.

"Thanks, Molly-moo." His face falls fast. "Sorry. It's harder than I thought. Now that we're here."

My jaw aches. If the bears get him, I'll have to pretend it hurts. Return home with what's left of his body. And I'll have to tell Hank what happened.

There, I find it. Like my mom would say, it's *the very last straw.*

I can't let rogue ursids have Tray and I can't tiny-folding-shovel-murder him even if it's one thing I'm sure I want, Traylor gone so I can walk these 4,265 kilometers alone, because that would destroy my brother.

Again.

Weeks after the accident, my seventeenth birthday hit. No one was in a celebratory mood, least of all me. Now that I've made it and I'm a graduate, I want to go back. Maybe to thirteen, almost fourteen, to that ice-climbing trip, to pizza that's probably dusted with some kind of magic it's that good, to my brother and my best friend when we were kids. When we believed we were safe. From the world's terrible indifference and all these questions.

SIX MONTHS AGO

Hank

AITA for not listening to my physical therapist?

I (18 yo cis white man) was in a pretty impressive but also horrible indoor climbing accident. The long story shortened is that I fell and hit my head. Also, chipped one of my front teeth. And I spent a little over three weeks in a coma.

Okay, backstory's done. Fast-forward to the rehab hospital. Where I'm being actively tortured by, let's call him Fred (30-something gay, Japanese-Canadian cis man), who must be a masochist because he gets off on my pain. Fred tells me I have to do the fucking exercises if I want to get out of this place, but the fucking exercises are, yeah, remember that last plot point, torture.

So, is Fred, the probable masochist, wrong?

Someone tell me Fred's wrong.

[TheSkyIsBlue]: Sorry, Fred's NOT wrong.

[OpinionatedAardvark]: Fred might be a masochist but he isn't wrong, dude.

[GillianXR95]: Fred is all that is right in this world.

[catralover5]: No pain no gain. That's a vote for Fred. But sucks about the tooth.

[IDinoWhatToTellYou]: Neither of you are assholes. But yeah, I'm with the rest of them. Go Fred!

[Hank-Is-Back]: Did he pay you or something?

    [NotFred03567]: I only paid the first five of them.

        [Hank-Is-Back]: That's cheating. Moderator! @Not Fred03567 is cheating!

            [NotFred03567]: I never said you couldn't cheat, just that you needed to do the exercises.

                [Hank-Is-Back]: You win this round. But I am not defeated.

[floss-ophy]: I'll say it. Fred's wrong. It's your body. You do you.

    [Hank-Is-Back]: You're my only friend!

[someone]: Fred is wrong!

    [Hank-Is-Back]: I have two friends! Joyous day!

VERSE I, OR THE SECOND STAR

The mouth-organ, commonly called the harmonica, is portable, adds depth. Without it, a song flattens, a design falls. On its own, the fiddle has too much to carry. The mouth-organ compliments, holds part of the melody fixed so the fiddle can thrive. If the fiddle is an agent of chaos, the mouth-organ is certainty.

And here you thought they were only instruments.

MILE 26.4

Traylor

If Molly wasn't overheating, draining her water supply from the campground at Lake Morena fast, yeah, this thing we're doing would only be monotonous. Instead, it's the goalie out of the crease because we're down a player on penalty. It's the way a fiddle can screech and cry, mimicking a sound hardwired in your brain to signal danger.

Water. One thing the body can't survive without for long.

Still, the two of us trek in awkward silence along the Laguna Mountains like we've trekked in awkward silence for the past day and a half, only interrupted by US Border Patrol helicopters hovering overhead. This is the driest section of the entire trail. And it's thirsty work, walking under the June desert sun, this sun almost unknowable to somebody who grew up in Alberta, where in June, it's still within the realm of possible things for a snowstorm to shut the province down. The year the streets iced over, and I played net while Molly tried and failed to score. That weekend we were supposed to hike the Wood Bison Trail but ended up snowshoeing across the neighborhood instead, loudly pretending we were

52

witnessing exciting acts of nature: The elusive snowplow! The man who thinks winter tires make him invincible!

Hank's usually our water man, proclaiming *When you feel thirsty, you're already dehydrated*, in the voice he uses to mimic his mom.

He told me the night before he told Molly. We were sitting in the grass, the nice chairs his parents bought the summer before unoccupied. Hank cleared his throat, ran a hand through his short-cropped hair. "Tray, buddy. I'm not coming."

"What, now?"

"It's not . . . I can't . . ." Hank stared at his feet, his toenails painted with black polish. "You're going to have to keep an eye on the canteens," he said, and for the next few minutes, Hank spoke like he was imparting some knowledge about the early part of the trail that I didn't already have. "You'll do this, right? For me?"

"Of course, buddy."

The afternoon turned to night, and though there was no snow in the forecast, a chill settled in. Neither of us moved inside. Coming to terms with the fact Hank wouldn't be hiking with Molly and me, I also promised I'd be the point person for general dental health.

And here we are just a day and a half into this, and even with my vigilance, the last reported water source has come up dry. On the map, the next option is considered *unreliable*.

To my left, there's movement in the brittle green brush. I wait.

A chipmunk. No, two.

Playful joy exists between them. I smile, wonder if I'll ever get back to that state with Molly. With her brother. Who has been nothing but serious since he woke up. He's still my best friend, yeah. No doubt. But he's focused in a new way. The summer-school thing, not graduating until December, might be getting to him. It's more high school than any of us, even Molly, would have wanted.

Ahead on the trail, her shoulders are tight.

Walking like this, she'll be sore for days. She's already acting like what happened at the zoo, us laughing at the sex antics of the bonobos, meant nothing. Like our conversation last night didn't happen. Like the past seven years of friendship are nothing but a mirage a man dying of thirst might dream up.

I know better. And yet, my own muscles tense, drawing the strings in my heart taut. I throw myself headfirst into an acoustic, way-too-slow version of Tay Tay's "Bad Blood." It's calming to me. While we're walking away from the border and those helicopters and everything they signify, something about the dry growth, the way out here the world is sparse, faded, has got me on edge.

I force relaxation into my body, exhale out worries, including graphic images of what will happen to us if we don't find water, reminding myself that, yeah, loaded with too much tension, even steel-lined nylon will snap. Today, we have only 13.2 American miles to cover. And Molly will feel like she's gone three times that. She'll be miserable.

As if in slow motion, she trips. I'm too far back to help.

"Fuck," Molly says, landing, one hand out, one knee in the loose dirt. "This *would* happen. You're laughing, aren't you?"

It's a question, but she isn't talking to me.

Maybe she's speaking with the land. Or the skinny crows off

54

in the distance, the ones following us like we're interesting. Something my dad said has stayed with me even if I think it's mostly a thing old men say once in a while when the youth are listening: *You can't trust birds, yeah. You know, the ones paying more attention to you than a bird should. Damn birds!*

My dad's good on the land, knowledgeable. Also, paranoid.

Upright now, Molly mutters under her breath. "Freaking rocks, freaking trail and its ridiculous rocks."

So cute.

Even in my weird mood, I can't help but smile. Glancing at the gently sloping mountains, I reaffirm what my therapist has gone to good trouble to drill into my head: I won't stop living even if I'm being offered one of the things I've wanted since I knew what it was to want something just because it's not perfect. I can handle imperfection. The world is imperfect. And that's beautiful. It's all these rocks and the world a step off this trail.

It might be naive, yeah. But I honestly think things will get better. Between me and Molly. With Hank as he keeps healing. With the land. The planet. I even believe that water will show up when we need it, maybe right around the next bend.

Shit like that, like love, it trends upward.

Always.

"You okay?" I ask.

"Yeah, yeah, I'm fine."

"Molly." I'm louder, firmer, so she knows I'm not playing around. That I need her to be straight with me. Not as a friend but as the person she's hiking with. "Tell me that you're okay to keep going."

She glances back. "I'm okay. I just lost my footing."

"Thank you," I say.

Now she's picking steps carefully, her sixty-liter pack loaded down, every centimeter of space used and used well. Her hiking pole with the beaded detail on the strap is stowed. Hank has the other one. Like it made perfect sense, they split the set. The Anti-Fascist, Anti-Capitalist, Clean-Your-Teeth Horse Force patch Hank bought for each of us is sewn onto her pack left of center with orange cross-stitch floss. My work since I'm the only one of us who can sew.

Which is bear shit. What self-respecting person doesn't know how to sew? My best friends, that's who. And I love that they don't. That they need me.

At twelve, I knew Hank was going to be my best friend until the end of time immemorial. So, fucking forever. Even though he was a white boy with a too-fervid obsession with Pokémon, one who didn't even think my jokes—a Pikachu would taste like chicken but a Popplio like that good salmon—were funny. By thirteen, I knew when we were grown, I'd marry Molly and that she'd be my best friend until the end too.

My mom laughed, molars on display, when I dropped that news, in the truck during a late-for-practice drop-off. "You'll probably change your mind when you're grown, Traylor."

I swore I wouldn't, and she laughed again.

"It's like what you said about when you first met Dad, yeah? You knew you'd end up with him. You just knew it."

We were at a red light, snow falling heavy outside. My mom raised one eyebrow, turned to stare me down. Then she hit me with evidence that didn't back up my claim. "And look how that turned out, eh?"

My parents divorced when I was ten. My mom wasn't going to move to the language camp and my dad refused to stay in the city. All I wanted was to play hockey. Which is hard to do when you're the only kid on two hundred acres in the northern bush. My parents are still friends, just happier apart.

But this thing with Molly, it's always felt right to me, in the same way it feels right to dance a jig, showcasing my skills for the younger Métis kids. To sit on the Norris-Norquay back porch and watch city deer wander into the yard, eating what the land provides. Or to skate around at negative forty, goofing off. Which is why the unright between us pushes the same nausea, the same dizziness into my body as when I think about performing songs I've written myself in public.

Original music, it's too much exposure. It's sharing a thing that shouldn't be shared outside of community spaces, like telling stories that ought not be spoken unless all the conditions are right. On Molly's behalf, I kick at a rock lodged in the middle of the trail.

Well, we're older now. All three of us.

At the most fundamental level, I still want exactly what I wanted back then.

Hank and Molly as my best friends. Eventually, Mollycakes as my person. I'm not in a rush. I'm good at patience. We have time for slow. For our minor disagreements, for making up. For university degrees. At the wedding, Hank will be both bridesman and best man. The deep freeze will always be full enough to share with neighbors. The house big enough to welcome those who need it, but small enough to hold them tightly. And everyone is learning how to skate, even if all they ever want to do is have fun out there.

But that big dream, it all hinges on one massive thing.

If Molly can forgive me.

For something I didn't do. It's the Grade 8 field trip all over again. I only came out the other side of that disaster because of Molly. She'd been furious, indignant at the racist BS the school was trying to pull, blaming the minor theft on a visibly Native student without any evidence, except that the girl whose necklace went missing thought she saw me near her things.

Molly fought.

Insisted on an apology when the girl found the necklace in her backpack.

The wind picks up. But it doesn't offer comfort. I'm itchy under my skin. I'm butchering this Swift song because it's too close to what I'm feeling.

Britney's "Toxic" would suit too.

But it's angrier and I'm not that angry. Wouldn't even use the word. I'm . . . unsettled. I'd do almost anything to take that day back, to have been paying closer attention to Hank's setup, as if that would have altered things, to have grabbed the battered old belay instead of the pink, or to have said, *No, Hank, let's stick to bouldering*, and for him to be here with us, enjoying this dust, this sweat.

In Grade 9, shortly after my first and only girlfriend, Amanda Exeter, dumped me absolutely according to plan in the cafeteria, Hank guessed things. And he has been teasing me outside of

Molly's presence ever since.

I miss even that.

Since he woke up, Hank hasn't mentioned it once.

Another thing he doesn't recall, yeah. A tiny, insignificant piece in the large scheme of his life that got erased when his brain had to heal up. During those early chaos hours in the hospital, I tried to set the story straight. To tell Molly everything that happened, beat by horrible beat, because she was the only person I wanted to talk to. Only she didn't hear me. Not that I blame her. The hospital was . . . horrible. Later, when Hank woke, he didn't remember.

Traumatic brain injuries come with a slew of post-concussive symptoms. I know from my days on the ice. Memory issues are only one. A concussion or a TBI can change your life. And what Molly doesn't get, can't see, is that what happened to her happened to me too. That the blood spilled between us is not only Hank's or hers—some of it's mine.

What used to be easy now takes work. And I'm thankful to do that work. Hank is always going to be my best friend, no matter what.

This time, I'm the one stumbling.

Molly turns back, snorts. "You okay?"

"Yeah. It's hard, but I know I should have my eyes on the trail and not the view."

"A lot of things are hard to do," she says cryptically.

I didn't watch Hank run through gear check, that's true, but after the accident, it seemed to be working properly. Now the belay device is in line at some government facility waiting to be tested. It has been for months. Some days, I worry I was daydreaming when Hank geared up. Molly had been freaking all week though she was the girl who aced texts without studying. Her worry, it got to me.

She stops abruptly. When I catch up, I think, finally, water. But no, under some scrub lies a sleeping rattlesnake.

"Found one," she says, like it's a competition. Get the best grades. Gather up fault and assign it. Find a rattlesnake before Tray can.

It's not the snake's fault. I pause, snap pictures on my phone without disturbing its rest. Molly pulls out her mostly empty secondary canteen, and when she misses her mouth, liquid runs down her chin and wets the collar of her T-shirt, and I think I might have a heart attack.

It's ridiculous how much I adore her.

And equally ridiculous how much she's never noticed. How much she can't relax, can't be herself with me these days. There it is, my not-anger, all nausea and faint dizziness echoing through a flat, soured note. Still, she stopped to point out the rattlesnake. She knows how much I've been anticipating seeing one.

"Maarsi," I say, backing away with care.

"Was it everything you ever dreamed?"

There's a layer of bite, of sarcasm in her voice. But that's normal for Molly. Or it was before she started offering me this really worrisome calm, this all-her-edges-missing treatment.

I crave her playful sharpness like I want that pizza, like I want Hank-the-Tank here with us. Like I need a flowing river, an abundant, cool lake, in these dry mountains.

"More," I say. "It was more."

She laughs, unsteadying herself.

I reach out.

Molly brushes me off. "It's not like we don't have rattlesnakes at home."

"Yeah, the prairie rattler," I say, forcing the nausea down. "This one, I think it's a Colorado sidewinder. I'll have to check the guide to be sure. But the landscape's right. And the color combo by the rattles looked textbook."

She snorts. To Molly, a snake is a snake is a snake no matter what ground it hunts on. She cares about people, forgets that humans are mammals too, forgets that the hierarchy settlers believe in between humans and other living beings is complete bear shit—no hate on bears. And that most of what we learn in high school biology class is settler hierarchy.

I don't know why I say it. Blame it on the dehydration.

"In fact, I'm so happy I could kiss you, yeah."

She flinches.

Before, Molly would have laughed this off. Not that before I would have ever joked about kissing her. She turns, stares at me, and for a minute I think, here she is, Molly's awake. For the first time since the accident.

Then she obliterates me.

"And maybe I wouldn't be a total stumbling beginner at it. I've been practicing."

"When?" My heart barrels in my throat. "And with who?"

She shrugs a shoulder like it's immaterial.

Molly smiles with teeth and walks onward, like she didn't just do that to me. Like my jaw isn't tight, too tight, in a way that would piss her brother right off.

The only thing that makes any sense is to ratchet up the tempo on "Bad Blood" until I'm singing a straight Swift cover. Farther along, past another place where the guide says we might find water but don't, Molly joins in, a line here or there, in her low voice. That's when I know it's time to change things up.

"'Shake It Off.' Slow or fast?" I ask, like I used to do when we'd hang out after school on the Norris-Norquay porch. When we shared Pop-Tarts or something equally delicious and processed. When this was effortless. When I knew Molly wasn't kissing anyone else because she spent all her time with me.

"Eighty bpm."

"So precise. I love it," I say, because I can't say anything else.

She laughs. And I don't ask her to tell me who she's been kissing. When she's had time to kiss someone else, when for months Molly lived in hospital hallways.

I'm hollow inside.

Hollowed out with a spoon.

Nothing is perfect, Traylor. Nobody is perfect. That you seek it so often will only result in disappointment. Remember this. It is possible, Dr. Yaliza said offhand, like I wouldn't jump on it, *to ruin a good thing because you expect it to attain impossible standards. Nothing real stands up to being compared to something perfect. Yes?*

This hike isn't perfect, the guidebook isn't either, but I still want this summer. Even if it hurts, today's already better. We've exchanged a handful of words. And we don't mention Hank. This is almost okay.

As we pass by, the crows in the low trees make a racket.

They know where the water is at. They just aren't sharing.

Maybe this is what Molly and me can build on over the summer: almost okay, waking up in a tent, bodies touching, bodies trusting, sweetgrass prayers sent up for harmony and healing, with intent, hoping for another good day where we find water when we need it, but not before.

Three more miles, give or take, stand between us and our plan to set up camp, to eat trail rations, to sleep. For now the ugly mess of emotion inside me is coiled, like a rattlesnake, tail wrapped around itself to stave off the rest of the world. She's been kissing someone, someone who isn't me, I whisper to the sour note, to the snake-that-isn't-a-snake.

Yeah, walking today I've changed my mind. I would give it all up, all the chances, the possibility, to become colleagues with the songwriters I idolize, the way I gave up hockey for this girl and her brother, if Molly would only forgive me for being there when Hank fell, forgive herself for not being in the climbing gym that Saturday.

After I stop looking so hard, we find water.

It's a lesson, yeah, but I'm too thirsty to take it in.

FIVE MONTHS AGO

Hank

AITA for refusing to embrace the narrative that says recovery after injury is the only sensible way forward?

Okay, some summary here. I (18 yo cis white man) am a few months out from a climbing accident that left me with what the doctors call a traumatic brain injury with post-concussive syndrome. Basically, in regular-person-speak, I hit my head really hard and that effs you up. I have some minor memory loss and walking is a pain, but yes, Fred (30-something Japanese-Canadian gay, cis man), the physio exercises do help. I'm working on balance and staying away from screens—I know, I know. I see the irony. We all have a tragic flaw!

So, onward to the point. Everyone says it, that the only way to come back from an injury is to recover. Completely.

I mean everyone. My mom (42 yo white cis woman) talks about *getting back to normal*. My sister (17 yo Native cis woman) won't stop asking me *How are you?* like the only answer she'll accept is *Better than before!* Our dad—who isn't my bio dad, but is my dad in all the ways that count—(55 yo old Native cis man) is weirdly obsessed with telling me what *progress* he sees in my recovery. Even the staff at the rehab hospital, even good old Fred, who otherwise is a cool guy, they push the recovery narrative, as if recovery means returning to where I was before.

That's fucked up, right?

The story says I have to recover.

But you don't overcome a chipped tooth. Even if the surface damage gets repaired, you still live with a tooth that was chipped, will always be chipped.

Insisting on repair, on fixing me when I'm not broken, just changed, that's violent, right? Am I in the wrong for wanting to tell this to all the people in my life? For wanting to yell it from some mountaintop, that is, when I can climb a mountain without losing my fucking balance?

[OpinionatedAardvark]: Society is incredibly ableist. It's messed up how I bet you didn't notice this until your accident? Not to take away from your point. Really, your point is excellent.

    [Hank-Is-Back]: Wouldn't it be great if a guy didn't have to fall 30 feet and hit his head really hard to see what's what?

        [OpinionatedAardvark]: Long live the revolution!

[Hank-Is-Back]: Did I just join a revolution?

[OpinionatedAardvark]: Yes, sorry. Your membership card is in the mail.

[NotFred03567]: I'm going to stop doing this. Shit, I'm the asshole.

[Hank-Is-Back]: Can I get this on a t-shirt? In yellow please? But a nice yellow. None of those muddy or banana yellows for my apology t-shirt.

MILE 130

Molly

The trail is a mild sandy consistency now. I sink down into it, my pack still secured on my shoulders, and drink the stale yellow water we found in an honest-to-god horse trough affixed with a large *NOT POTABLE* sign. But we have a top-of-the-line filtering system for exactly this reason. We've been on the trail only a week and already my absolutely everything hurts. From the low-key constant headache I think must be like the one Hank can't shake to my toes.

Especially my toes.

I thought we'd trained enough, even with the interruption, those weeks where I did nothing but make promises I couldn't keep and later, in the rehab hospital, where I sat in a different chair, hoping Hank would remember. Not just the accident. If he fucked up or if Tray did. No, I wanted my brother to remember everything about us. To call me Molly-moo or Guacamolly or even Mollycakes. I blew off everything, class, shifts at MEC. For a month and a half at most.

And that tanked my bio grade.

Though I stopped only a mile ago to do the same thing, I need to relieve the pressure. I unlace my boots with swollen fingers. Before today I didn't think toenails could hurt. Before today I've never been freaking homesick in my life. Things are beautiful out this way, but these aren't the trees I know, towering in my backyard, or the land I love, the walking paths along the banks of the North Saskatchewan River.

Tray ambles up behind me. "You okay?"

He's taken that spot on the trail. It means I hear him singing almost all the time, but he probably can't hear when my thoughts get too big and I speak them out loud.

"You know I'm getting a little tired of that question."

Tray only laughs.

I shake out my ripe hot-pink merino-wool hiking socks. I'll wash them tonight. I might sink my whole self in a creek.

If there's enough water.

He's staring, so I add, "I'm good."

Sweat rolls down my back. It's hot, too hot to rest for long without any shade. But last night was cold. The part of me that doesn't want to offer Tray any bones fights the part of me that would have frozen to death without his body heat. In the end, living in order to suffer later wins.

The boy throws off warmth. His body temp must run a few degrees hotter than mine. It's interesting. In a science way.

"You sure?"

"Very."

His give-a-care toughens me up. Even though my mom doesn't abide by *boys don't cry*—she believes it's harmful to the production of happy, emotionally healthy men. But that doesn't mean she hasn't always made it clear to me that I have to be strong enough to play with the boys.

Tray crouches, places a hand on my shoulder for the briefest second. "When we pitch camp, you can eat dinner with your feet in the water."

"You not worried we're going to die of dehydration anymore? Or have you moved on to thinking about death by dysentery?"

We definitely purified the horse trough water, but even science can't filter out the smallest most hurtful things.

"You need it." Tray shrugs. "So the water will be there."

I soften. "That thought will get me through this day."

"You're welcome," Tray says with a laugh.

I replace my socks, pretending they don't stink. Pretending I don't hurt worse than I ever have. The only good thing about my toes throbbing is other aches dim. My shoulders have been upset for days. My left hip, sore from side-sleeping on hard ground, all my extra padding there doing nothing to help.

There are tracks in this small clearing. Impressions in the dirt. I don't know enough to know if they're mountain lion or a large dog, but no part of me wants to fuck around and find out.

Clouds blanket the stars, so it's full dark. I wake cold, covered in sweat, my sleeping bag zipped to my chin. When we reached camp, while my feet screamed bloody murder, I half-heartedly ate what Tray cooked, more rice, beans, and rehydrated moose meat, our fresh veg gone now, by slathering the mess in hot sauce. My jumbo-size bottle is a luxury item, worth every extra gram.

Now dinner isn't sitting well. Tray is still the warmest thing. I struggle to the main zipper before he wakes.

"What's wrong?" he asks, and in the dark, out here, for a second I think he's asking me what's wrong between us.

Only for a horrid second.

"I need to pee."

He rubs at his eyes, exhales loudly. "Want me to come with?"

"In your dreams."

He turns over again, but I hear the smile in his voice: "Holler if you're being eaten by a family of bears."

"What's with you lately? It's bears this and freaking bears that." I snort, the reverb tightening my abdomen. Out of all my aches, my stomach protests loudest. I shove my feet into my camp sandals before he can reply, like I don't even care.

Because I don't, right?

Standing, I feel everything all at once and wish the clouds away so I can ground myself under familiar stars. The ones I memorized a long time ago from stacks of library books my mom, who wanted to feed my growing brain, trekked home on the bus. It's been with me a long time, this quiet voice, these specific words: *memorization isn't enough.* Maybe I'm not doctor material. That could be what the gods want me to learn. And if it's true and this is fated the way things are in stories, it won't matter what I do out here or back home, I'll only disappoint my parents. And I know how that hurts. It's on my dad's face every year I choose science camp over Back to Batoche, the annual gathering of Métis people across the prairies; the way he can't help feeling sad that I'm not interested in how a fiddle makes its song. It's my mom telling me how as a doctor I'll be able to effect change, to fight for abortion access, for trauma-informed medical care for trans people.

Struggling to pee in the middle of nowhere, my thighs scream that they can't hold this awkward squat. With a hand on the ground, I steady myself. Then I speak out loud, "No big deal, eh."

I know all you gods are listening.

Chew on that.

When I wake next, Tray's outside, braiding his hair like he does every morning. I stumble into the light, my body unwieldy, muscles uncoordinated. It's like I'm high-altitude loopy, cells starved for oxygen. But we won't be high like that for weeks. And we'll acclimatize because we planned it out. *See, we'll stop here for the night,* Hank said during one of our sessions crowded around the big map, only six days before his accident.

Dinner is still rolling, my abdomen hard, achy. I drank the rest of my secondary water supply before going back to sleep. I desperately need to pee again.

The stickiness between my thighs doesn't register at first.

With one look at my blood-stained wool pants, the ones that function as daywear and sleepwear all in one, Tray pushes off the rock where he's been sitting. He guides me over like I'm injured.

And I sort of am.

I'm pretty certain I'm going to lose a toe.

"Do you want water to clean up?" he asks. "Or breakfast first?"

I shake my head. "Big no to food."

"That bad?"

I can't lie. "Yes."

"Let's take a zero day, yeah?"

It's all I want, but I'm no good at giving in, at giving up. "I'll be ready to rock and roll in fifteen."

Tray ignores my absolute false bravado. "Where are your supplies?"

"Left side of my pack, with the first-aid kit."

I talked to my family doctor about birth control options that would stop my period for the trip. He listed side effects in an almost-bored tone, and then he stared at me for a minute like he wasn't sure he wanted to say any more before he told me there were increased risks of blood clotting in overweight and obese patients. I left without a prescription.

Tray delivers the case holding my menstrual cup and Kula Cloth as well as my second pair of merino-wool pants and our communal TP.

I nod at him. It's a kind of thank-you.

"Strip. I'll clean those for you."

"Not happening."

He stares right at me. "Don't fight me on this. Save your energy for tougher things."

He hasn't looked right at me in months.

Or I haven't let him.

Here, I'm too tired, too hurt to argue. I slip out of my pants and my dry-fast hiker undies, nodding again. I limp toward our backwoods latrine, pulling my too-big Electric Pow Wow hoodie all the way down until it hangs mid-thigh. That's one thing I'll say for my first and second kisses. They looked right at me, and I looked right back at them, my eyes open the entire time.

This hoodie, it used to belong to Tray.

Used to be a thing my brother teased me about, all covert like he didn't want anyone else to know. After everything that's happened . . . I hate myself for bringing it along, for sleeping in it like it's comfort when something technical would keep me warmer, take up less real estate in my pack. I'll dump the thing in the first hiker box we find, you hear me. I'll do it. As long as I can trade for something else.

By the tiny, barely trickling stream, Tray's singing again. Because Tray's always singing. Unless he's in conversation, and then he's there 100 percent. This boy listens so well. And because Tray is a great listener, it's been rage-inducing that he didn't listen, not one bit, when I told him everything. How I said *I know it was an accident but it still damages me that you damaged my brother.* The hurt doesn't care it was an accident, hurts more that something so bad can happen *on accident*, like the universe isn't run by a set of predictable principles. Like science is lying to me.

This is a promise: I won't ever touch rye again.

Today's song isn't familiar. Not a pop anthem, which are this boy's go-tos. Not even "Don't Stop Believin'," Tray's favorite, even though it's too epic, too cheesy, way too '80s sincere to qualify as good music.

He's singing about a girl. Her sharp tongue, her laugh gone missing the way the bison were eliminated from the plains, violently and with intention. *Sharp girl can't outrun / Even a sharp girl can't outrun what's coming.*

It's haunting.

Upsetting.

But I hang on his words, on the melody. My heart wants to listen, like I could forget, like I could heal, if I let the music balm me, hold me, and—

A while later, I return to the clearing, limping worse, wearing a hoodie I can't think of as anything but his. "Knock. That. Off."

"Are you going back to sleep?" he asks with the same degree of intention.

"If you don't sing a single note for the rest of the freaking day."

Impossible. He'll never manage it. And I'll push forward, keep walking somehow. After all, it's nonnegotiable. We have a plan. My mom expects us to meet our goals, to check in regularly.

"It's a deal," Tray says, and he knows he has me beat. We've been friends long enough for that to be clear as crystal, strong as bone.

My pants and underwear hang, drying in the early morning sunshine, between two skinny trees on our utility rope. I should thank him. But that will leave me too exposed and like a frayed nerve, I already hurt in impossible ways. So thanks but no thanks, sorry not very sorry at all.

"Don't think that doing the wash makes you a feminist or something," I say weakly, and turn, struggling toward the tent. This would be more badass if I could storm. If after behaving badly, the rush of shame didn't ruin things.

All Tray says is: "You're welcome, Molly-moo."

Though I want to hold on to this, as if holding it will save me, I hate my nickname on his tongue less than I did yesterday. Lying in this hoodie on top of my bright purple-and-red sleeping bag, his green one pulled over me like a blanket, I think the old Tray would have been fine with me deciding I could walk. The old Tray trusted me when I said I could keep going. He was the only person in my life to truly believe I could handle myself. Like everything else, this is different.

Some other thing that's changed.

Eventually, the noise around me quiets and, pain throbbing in sequence with my heartbeat, I become weightless and sleep.

The next morning, I'm finishing a double serving of oatmeal with dried fruits and nuts added in, about to put socks on when Tray comes close, squats down next to me. "Those look bad, Molly."

"No shit, Sherlock."

"Your feet moving around in your boots?"

"I don't think so. Are yours?"

He shakes his head.

There's no good reason for my big toes on both sides to be bruised under the nail beds or for my legs to ache except that I've walked 130 miles in seven days. Every guidebook says it gets real bad sometime in the first two weeks. I'm only hitting that granite wall early.

"Can I tie your laces different?"

"Tray, I worked at the same store you did. I know the tricks."

"Then why haven't you done something about this yet?"

I ask because I need to know: "You're not feeling rough?"

"Not this rough. My feet are prettier than yours. Even without the pink." He brushes a finger against my middle toe. The only one where the polish isn't ruined, where my toe isn't swollen, blackening under the nail bed.

I glare at him.

"I mean, like, yeah, my feet hurt and probably, eventually, I'll lose a toenail or two, that's just what happens on these kinds of hikes," he says, like I didn't read the same blogs as him. "But I'm not also shedding my uterine lining."

I glare louder.

Yes, it's cool that normal bodily things don't freak Tray out, and yes, Tray's a feminist, probably a better one than me. I'm starting to see a pattern, and patterns form strong hypotheses, develop into asking smart questions. Where Tray's good at stories, I am good at hard science. The two exist in separate spheres. There isn't a Venn diagram in sight.

And this, this is basic biology.

"That has exactly what to do with my toes hurting? Are those systems connected or something?"

BIO10 was the first and only science class Tray and I had together. I carried his ass in that room. Me, the girl who skipped right over Grade 9.

"I don't know, Molly-moo." Tray shrugs. "You're the brilliant one when it comes to bodies. You tell me."

I'm saving all my energy for the trail, so I can't berate him for using that nickname yet again. And I hate that it comforts me. That he's not *Mols this* and *Mols that-ing* me. The way Hank does.

"Give me your foot."

"Let me get a sock on first."

"Yeah, yeah."

Once I stuff my poor tortured toes into my crunchy wool socks, the ones I purchased because they had extra padding for intense hikes, I pass my boots to Tray. He pulls the laces out, the same way he would have done for a customer. At MEC, he's re-laced a million pairs of hiking boots. Normally he'd hand the shoe back. Instead, he pulls my leg, gently enough, onto his lap.

And my body registers his heat.

I close my eyes hard. This care, this touch, it's everything. My body tingles in that good, good way. The hurt retreats. I want to run from this small comfort, from my best friend. At the very same time, I miss him. He's right here next to me and I miss him.

That should be impossible.

It's not that we didn't touch, didn't hug or get close climbing and camping. But I've made a point of taking space for myself, after the accident, but especially since the night Tray ignored me. Because even if he doesn't agree with me, he's never ignored me before. That morning I woke surrounded by every pillow in the house, even the decorative ones with the cross-stitched florals my mom keeps in the living room. He was the only other person at home, so I know it was Tray who ensured I was safe that night. Which only makes it worse that he hasn't said a word since.

He washed my things when I was too miserable to do it for myself, but he didn't listen to me when I was hurting.

"There you go," he says.

I push the words out: "Thank you."

Tray shrugs again. "It's not even a thing."

We break down camp. In a few minutes we're ready to go, leave no trace and all. But Tray's got his phone in hand and his pack at his feet. His face slowly blossoms into a smile. That gorgeous dimple comes out to play. I used to love when I said something to

77

draw it out. It was how I knew I was winning, was in first place, held the high score.

"I got service," he says. And then Tray hits me with exactly what I thought I wanted: "Hank changed his mind, yeah. He's flying out to join us."

This should make me happy. Should right wrongs.

Sometimes, in the noise around me, gods of the known universe, I hear you laughing. Right now, it's in the chatter of a hungry squirrel. Tray joins you all, typing on his phone.

He's thrilled.

I'm caught in a trap, like the kind Traylor and his dad use up north. I'm caught, waiting. Anger is freaking easy, yes. And I know I'm being mean, that this isn't sarcasm or speaking plainly, and even though I know it, I can't stop.

"Great," I say eventually. Ignoring my feet, I settle my pack's straps against my bruises and start walking. The greenery is low to the ground, spindly, doesn't offer shade. A crow is tracking me, following us, watching a little too closely to assume it's only curious about how we've gotten here.

Tray's far enough behind, still on his phone because who knows when our service will drop out.

"Forgetting doesn't mean I need to forgive," I say, looking right at the crow. "Now does it?"

And I swear, the freaking bird nods in agreement.

NOW

Hank

Me: Breaking news!!! *disco ball emoji*

Me: Nothing? No answer? Don't drop the disco, buddy!

Me: I mean, you probably don't have service. That's
a better explanation than you leaving your bestie
hanging.

Best Friend *disco ball emoji* *tooth emoji*: Hey! We
have service! Mountaintops are good for that!

Me: So . . . you disrespected the disco? Ouch.

Best Friend *disco ball emoji* *tooth emoji*: Come
down here. Make a guy regret it, yeah.

Me: Actually . . .

Best Friend *disco ball emoji* *tooth emoji*: Don't
joke, Hank.

Me: No joke. Short story instead. Ditched summer
school, rebooked my flight, packed my bags.
Updates once I get to Los Angeles. I'll be seeing
you in a few. Unless I meet a man with perfect teeth
at the airport. Then I might drop out of high school

and become someone's fancy househusband. Goals, am I right?

Best Friend *disco ball emoji* *tooth emoji*: Didn't I already ask you NOT to joke about this . . .

Me: *sends link to flight rebooking* *sends photo of stuffed pack*

Best Friend *disco ball emoji* *tooth emoji*: Bring that tent I left behind, yeah?

Me: What, buddy? Don't want to cuddle puddle with me and Mols?

Best Friend *disco ball emoji* *tooth emoji*: . . .

Me: *skull emoji* *tooth emoji* *toothbrush emoji* *disco ball emoji*

Best Friend *disco ball emoji* *tooth emoji*: *head-desk GIF*

THE CHORUS STAR

The star that makes it obvious you're seeing something whole. The first time your heart notices something larger, grander than you thought possible. Enter the throwback.

Outside of the blues, the accordion is not well regarded in modern music. It's loud, crass. We expect it to behave in certain ways—many of us have relegated the accordion to the past, as if the past isn't central to what's now, to what's to come.

As if everything isn't doing its part. As if music isn't about bringing instruments together, even the ones you think don't belong in symphony. As if song isn't a marriage of unexpected sounds, a constellation.

Yeah, yeah, now you're starting to get it.

Sing on, shine on.

MILE 248

Molly

I've been doing such a freaking good job of forgetting. Food is a neutral topic. So Tray and I, we've talked about cake, yes, but about wild raspberries too. How we hunger for them. Only the moment I see Hank, standing in the doorway of room six at the Starry Skies Motel, in Big Bear, California, his hair freshly buzzed, as if he's trying to hammer something massive, absolutely life-altering home, like an uncontrolled fall from thirty feet, I remember.

How I could taste bleach for weeks after.

The flash of emergency room lights stinging, the fluorescents almost pulsing, and someone, not my brother, screaming, and Tray wrenching his hands, a spot of blood near the collar of his T-shirt like this was only a minor accident. A nosebleed needing cauterization. At worst, a broken bone breaching skin.

Neither the memory nor the pain stops me from dropping my pack on the concrete and following this instinct: to run, dirty, sweaty, properly gross in a beeline toward Hank.

Remembering doesn't mean I miss my brother any less.

My muscles rebel at this attempt at enthusiasm, and I slow even more to jump for a hug. My brother steps back to steady himself, but he catches me. I haven't done this in forever either.

Hank hugs me for a long while.

This is better than before . . . The thought is unwelcome. I tell it to get lost, mind its own freaking business.

I hear laughter.

But it's only Hank.

"Missed you," I say.

"Missed you more," he responds as if this too is a competition. Still holding on, he steps closer to the motel. Hank leans our combined weight against the wall, exhales, wrinkles his nose. "Mols, not to be indelicate, but you . . . um . . . you stink."

There's a beat. We're both unsteady, dizzy, worried the ground will fall out from under us a second time. And then we break, laughing as if we're high on the gas you get at the dentist. I sink down until I'm sitting on the hot concrete. So does Hank. I lean into a potted plant, filled to the brim with plain white daisies, an arm thrown over my head dramatically.

He's right.

Natural deodorant is not keeping up on the trail.

When I glance Tray's way, he's watching us the way he watched that rattlesnake. Like it was the very best thing. He collects my pack, shoulders the extra weight, this new look on his face. Half confusion or half hurt, I can't tell which, and half unexpected joy. "I like how she smells," he says with a shrug, and then he's pausing, lowering both our packs to the earth. He sits in the parking lot, legs crossed, elbows against knees, as if he's made a critical mistake.

Like he's lost the whole freaking hockey game. Worse, a championship. Now a bunch of rabid, fickle fans will tear him limb from limb.

Hank points at Tray like this is the funniest thing he's ever seen and laughs harder than before. With his other hand, my brother pushes me farther into the daisies. "He likes your smell."

My face goes red, burns.

It's the coward's move. I should say something calm, collected, and utterly devastating. But all I'm thinking is how the nasal bone is actually two oblong bones supported by cartilage, not one, like everybody thinks. And that's not devastating at all.

I untangle myself from my brother and the sad flowers before leaving the boys to sort out their own reunion. Now that I have Hank here, the only thing I need, really, truly is new deodorant.

The powerful chemical stuff.

I stay in the shower a long time. Long enough that one of the boys knocks on the bathroom door, cracks it open.

It's Hank. "Want us to wait for you to get pizza or what?"

A small part of me never wants to leave. It's warm, comforting here. My body hardly hurts in the shower. All I say is "Pineapple, please."

"That's not really an answer, is it?" Hank throws his voice back into the main room.

"Course it is, buddy," Tray responds. He gets closer. "Hey, Mermolly, want anything else?"

Too many things. Half of them impossible. "No . . . That's okay, that's freaking enough."

There's a pause.

"Your pack's on the bed when you're ready to leave the ocean again."

The water never goes cold, neither of the boys boots me out for their turn, and I think I fall asleep in the bathtub, knees pulled tight to chest, head bowed under the water's spray, for a few minutes. When I emerge, because no matter how upsetting or awkward your life is, it's not sustainable to live in the shower, there's a pizza box on my bed. Next to it are two full water bottles and a farmers market basket of the best-looking raspberries I've ever seen. They almost glow. There's a note in my brother's horrible handwriting: *We're doing laundry. Yours too, stinky.* Next to the note lies a brand-new thing of men's deodorant. Old Spice. Jumbo-size.

It's obvious which gift is from which boy.

Because this is what you do for your friends. These raspberries are what friendship looks like. Because you can lose a partner, a parent, but this kind of friendship, it's supposed to last. You can kiss a stranger safely, but it's untenable to think of ruining a best friendship, even if it is shaky these days, with kisses.

Wrapped in a towel that barely stays closed, I scarf down the whole pineapple-and-green-olive pizza, recognizing that although I didn't ask for the olives, I wanted their salty goodness. Afterward, I dig into the raspberries. Even clean, full, content enough, when I stop to think about Hank being here, about the next five and a half weeks, about the weeks after that, Tray liking the way I smell, those green olives I didn't ask for but he knew I wanted, the noise filters in. The alarm clock in this room is digital, but it crackles. The shower drips irregularly into the tub. This towel is noise too: *you don't fit, you're too much.*

It's not my fault the world expects girls and women to be smaller. Not to grow, but to shrink. Not to take up space, but to make space for others. To look pretty, fall silent, above all, be small.

My skin heats like I'm suffering a sunburn.

I drop the towel, search for clothing.

But since the boys are doing the wash, there's nothing in my pack except my town dress. It's lightweight cotton with cap sleeves, a clearly defined waist. The skirt skims my hips, the bodice hugs my chest, my too-wide shoulders.

I know what you're thinking. It's pink, right?

No. This dress is an ugly yellow-green. Found on sale because it washes most people out, so even normally hard to find sizes like mine were still on the rack by the time we were cutting steep discounts at MEC.

The air is heavy with humidity and something else, so I throw open the door. Down the way, there are picnic tables set up with views of the lake, the mountains around us, where if it were high season, just a month ago, the field behind the motel would be filled with tents for PCT hikers who wanted town conveniences but couldn't afford a room.

The boys can manage this, but my money needs to stretch further. Through Oregon and Washington State and to the border.

Hank's and Tray's voices are gentle.

That's enough for me to dial it all down. With the motel room door open, listening to the boys talk without hearing their words, I fall asleep on top of the covers. It's all a blend of fresh air, sweet comfort, voices I know, voices I've loved, and nothing more.

I wake once, in the middle of the night. Now I'm under the blankets. The alarm clock glows red, brightening the room too much.

I can't ignore it any longer.

These two hundred and forty miles have changed me. Already. I would have never noticed this before. Light that shouldn't be, that interrupts nature. The heaviness of interior walls. A carpet that holds too much biology.

In the other bed, the boys are cuddled together.

Some things are unclear. This isn't.

For twenty minutes, I think about how now that I'm in a bed, a decent one at that, all I really want is to be back on the ground in our tent next to a body that runs hotter than mine.

Anger is too easy.

Somewhere, maybe right outside this motel room door, spirits, gods, and other night creatures have sent their proxies to laugh at me.

At Onyx Summit, off Highway 38, we wave goodbye to our ride with thanks. They saved us a bunch of bonus miles hiking back to the trailhead. And since it's Saturday in the real world that means day hikers.

And that equals distraction.

A mom is dragging her two boys out of a red Jeep. She spots our filled-to-bursting packs and smiles. "Through-hikers?"

Hank's half-asleep still. Tray's adjusting his load, unhappy with how the weight is balanced.

"We are," I say, and smile back.

"I did the PCT with my college boyfriend when I was about your age. We made out all along this trail." The woman laughs. "A lifetime ago, I was called Sunshine out here."

I'm not afraid to say this is what I need. Because being angry at my brother feels wrong and throwing it Tray's way isn't right. Not after the raspberries. The green olives. All that care. Only, the anger needs to go somewhere. Holding it inside me would be disastrous, like a musician or a hockey player breaking every bone in their talented hands. So each time we come across day hikers, I'm saying hi and asking their story. For a moment I forget that you all can get to me anywhere. That you'll let me think I'm winning.

For a little while.

Sunshine's kids are surly and, respectfully, it's hilarious. The younger one claims there aren't even any good *Pokémon Go* caches, as if that's the only reason he came along. Eventually, Tray warms them up. They talk about K-pop and which are the best pocket monster evolutions until the family reaches their turnaround point.

"I wish you loads of trail magic," Sunshine says, passing me a bag of hard candies. "It's obvious my kids don't get it. The draw."

We're looking at the sparse but tall trees in this dry, grassy meadow. The way this place feels so far from all the noise.

"They seem more into anime right now."

Her eyes crinkle. "God, that boyfriend? We broke up a week after we made it to Canada. And I love my partner. I really do. But I was with the right person to do this. Like I couldn't have done it with anyone else, certainly not with my partner, who is happier in a greenhouse than in unmitigated nature. This hike, it was amazing. And it was . . . Well, some days I was certain I wouldn't make it another step. You understand."

It's not a question.

I nod because I'm pretty sure if I'd been alone the day everything hit me at once, I'd have given up and embraced easy. Across the whole rest of my life. *Easy as pie, easy as all that, easy-peasy,* a litany of my mom's sayings. The easiest thing, it's calling my parents, coming clean about how I only applied to one school, and then, when the acceptance came, I let the deadline to respond pass, how I'm ignoring follow-up emails from admissions. Maybe I come clean about how their months of thinking, obsessing over Hank let me break out. But no, the easiest thing is to follow my mom's plan. To respond to the latest email from U of Calgary and say, yes, I accept.

To think, back in Edmonton, when Hank changed his mind, I wanted to spend this summer alone.

"Know what helped?" Sunshine asks. "On those total shit days."

The younger boy chimes in: "Mom said shit!"

The older one laughs. So does Tray.

"No idea," I answer.

Days like that are ahead of us, I know. The last time my life went to the bears, my brother, me, and even Tray, we almost didn't make it to the other side.

She's deadpan, ignoring the way her children get a kick out of their mom cursing: "Sugar. Candy. Chocolate bars."

89

I laugh, unsteadied, realizing I haven't thanked her. So I do.

"Try it," she says, and waves goodbye. As the family branches off, they start singing a K-pop hit, all off-key, and I have a feeling that Sunshine's boys will remember this, will fall in love with the trail too, in their own ways.

So close to a tourist hot spot, in this section the PCT signs are easy to follow, not overweathered or knocked down or straight-up missing like they have been elsewhere. My legs are sore, heavy and tight, but my toes are happy. Switching the lacing on my boots really did help.

We're alone again. My brother is too quiet, leaning hard onto his hiking pole, the one that's the twin of mine. Tray's still too loud. *Leave her, Johnny, leave her / Oh, leave her, Johnny, leave her / For the voyage is long and the winds don't blow . . .*

It's not what I expected. How I thought our summer would go. Before or after the fall. I crunch on hard candies and wish for more short-term fixes to a long-term problem. I've got nothing else. I send an unspoken thank-you into the ether.

Maybe I've turned the gods to my side. Maybe you understand now.

We're above Cougar Creek Trail, another one of the options for getting down on foot to Big Bear, when we meet the hilarious kids dragging their parents along for the day. They're full up on energy, throw out facts on the trail like they've been excited about this trip for weeks. We're vibing until the dad says that he's a doctor and he'd be better off in his office.

"I'm wasted here," he says. "I could get injured here."

It crushes his kids, the general mood.

No one knows what to say, so we all fall silent. We watch chipmunks playing in the boulders.

"That's how I pay for these things," the dad continues when the silence becomes too much, as if his kids aren't wearing basic running shoes and worn sport shorts, carrying their sticker-clad water bottles in their hands. There's no fancy gear anywhere in sight but on me, my brother, and Tray.

I'm sure Hank doesn't mean to launch me under the bus. I cling to that even as he says, "Mols is going to be a doctor."

And somehow, that frees the kids and mother to hang with the boys.

While I'm stuck with the dad.

Woo-hoo.

Suddenly he's more comfortable out in the woods. "So what specialty are you planning? I'm a neurosurgeon."

Even if I'm not sure a thing I'll say in this conversation is true any longer, I can keep the peace. Give these kids one freaking afternoon without their dad's BS. Because we all know, this is what he's like all the time. And though my parents being super focused on Hank happened for the worst reason, it was also breathing space I desperately needed.

"Family practice," I offer.

We climb a particularly tough hill.

"You seem like a smart girl," he says, wheezing, at the top. "Can't you do better?"

As if taking care of people when they have a cold or need vaccines isn't good enough. As if figuring out what's causing a working parent's fatigue or how to help someone with high blood pressure or even assisting a family in eating well on a limited budget isn't critical to everything else.

Health isn't a hierarchy.

It's holistic.

I bet that word spikes this dude's freaking blood pressure.

I've been trying not to be rude, but also, I don't care enough not to tell this stranger straight up what I think. I haven't felt this free in months. "Yeah, people need a neurosurgeon when they need their brains cut into . . ." I pause, thinking of the scars, the ones you can still see because of how short my brother keeps his hair. Today everything's hidden under his green-and-white Saskatchewan Roughriders ball cap. "But people need a family doctor all the time. You know, because the brain is only one part of the body."

The man's laugh isn't nice. His eyes get hard. "General practice is a better fit for a woman anyhow, even a smart one. Since you'll want children and there's a reason my wife stays at the house, and that reason, it's those kids. I can't be picking them up because they have a runny nose and need to see the GP when I'm scheduled to save a man's life in the OR."

The subtext is barely buried. *When I, important man, am needed for more important things.*

I wish Hank or even Tray were listening. But they're ahead, pointing out something in the trees.

"Cool!" the girl says, and jumps up and down.

"It's so pretty." This from the boy, who is more understated. Calmer.

It would be exactly like Tray to show some preteens a sleeping snake like it's the best possible thing and not a total nightmare. He's good with kids. Always in high demand at Métis cultural events and on the ice when he makes it out to free skate. Sort of like a rock star who can do a jig while expertly handling a puck. Tray makes his skills seem impressive but reachable. Something I've never managed.

We come to a standstill a few feet away from the man's family. He's smirking like he thinks he's won an argument against a seventeen-year-old and it's fulfilling or some such. He has excellent teeth. It fits the tan, his golf course clothes, that better-than attitude.

"You don't sound like you like your life that much," I say, and start walking faster now because I don't want to spend any more of my day with this person.

I'd rather hang with Hank, even if he's off, and Tray, even if he's . . .

Distracted from finishing my thought, I catch sight of the hummingbird. Tiny and green and purple, its wings move too rapidly for the human eye to properly understand. It really is pretty. I say so, loudly, and the kids shine.

The dad, he shuts up.

Maybe I won. Maybe there's no winning.

Later, when we stop for a quick lunch in the shade, the dad forces his family to turn back. He checks his phone three times. "Our Uber is scheduled for two o'clock, and we can't be late."

I'm happy to see him go.

And I'm sure I never want to be around someone like that again. I bet med school is full of cis dudes who think family practice is lesser, that some of us aren't cut out for the job, at least not their specialty. The surgery-over-everything-else crowd. The ones who think people like me only get in to meet some diversity quota.

The fat, probably queer Métis chick.

I wouldn't make it through med school without cracking, forming a fist, and doing what I wanted to do to Emma C. at graduation: discover if there's enough force inside me to break a nose.

That's generally frowned upon.

Even now, it simmers inside me. That easy anger. I don't know what to do with all this tension. Before, I would have ignored that man and his unwelcome opinions. Before, I would have let it go, only shared my thoughts, sharp as they might be, with Hank and Tray.

Now, for some reason, I can't ignore a thing.

Hours after that man goes back to his important life in Ohio, which, frankly, sounds to me like a made-up place where storybook characters and villains moonlighting as neurosurgeons live, we reach our stopping point for the night. A crew of hikers are set up near the water source. There are five of them. All young men. Two are hoisted into hammocks strung between knobby pines, all the lower branches snapped off. The hikers drink beers they carted in. All that liquid, it's extra weight. Especially on this part of the PCT, where water is hardest to come by. Where only a week ago, it seemed like we might not find water at all.

One of them announces the obvious: "Guuuuuys, we have guests!"

He's the dramatic friend. I can already tell.

Even though Hank's the dramatic friend in our group, my

brother stares at me with a serious glower. "Want to keep hiking? There's another decent place a few miles along."

That's our backup plan. In case of emergency and this isn't one.

"She's a good stopping point," the dark-haired hiker says, a beer in one hand, a protein bar in the other. By his bare feet, discarded wrappers litter the ground. "There's a creek back that way with the wet stuff in it and everything."

It's sarcasm, a language I understand.

While this clearing stinks of weed, it has water and plenty of space for both groups.

"This is fine," I say. Because it is.

We haven't had to share a campsite yet. Even with the herd a month ahead and getting farther after every unplanned zero day or town stop we make, some people will be doing section hikes. Going for days, even a month or two on end, but not finishing the PCT this season. Technically, that's what my brother and Tray think we're doing.

Tray walks a few feet back toward the trail and calls me over with a nod. "You sure, Molly-moo?"

That name. Not all pain is equal. It's like the bruises on my hips, the ones I keep gently pressing against at night to remind myself that some hurt can be good for you. That muscle fibers tear before they get stronger.

"Yes. Let's set up. I'm beyond ready for food."

While we get our tents together, the other guys are doing what guys do. Getting loud. Roughhousing. Making sure that we know they're here.

Even far from Edmonton, I can't escape those people. The girl who said unkind things becomes a grown man who tells me even though I'm smart, I'm not enough. And we're sharing camp with men who have the same energy as Shawn E., who hollered his name throughout our grad ceremony.

The noise, it crawls up my spine, carving an itchy trail.

But we have dinner to whip up before I can crash. We've taken a break from rice and beans, not that Tray or I talked about it. Some things you simply understand on a hike like this. At least that's what I'm telling myself. It's not that Tray knows me well enough, cares enough to pay attention. Tonight, we're having ramen with fried eggs. As a surprise, Tray's been carrying a full dozen.

We get two each, today and tomorrow.

I don't say thank you, but I think it.

Give me some credit.

Once we've turned the camp stove off, the guys invite us to their fire. "Make room, make room, you heathens," the dramatic one says.

When we were in town, the no-burn signs were everywhere. If it's not directly for cooking and, even then, you're supposed to use a stove whenever possible. Maybe these guys haven't been off the trail lately. Maybe they don't know.

I sit next to Hank, inhaling my dinner, my giant bottle of hot sauce resting against my thigh so I can top off as needed.

"This is Doublecross." The dramatic one points to a bro in a San Diego State sweatshirt. "That's Lucky Strike." He points at the dark-haired one.

Russ is next. He's the tallest of the bunch and the only

non-white guy. He gives Tray and me the chin-up nod, leaving my brother out.

I guess he can tell. Tray's braids are a giveaway, and when I caught sight of myself in the mirror at the motel, I'd tanned up enough that mixed with my brown hair and the #MMIWG2S patch on my pack, it's not too much of a guess to assume I could be bicultural. Both white and not.

Joey is shortest, pleasantly rounded through his chest and stomach. He raises his beer at us, miming cheers.

"And I'm Fresno. Who might you be, beautiful?"

I snort and finish my second egg, wishing for more. "Molly. That's Hank, my brother from the exact same mother. And on the end there, that's Traylor. He's . . . a friend," I say, finishing weakly.

The guys mishear Tray's name, and I swallow a laugh.

"Oh, no, no no. That won't do," Joey starts off with a grin. "Trailer gets a pass. Hank is fine. It's not anything special, but not everyone can have an absolute baller of a trail name. But you, girlie, that won't do."

"What are you thinking, Joe?" Fresno asks, like I'm not even here.

"Three words: Hot Fucking Sauce."

The guys laugh, even Hank. The only person not joining in is Tray.

I like how she smells.

The way he said it and then wished he hadn't.

"She's got solid nicknames already," Tray says, crossing his arms in the most defensive position ever. But it was something we were excited about back in the day. Our trail names. "And that's just on the nose, right? Just because she—"

Doublecross crushes his empty beer can, tosses it with the rest of his collected garbage. "Yeah, man, but what does girlie think?"

"Her name is Molly," Tray says.

I could do without the way it feels like these guys are littering, even though I'm sure they'll gather their trash before they go to bed, and Tray is right about one thing: if this guy calls me *girlie* one more time, I might do some damage. But the trail name, it works for me. It's not *Mols* and it's not *Molly-moo*, both of which sting differently. All I say is "I like it."

Traylor shuts ups.

And Hot Sauce, f-bomb optional, sticks. Scribbled in trail registers, included in introductions when we meet with day hikers, the name stays all the way to the very end.

Soon after, it's hiker midnight, you know, nine o'clock, and we head to bed. Tray's grumpy. I'm not sure if it's because he's finally getting worn down by the miles or because he hoped I'd let him give me a trail name. After all, he's responsible for more than half of the nicknames I've found myself answering to over the years, the ones nobody but him uses anymore.

Like the love ran out when Hank got hurt.

Sleep is a long time coming. In the boring green tent my brother brought along, Tray tosses about.

The other guys, they stay up drinking, roughhousing like this is just another night in their world. Like the stars, nights in these wild places aren't the very best thing. Like we don't have to walk twenty and a half miles tomorrow.

MILE 272

Traylor

Yesterday grits in the space behind my eyes. I haven't slept enough to be happy I'm awake, yeah. But I want to vacate this campsite before our neighbors drag their hungover selves from bed. These are not the people we want to be spending too much time with. Already, they've run out the clock in my books.

When I subtract the drinking, and the smoke, it's a feeling. Nothing more.

But the feeling's a bad one.

While I wait for Molly and Hank to wake, I eat and I eat. Underneath everything these days there's a hunger. I know a lot of stories about hunger. It's never good when things get so bad someone needs to tell a story about it.

So I chew slowly.

It's not jealousy, not about Molly's trail name at the core of it. This is that mood, the one you get when you're out on the land. When you know it's time to go home from the hunt empty-handed. It's the two seconds of dread before your best friend's accident, those moments not long enough to do anything but grab firm the rope that should in combination with the belay device hold his weight, but instead runs fast through your fingers.

Tore right through calluses.

I picked nylon fiber from my skin for weeks.

This morning, I'm stuck in those two seconds. I tell myself that's why the music won't come. Not the way it usually does. There's something, a melody. It's less than half-formed. The sour notes are the only clear thing.

I fill our water stores, braid my hair. Gather empties and protein bar wrappers, the remains of the cigarettes these guys were smoking once the weed ran dry from around the campsite. Without the music to tether me, I'm off-balance. Like Hank. While I stretch overtired muscles, I tell myself today is for listening, not for making sounds. I'm hanging the accordion, the fiddle, and the spoons on a shelf in the kitchen.

But this keeps sneaking through. It's the kind of hit you feel through the pads, the kind that jars your teeth, your joints, your bone marrow. A lyric, a mantra: *My sharp girl's been kissing someone. Someone not me.*

I find a good sitting rock and sit.

I watch the sun come over the trees, the day greeting the land, the way the colors move from muted shades to brightened greens, browns, and silvers.

Molly wakes before Hank.

The others roll out of their racks before Hank.

He's never been one to laze about. But while Molly and I have hundreds of these gorgeous, desiccated desert miles under our treads, yesterday was Hank-the-Tank's first day. And in September, he was in the hospital with swelling, bleeding in his brain.

The music's making a fuzzy point with its shadow melody, its refusal to offer me anything but tonal ghosts. That Hank's here at all is beyond what we hoped. There was a reason we never canceled this trip outright, why we kept planning, bought three very refundable plane tickets. He needed this.

And Molly needed this.

And yeah, I did as well.

Before I get too anxious over the miles we need to cover and the cooler early hours getting away from us, Hank's emerging from the tent, his toothbrush shoved in his mouth. "Are we set, or what?"

"Let's hit the road!" the loudmouth from the other group says. His buddies rally enough to cheer.

That's how we end up hiking with my bad feeling.

For the first hour, we're all quiet, even the loudmouth, working our way through the San Bernardino Mountains. At the bottom of the switchback we're tackling, my calves burn. Molly strips down to a hot-pink tank top now that it's sweltering and rolls her merino-wool joggers to her knees. The top half of her hair is ponytailed high, that red bandanna tied up around the rest. These days I'm watching her in a new way and asking a question I can never ask: *Who?* Another: *Why?* Because once I ask those questions, what would stop me from asking: *Why not me?*

All this, it's fodder for a song I'll never perform.

Suddenly, everywhere I look around me, huge mounds of pine cones take up space. Fallen and settled in crevices and low points on the mountain. Along the trail, they're gathered where hikers who came before us booted them out of the way.

I spot cones from sugar pines and the Coulter pine's spiky ones. Our guidebook says its seeds look like sharpened bear claws, and I have to agree. They've got deadly vibes. But they're beautiful too.

It isn't fair not to acknowledge both sides.

I want to share this with Molly—no, I need to, like we've shared almost everything else since I moved to Edmonton. But she's hanging ahead with Joe, the short guy with the glasses.

They're hiking and talking and Molly's laughing. The way she did before her brother's accident. If she offers Joe her sharpness too, I won't be all right.

Even if I'm not okay with her now, that doesn't matter.

She's my pine cone.

I laugh under my breath, bitter. There won't be any working that into a song, not even one I'll never sing because it's too personal, too much exposure.

Hank catches up from the back end of our not-so-merry band, his hiking pole strap secured around his wrist, the sunrise beadwork gradient catching the light as he uses it to steady himself. "Think that guy likes the way my sister smells?"

Hank elbows me.

I elbow him back, continue hiking. Just because he can read my mind doesn't mean I need to let him play me. I'm not a guitar string he can pick at. "Thanks to you, buddy," I say slowly, "she smells like a man now. Maybe that guy's into dudes. You should go and find out."

Hank snorts. "Mighty binary of you, buddy. Why can't anyone, gender set far aside for this conversation, decide they like the classic power scent that only Old Spice provides?"

"Power scent?"

"Don't act like you don't know what's what."

Hank's right. I ignore him anyhow.

"Do you still think my sister smells good? Even covered in *manly* deodorant."

I don't think, just answer: "Yeah, affirmative."

"Just checking. And you're right," he adds. "Joey's gay. Super gay. Even has real nice incisors."

"That's, like, your number one."

"Teeth are my weakness." Hank sighs, exhaling until his lungs are empty. Then inhales swiftly the way cartoon characters do before they clasp their chest, their eyes turning to beating hearts. "Dr. Bell really fucked me up. Too bad the guy was three decades older. We would have never worked out."

"You were what, eleven?" I ask.

"Eleven and a half. Thank you very much for remembering my important life events with precision." Hank smirks at me.

I laugh and I'm lighter.

Would have missed Hank if I'd chosen hockey.

I never once told my therapist about quitting, about deciding that I wanted to be in my friends' lives, not give up on what could be ours, on our future, because I was always on the ice. To be great at hockey it has to become everything.

My coaches tried talking me out of it. *This is your one chance to play at the highest level. If you stop now, you'll never get back to this* point. *Don't throw that away.*

My mom rolled her eyes and said, *You certain, Tray? Really certain?*

When I nodded, she asked me if I was doing this for the right reasons. *Family, yeah.* She might still bring it up when my uncles come to town for Easter, but she didn't try to stop me.

My dad, he looked out at the land, pointed off toward the farthest trapline. *We have to go up there tomorrow, eh? No more putting it off.*

When I told Hank, he said: *Thank you for placing your teeth first, for once in your life, buddy. Do you know exactly how many falsies the average professional hockey player has in their mouth? Respectfully, too many.*

And Molly, who I knew would be happy for me, she jumped up and down, her T-shirt climbing, revealing a patch of skin above her high-waisted tights. She pretended to brush something like lint off her shoulder. *So, I guess you're free next weekend, then? You know, climbing ice is way cooler than skating on it. Let's see if that guide is still available.*

Oh yeah? You're that happy? I smiled because this, this was why I quit. For this moment. For all the moments that would follow with my friends.

The voices that have stayed clearest, they belong to the Norris-Norquay siblings. The way Molly jumped in the air, didn't miss a beat dragging me into her adventures. The way Hank was saying *yes, thank you, I'm happy for you* in his code. Because I've missed this, having them both close. Talking to my best friend. Even if half the time Hank's talking about teeth.

"Why haven't you . . . said anything, yeah. About Molly."

Hank scratches his head, dislodging his ball cap. He hasn't tried to drag me to a Roughriders' game in too long.

"I, ugh, forgot. Until you awkwardly outed yourself at the motel like a simp. Then it rushed back. Your not-so-little crushy-crush on my baby sister."

Makes sense. Hank has had memory issues. It's the reason he told me he was backing out. He didn't trust himself. Not with the physical stuff. That was getting better and better. The hiking pole and making sure to sleep a solid eight a night would help with lingering balance issues. No, Hank-the-Tank worried he wasn't up to this hike mentally. Like in the aftermath of the accident he'd forgotten something critical.

I told him it was BS. Not to try to change his mind. But because I needed him to know I trusted him, even if he didn't trust himself yet.

"You don't need to say. But why'd you change your mind?" I ask. "What happened to summer school?"

"*This* is my summer school, buddy." Hank looks at me like I've been hit in the head with the puck one too many times. "If I have to do another semester anyhow, why not go all out?"

I let it pass. He's allowed to keep things close to the chest. And in the end, what we're doing out here is putting one foot in front of the other, on repeat. It's only daunting if you think further than one step ahead.

Hank stops in the middle of the trail, forcing me to stop too. "Have you told her yet? Has she crushed your soft heart like a Cheerio under her hot-pink hiking boot? That why she's all awkward around you? Why she's hanging with Joey of the shapely incisors? Because something's up with that girl."

I thought I'd be Molly's first kiss, that music was my home, that I chose to make music that home, that I was protected from missing Edmonton because I had Molly with me, and now I'm starting to wish for the too-early Saturday-morning bus rides to MEC for opening shift. Hank's hair is shagged out, so this moment I'm homesick for, it happens before the accident.

Before Molly's first kiss too, I bet.

I don't get a chance to answer Hank. To say, that for my pine cone and me, it's complicated.

Ahead, a few voices yell out. Then Molly does.

We take the rest of the hill at a run.

At the top of the rise, Molly is on her knees, strapped into her pack, leaning over a cliff. There are pine cones all around her, sharp and beautiful. I wish for the music because I don't want to forget the way she looks, surrounded by all this. That's what I notice first, what I cling to.

Instead of what's happening.

"Fuck, fuck," one of the guys says. He vomits into the tree line. It reeks of alcohol.

"Molly?" I manage.

"Joe fell. Slipped," one of the others answers. This one, he sits on the pine-needle-encrusted ground, puts his head in his hands. "And I have a bloody fucking migraine already. I didn't need this."

Molly shifts, presses herself flat in order to lean out farther. "He hit his shoulder, his neck. Maybe his head," she says. "When he fell."

Next to me, Hank freezes, then backs as far from the edge as he can until he crushes himself against sap-sticky bark. Starts breathing hard.

"What do you need, Molly?" I get closer, lean over the cliff.

It's not too far down, which is all sorts of luck. Joe is moaning, eyes closed, glasses askew. I can't see bone, anything to suggest a critical injury. But that doesn't mean a thing.

And even though it's nothing like what happened to Hank, I'm caught in a flashback.

Chalk, I taste chalk.

My ears hollow out as if I'm underwater. It's seconds, maybe four dreadful beats, but I must miss something.

Molly's pissed. Her pack is a few feet away from the drop-off now. She's got our all-purpose rope unraveled. "Jesus fucking Christ," she says. "You people are useless."

She's yelling at the other guys, at her brother too, maybe even my way. But it knocks me out of whatever that was. We coordinate, secure the rope, slip down the cliff side, scurrying against prickly brush, until we stop at a massive old pine. It grows out of the mountainside diagonally. It's what braced Joe from falling farther.

There are pine cones everywhere.

"Well, that stung a bit," Joe says, groaning.

Neither Molly nor I laugh.

He's okay, says he's only stunned.

The two of us help him up the hill. He's on hands and knees, but so are we. The grade is steep, the groundcover loose, dry. And while Joe's coated in sap, has a scrape on his forehead, and his glasses are bent enough he can't wear them, he's mostly fine. Because that pine tree decided it didn't care if the pitch was awful, it was going to grow right there. I thank the tree under my breath. Should thank it properly, but I can't around these people. Later, I'll burn some sweetgrass.

"His eyes look good," Molly says after she's checked Joe out. His pulse, asking him questions and whatnot.

With the cut on his forehead cleaned care of our first-aid supplies, now Joe's laughing like he didn't have a too-close call. When we were down there, I leaned over the edge. Free fall, unforgiving rock face. If Joe went two feet to the left or the right, it would have put Hank's accident to shame. These guys are retelling the story like they did something, making fun of their friend for, shit, taking a swan dive off a mountain to impress a girl when he doesn't even like the species.

I don't remember any of their names. They all sound alike.

"And the next thing, whoosh! Our boy's gone!"

"Fuck if that was elegant, bro. Nothing out of ten for execution."

"But first scar of the trip! Cheers to that!"

"It's a scar on the face. That's points, right?"

They all laugh, even Joe, who wants to know exactly how many points he's earned.

Hank-the-Tank hasn't moved since this whole thing went down. His eyes are distant. Like they were in the early days after he woke up. When I worried he wouldn't drag himself out of bed for his physical therapy sessions. When it looked like he was deciding his changed life wasn't worth fighting for.

And I'm watching Molly get angrier and angrier. The color in her cheeks deepens. She's crushing her nails in tight fists. When I ask if I can help, she throws our diminished first-aid kit at me. No underhand tosses for this girl. She's always overhand, throwing things like it's serious business.

I love this about her.

But today, here and now, I wish she'd act like we're on the same team. Throw me an easy pass. Instead, Molly always plays like she's going to win the whole game on her own. That even the people on her team are her competition. Back when I lived and breathed nothing but practice skates and weekend tournaments, I hated guys like that.

I wonder if that's the kind Molly kisses.

She checks on Joe one last time, says to the guys, like it's obvious but they won't understand unless she speaks plainly, "He hit his head. He should rest."

"Yeah, yeah, Hot Sauce. We're gonna make camp just down the hill."

There's a clearing. It's wide enough. Not the best spot, but it'll do.

"Trust Joe-Joe to try for a shortcut, wind up on his ass!"

They all laugh again.

Molly wants to punch half of these guys in the face.

I wait.

Instead, she picks up her bright bag, hoists it onto her shoulders, and takes to the trail again. "And none of you , . . absolute dickheads should be out here hungover," she offers, like she's trying real hard not to chew them out and completely failing.

"Later, Hot Sauce," one of the guys throws back her way. "Thanks for the fucking Band-Aids."

As we're walking off, I smell weed again.

Eventually, we're far enough that it's just trail in front of us, sloping consistently downward, my best friends and the pine cones. Still the music doesn't come for me. This time, I'm thankful. I don't want to remember any of this.

Fifteen miles later, we stop for the night. For the last six of those, I've been promising myself that once everything is set up, I can open the Snickers bar I bought in town. These days, walking this much, I'm always ready to eat, and even if it's a little scary, caring about food so deeply, that thought is about the only one keeping me upright and in motion.

Over where we agreed to put the tents, Molly's throwing things around. Being rough on her pegs, like extra force will finesse them into tough ground. Without recent rain, the earth is holding tight.

"Let me," I say, brushing her shoulder accidentally when I reach out to help.

She explodes. "Back off, Traylor."

I do.

"Jaysus," Hank says, but he's smiling. "Miss Mols has claws."

She speaks so quietly now. "Fuck you too, Hank."

"Oooh-eeeey, what's up your butt, Mols? Got a rock in your boot?" Hank's overplaying this.

"Or something." She returns to murdering her tent pegs. When one of them bends right in half, she screams.

Just screams.

Hank rolls his eyes like this is a big joke. Which pisses me right off. His sister is clearly upset, and he's acting like this is a temper tantrum, thrown entirely without reason. Like his sister isn't one of the smartest people we both know.

"Molly, what's wrong?" I ask, tempering my voice.

I ask because I love her.

She inhales.

And even though I bet there isn't one within a hundred miles, I hear a fiddle. It screeches.

"If you really cared," she says, the way you test the edge of a blade to know if it's sharp enough to do damage. She's looking me right in the eyes. I love how hers are flecked with green in direct light but seem only one color at first glance. "If you really fucking cared . . ." Her voice breaks. "You wouldn't have gotten my brother hurt." She turns to Hank. "And if you fucking cared, you wouldn't have gotten hurt at all."

That's a big pile. And I'm sick of this. "Molly, I know we haven't talked—"

"We did actually. Do you remember the night my brother was transferred to the rehab hospital, where he had to basically learn how to walk again? Remember that? I freaking do!"

I'm dizzy. "Then you have to know that what happened, it wasn't my fault, yeah?"

Hank is silent, rubbing his short-cropped hair over and over. His ball cap is on the ground, next to his pack. Without it, I can see the scars a team of doctors cut into his head.

They said they did it to save his life.

Even then, it seemed radical. Too much. The way doctors

sacrifice healthy cells to carve out a malignancy.

"I know," Molly says, whisper quiet now. "I do know and I'm still so angry. It might be easy. But I'm pissed at you. For letting it happen. For not stopping it. For being there when he fell! For not making me come with you that day!"

Up until this moment, I've been operating under a very different assumption. I was sure she didn't really get it. That the pain of what happened to the brother she loves so deeply threw up a block in her head, one that would crumble eventually.

But I was wrong.

Molly knows and she doesn't care.

"Okay, then," I say. "I'm angry with you too. Because that's utter bear shit. You're holding someone responsible for something they didn't do. That's absurd. That day, yeah, I was distracted . . . thinking about you. And so maybe I didn't watch Hank run through equipment testing closely enough and maybe I didn't see whatever invisible thing you expected me to catch. I was thinking about you! And that test you were obsessed with, like you hadn't aced every single other one ever. But you were worried this time! So I worried too!"

"I didn't ask you to do that, to do anything at all!"

"I know!" I yell back. It hurts my throat. To yell. At Molly. "And that was my mistake."

It's finally quiet.

We've finally said enough.

It could have gone another way. We could have approached each other gently, said: *We need to talk about what happened, really talk, so we can get over this. So the two of us can have a future.*

That we didn't hurts.

Resentment speaks with a voice much sweeter than I'd have figured: *someone who loved you wouldn't do this to you.*

Hank cuts in. "Hey, what about me? I'm the one who got hurt. Either of you remember that? The weeks I lost? This constant headache? Or my incredibly annoying chipped front tooth?"

Molly starts to cry.

This girl doesn't cry often, hasn't cried since September. At least in front of me.

"That's what I thought. You've been making this all about you. Well, I'm done." Hank gathers his bag, dragging it farther into the clearing. "I'm cowboy camping. You both have until the sun comes up to figure your garbage out. Seriously. After that, if you're not acting like the rational human creatures I know you both know how to pretend to be, I'm heading home. And brush your teeth after eating those candy bars," he yells. "And fucking floss because it prevents cavities."

I want to laugh. But my body won't let me.

Hank hasn't been that upset since he left a rare Pokémon card out on the deck back in Grade 8 and it got ruined in a thunderstorm. But Hank-the-Tank leaving sucks the vitriol out of the air. All we're left with is warm pine forest and decomposition.

I straighten the mangled tent peg, help set up for the night without speaking. Molly's going to have to apologize first.

She's in the wrong.

Even if I love the way she smells, after everything between us, I'm not sure I like this girl today. A flat and sour, unwelcome thought. I'm nauseous. But in this mess, a tiny melody announces itself. Notes banding together for the first time today.

If I don't like Molly now, when she's at her worst, I keep thinking, how could I have ever loved her in the first place?

And if I never loved her, I don't know anything at all. Except that I gave up hockey for this girl, for this lie I've been telling myself. Sweetgrass, as much as it offers, can't fix this.

VERSE II STAR

Because Michif people are experts in making do with what they have, the comb in our music is like the spoons, ordinary. As if the ordinary, the miracle of song, of stars peppering the sky, isn't enough.

FOUR MONTHS AGO

Hank

AITA for thinking my sister is overly invested in me and my "recovery"?

Okay, okay, find the summary of my horrible, terrible climbing accident <u>here</u>. Discover why I put recovery in scare quotes <u>here</u>. Now that you're caught up on my adventures, on to the new plotline! I (18 yo cis white man) have a sister, let's call her Mols (17 yo Native cis woman).

For reasons, I grew up with my grandparents. After they died, I moved in with my mom (42 yo white cis woman) and Mols. While moving in with my mom, who left me with my grandparents for reasons and almost immediately had another kid for other reasons, another kid who she kept and whose father she married, while all this was scary and, you know, emotionally traumatic and all that jazz, Mols was always, from the start, one hunny percent the best ever. She let me have feelings about our mother. She let me share her best friend. Basically, until this accident, I was always TeamMols.

Now she's clingy. When she visited the rehab hospital, I literally sometimes played sleeping opossum. But now that I'm home that method doesn't work so well. She follows me from room to room like she's going to break my fall if I lose my balance. The only thing she wants to talk about is how I am. Like the world hasn't kept barreling onward while I've been in "recovery"? She should be telling me about applying to university! Or complaining about her part-time job! She should get a life of her own. A life outside of me.

It sounds bad when I type it all out.

But that's what I come here for.

Is my sister a special kind of hell? Or am I?

[floss-ophy]: Have you looked up codependency in the dictionary lately or ever?

[quote text] a psychological condition or a relationship in which a person manifesting low self-esteem and a strong desire for approval has an unhealthy attachment to another often controlling or manipulative person (such as a person with an addiction to alcohol or drugs)

broadly : dependence on the needs of or on control by another

[BeanClub4Life]: Can we not arm-chair psychologize here?!

[floss-ophy]: Hi, you've reached AITA. I'm not here right now but leave a message and I'll get back to you when you start making some sense.

[Hank-Is-Back]: *upvotes this comment*

[getalifebot]: Get a life!

[TellsItStraight69]: Your sister sounds like a bitch.

[Hank-Is-Back]: Hey now!

[TellsItStraight69]: I tells it straight.

[YouBatterBelieveIt]: It's obvious the two of you love each other. Maybe she's just not dealing with what happened to you so well. Not to be all, mental health matters, but mental health matters. Has she tried therapy, y/n?

MILE 346

Molly

It's still full dark when I wake. My tent's zipper is opening itself. This isn't a bear. Heart thudding in my pulse points, I know it immediately. Mostly because they don't have opposable thumbs. A bear would just slice through this nylon, not open the zipper all polite like.

For once, the wind is quiet. And even though I know it's not a wild being outside trying to come in, I'm breathing too loud.

I'm wearing *my* hoodie.

Because after all this time, Tray can't still think of it as his.

"I know it makes me sound like a total baby, but it's scary out there," my brother says carefully, still squatting at the zipper like he's worried I'm the bear. That I'm going to surgically remove his arm. And chew on it.

Oof.

I bite my own cheek. Have I been doing this for months now? Settling into my easy anger? Hurting Hank because I've been gnawing on Tray? Even woken from deep sleep, I'm pretty sure that bears, those big mammals, are omnivores and on occasion maybe they let the anger get too loud. It can't feel good being a bear in a world that doesn't care about bears.

Where it's not safe for them.

I taste blood.

We're leave-no-tracing ourselves across the trail, picking up after other hikers, but we are the exceptions on this land. That, I think, justifies a bear's anger.

Hank exhales, slow and steady, giving me time.

But this is unlike me, more story than hard science, and I'd rather be sleeping. "Yeah, it is scary," I say, and roll onto my side so my brother can't reject me to my face. "You better get in here, then."

Maybe we're both thinking about bears now.

Hank clears his throat. "Yeah. I better."

That's all we say. It's cold. Maybe the coldest we've ever been to each other. But then Hank turns his back too and snuggles against me like I didn't freak out earlier. Like I didn't tell him exactly what I've been thinking.

With us back-to-back, absorbing each other's warmth, I pretend that I apologize. Pretend my brother accepts with grace.

Instead, since I don't apologize, things end up weird. They stay weird for three days, as we descend the San Bernardinos in an almost-constant decline; bright orange poppies, so different than the ones we use back home in November to memorialize fallen soldiers, are cheerful stars in the wildflower meadows we cross. After an hour on the trail the very first day, the boys made up, the word *sorry* flowing back and forth between them like water.

They've been treating me to, I don't know, not silence. The quiet between songs, when you're not sure if there's another coming or if the album's finished.

They linger behind, talking under their breath. It's private, but I don't try hard enough not to listen in. Out here, you're either in your own head or you're trying to get out of your own head.

It's day three.

I'm sick of myself the way I'm sick of the changing texture of the trail, peeing in the woods, my body revealing herself as not quite tough enough for these labors. And the boys, they're talking about me. I refuse to look back. Hank's probably all awkward, holding his hiking pole as if it's safety, as if it's what's keeping him from falling a long way down. That thing is only a tool. And they fail at the worst times—this he should already have learned.

Fool me once, it's your shame.

Fool me again, and the shame's all mine.

I twist my mom's saying until it makes sense.

"It wasn't your fault," my brother says to his best friend.

There's a pause before Tray speaks. "I know."

As much as I don't trust the hiking pole the way Hank does, I don't want to make him feel unsafe. Though he is, I don't want to make him feel it. Don't want to do that to my brother.

Because we are all unsafe, all the time.

It took walking this far, easy anger diffusing in messy ways, for me to understand. Maybe it took a still-drunken boy tripping over his own feet, pitching himself down a small cliff. At the start with Darlene, the trail angel, I understood safety in the ways you do when you memorize the world around you.

Now I understand it in my body.

"I'm talking about all those nights back. But I'm talking about my accident too." It's just like Hank to need to make sure everyone is on the same page. He doesn't like meaning to be muddy. Especially between his people.

When my dad and our mom got remarried, Hank was the happiest of all. But let's be honest: my dad is Hank's in all the ways that matter. And I've been a dick to my brother, using words like *my, mine*, refusing to share as if it's my choice to share or not when it comes to kin.

"Yeah, I know," Tray says.

There's a break as if they're done. We're cresting up again now. Up and up.

So much of what we do, these adventures in places where the land is still loud, are about being freaking good at communicating. Hank learned that lesson well. "We good, buddy?"

And Tray, like he does, shows up with comfort. "Always, even when we're not, buddy."

My brother, he laughs like it's that easy to forgive someone.

I don't need forgiveness. I don't need it.

I still mean what I said even if I wish I hadn't spoken it. Because anger isn't only easy. It's a breathing, lungs-expanding, blood-carrying-forward, pulsing thing. So, listen up, you all. Wherever you're hiding, here's my question: Would it have been so hard to pretend everything was fine, at least until the end of summer? When the boys will leave the trail and I'll keep going all the way to the very end?

When Joey went headfirst over the edge of the known world,

I held it together. Did all the smart things, the textbook things. Everything the Canadian Red Cross Wilderness and Remote First Aid Program taught me to do at sixteen.

At its core, first aid is about keeping calm, doing what you can until you can get to a hospital. Wilderness first aid is that too. But also, it's knowing help might be a long ways away, knowing you only have what you carry, what you can find, to solve incredible problems.

You need to be smart, resourceful.

Now I'm walking, first to wake rattlesnakes, to end up with spider silk in my hair, across my face, marring my sunglass lenses. I'm on the outside, forgiven-not-forgiven. As if it were my fault Hank fell. My fault we're falling apart. I'm starting to doubt the word *smart* has anything to do with the real me.

"Have you thought any more about what you're going to do?" Hank asks, a little too loudly, like he wants me to know Tray's got plans that I'm not a part of.

I've been wondering, of course.

His dad wanted to start a music program up at the language camp. I only assume Tray sent out his own university applications. Music composition paired with Indigenous studies. That he, in all likelihood, accepted a spot well before the deadline. But I don't know. Not anymore.

If it weren't for the obvious, and if we were good actors, we could pretend that nothing bad ever happened to any of us. But acting is storytelling, not a science. And I'm trash at that. Prefer formulas, the scientific method, taking things step-by-regulated-step. This universe is built on laws of nature because otherwise it would be untenable. I can admit that when Hank fell, more than one critical thing was severed. That I used to need Tray, want to be around him as much as around my brother. That, when Hank fell, we all did. In our own ways.

And three days ago, I jumped, knowing I'd break the last unbroken pieces of a delicate, imperfect thing.

"Nothing's changed since we last talked. I'm really trying to get through today. And then get up and do it again the next. What comes in September will come. I'm trying not to let the pressure of tomorrows build up until I'm not living my todays."

"Fair, buddy."

Tray laughs.

I've missed his laugh.

And even though I know I'm being terrible, still, I bristle. That plan might work for a musician, but nobody stumbles their way to medical school. Nobody stumbles out of promises given to gods. The scientific method is not a stumbling process; it's order.

"Hey, check out this pine cone," Tray says, and I hear Hank oohing and aahing like this is truly the world's nicest freaking pine cone. He's making fun. Because these days, Tray won't stop pointing out every other one like they're special.

These things the trees have dropped.

I hear a huff.

And I smirk.

Tray's elbowed my brother, not hard, but hard enough, like he deserves it for being impertinent. Something they'd have done without thought before the accident. To get back to where they were, it could be they needed me to yell. Maybe I'll be left on the outside, but they can hold on.

Is that enough?

I don't have to flail around wildly. I can be surgical, precise, if I know my freaking role. If I know the steps.

"Okay, okay," Hank backtracks. "I'm not cutting you down. It is a nice piece of tree, a very, very nice piece of tree. The best you've shown me today. Thank you very muchly for sharing it."

"How hard was that?" Tray asks.

"Respectfully? Harder than it should have been."

Tray laughs and then so does Hank.

They used to include me in these conversations. I used to laugh alongside them.

The trail cuts upward again. With mountains it's always up except when it's not. And up is better than down, I'm learning. Tonight, we'll see Los Angeles County in all its brightly burning glory. We'll be far enough away to notice how loud the place is, how invasive cities are. How quiet the land is forced to become. Tonight, we will see the noise.

Case in point: my phone has been buzzing nonstop. Altitude is good for cell service. Mountaintops are awash with signal.

It's Mom. She wants to have her weekly check-in early.

I text back: Everything's great. Daylight's burning. Talk later.

Shoving my phone away, I wonder if Hank's is as active as mine. Or if our parents lack trust in only one of us. Because our mom ignored me all last year, and it's fine—Hank needed her. But now she's doubling down, as if trying to make up for lost time.

And that's scientifically impossible.

***

A little more than a mile from our stopping point at the very top, where we'll have the best view, we run into Brynn. And this girl will change everything. I know it in my bones, but I fight it for a minute. Because I always have to fight.

Around her the boys go soft. Around her, I'm softer too.

That's terrifying. If you're soft, it hurts when your dad leaves you for a long time. When you love someone, it hurts if they fall. When you melt inside, you're not built to live in this world.

She's ahead of us, her voice warm, way higher pitched than my own. "One more damnit-all-to-H-E-double-hockey-sticks step." Breath. "Step and step and step and wow, this is boring. Stepping steps."

She makes the *damn* sound cute. It's her voice.

Hank whistles. "Absolute cosign."

She turns to find us watching her. "Oh, hi!"

The girl is wearing actual pink lip gloss and cutoff jean shorts, and even though she's bigger than I am, her shirt is tied into a knot at her waist, revealing a wide strip of skin. She's not hiding her body under her clothes.

"I know I'm not alone out here, but sometimes it feels like it, doesn't it?" She smiles at me in particular. "I'm Brynn. As for pronouns, she/her/hers fits, maybe like a pair of tights, the kind that only dig in when you sit down. But they/them doesn't feel right either. So yeah, she/her, please and thanks."

The girl curtsies.

Literally.

I'm slow to warm. I'm easy anger in a too-big body. A prickly girl with only two friends, and one of them is my brother. And this new girl is effortlessly charming.

"I'm an Aries, my favorite color is probably sunset, though sunrise is awfully nice too." Brynn pauses, but she's not done. "I'm eighteen. Well, eighteen and two months. I've just graduated. From high school. Like you do. And that's everything first-impression important about me."

Hank falls in love immediately. She charms Tray too. Suddenly the boys aren't leaving me out in the cold any longer.

In fact, Brynn is so dazzling, they seem to truly forget.

This is where I mostly give up, where I decide I could adore her too. Because even if I said those things, I don't want to be alone out here, not yet. I don't want to have to say goodbye to Tray or Hank even a minute before I have to.

Maybe I'm greedy.

My knees get weak. My whole body tingles. It's clear now. I do not like myself this way.

I want to be better.

Because I need something to change. Need it so badly I've abandoned all my plans, everything my parents want for me, everything I used to want for myself, to walk a really long way for nothing.

There's no accolade or grade or reward waiting at the end of the trail.

"Ooooooh, I'm a Pisces!" my brother says, like he's found a new bestie. "And while I respect sunset as a strong contender for best color, I would like to put forward the orange that construction workers wear."

"Oooooh," she says back. "I love a good construction-worker chick. Steel-toed boots are very fire." But then Brynn smiles like she's about to win at life, and well, she does. "But I didn't say best color, my new friend. I said favorite and excuse me, you gorgeous fish, but favorites are subjective."

That's how she wins over Tray.

Her shirt is covered in flowers. The kind that get mass-marketed for fat girls to wear. They're big, ugly daisies. Her backpack isn't overly large, is more like the schoolbag you buy to lug textbooks from class to class. But she's got a tent and a sleeping bag in a waterproof sack strapped to the exterior, and two full water bottles in the pockets by her hips.

"Doing a couple days?" Tray asks as we tackle the hill again.

This time we're a real group. I'm not even in front. Brynn is.

She smiles again, big and bright. "Oh, no, I'm going all the way to the end. I want to crush this boring, overly long trail under my little shoe."

It's funny. I laugh, the shaky sound unfamiliar.

Her shoes are small. Maybe a six and a half. They aren't hiking boots exactly. But they have tread. Some ultralight hikers wear sport sandals for parts of the PCT. So Brynn's way ahead of them.

"We're only going to finish California. If we somehow pick up the pace, maybe sneak into Oregon," Tray offers.

"So you're the real baddie here," Hank says.

Because I don't want to lie, and because I do want to like myself again, all I do is nod.

Tray smiles at me, his dimple on full display, and Hank bumps me with his shoulder. It's simple: with Brynn here, we're rebalanced.

A triangle might be a comfortable shape, most days. But a square is more stable.

I pull Hank toward me into a hug, whisper in his ear, "I'm sorry."

He whispers back, "I know."

I hug him harder. "Do you want to keep her?"

"Is she a lost puppy?"

"Hank, I'm serious. Will this overtly extroverted thing become annoying? Is this too easy?" I ask.

"It's not like we have to commit to anything here, Mols. Can't you relax, for, like, a fucking minute?"

He says it lightly. But it stings.

We pull apart.

My cheeks burn.

But we hike and we joke, even me. We finally introduce ourselves back, pronouns, star signs, and all. Before we know it, we're atop the San Gabriels. It's the fastest mile of the trip. Nobody complains about their feet or the way their pack digs in when the manufacturer claims it floats on your back. Nobody is thinking about what I said.

I drop my bag to the rocky ground, happy to be done. "What's for dinner tonight?" I ask with weird hope, like dinner's not going to be something drenched in hot sauce.

We make enough to share because that's the kind of people we are. And after dinner, Brynn pulls out a sleeve of Oreos that we devour.

I don't even like Oreos. But I eat them gladly.

It's a good night.

Three tents on a mountaintop. The one I share with Hank is hot pink, Tray's is boring green, and Brynn's is old-school canvas, spray-painted along the sides with big block letters: *CAMP HMMNGBRD*. On the flap, there's a tear that's been stitched and restitched a dozen times.

My phone buzzes. The parents, again.

But no, it's only my dad.

Dad: It's too quiet here without the both of you.

I laugh, thinking of how after he came back, after he married my mom again, how it was always *too loud* in the house, how he said it with a smile so we knew he was only teasing.

"Put your phone away," Hank says, "and admire all this with us, eh? Tray, buddy, was she this bad the whole time I wasn't here?"

Tray just shakes his head.

My phone buzzes again.

Dad: And you got mail. From Calgary. Do you want me to open it?

I type fast: No, it's okay. They email everything. Recycle it, please.

Dad: Such a waste.

Me: I miss you too.

Hank glares at me.

"Okay, okay, putting it away." I take my phone to the tent, throw it onto my sleeping bag, and because now that I'm not walking, now that the sun is gone and I'm cold, I pull the hoodie on, cross my arms awkwardly over my chest, and reclaim my spot in the circle.

"It's weird to see the stars and the city lights." Brynn is leaning against her bag, a blue pony stuffy with its rainbow tail in her arms. "Hey, don't judge, he doubles as a pillow."

Hank rolls his eyes, returns to doctoring his feet. "Look, there's the Smallish Dipper."

And Andromeda and Leo and Leo Minor and Orion. Hundreds more.

I know the Greek and Roman stories. They were taught to me in school, filled the library books my mom checked out when I was a kid. But I don't know what the Métis believe. Not about the stars. Not really. Stories are Tray's department, and Dad, who knows more than me, even though he was adopted out, raised by a white Protestant family, was gone from my life for a long time.

Maybe Dad was gone for the storytelling years. Even my uncle Dom isn't a big storyteller. They're both focused on what they love: music and those cows, respectively.

"The Little Bear," Tray says, strumming nothing songs on the ukulele he brought along.

The bear again. It's bears, bears everywhere.

I want Traylor to tell us a story suddenly, ferociously. But I can't ask and Tray keeps strumming, contributing to the noise.

Against the backdrop of sky coming alive with stars, Brynn tells us about her high school and how restarting the queer student org in Grade 10 was like asking the people in her small, Southern Californian town to embrace the literal devil. "Why do you even need that club, they said, it's legal now. They fought like Main Street would be drag kings and queens all day, all night long."

"Like a drag show isn't the most welcoming place ever," Hank says, exasperated.

Tray strums the same couple chords. "In California? I always thought that Cali was . . . better."

Brynn rolls her eyes.

It's funny. I laugh.

She's not just an extroverted shell, she's got grit inside.

"It gets worse," Brynn says. "It's this low-key-not-low-key-at-all racism, especially toward Mexican Americans. And my parents and their friends think if your body isn't perfect, doesn't conform, if you don't eat kale for breakfast, lunch, and dinner, do you have any value at all?"

Tray nods. I know he's thinking about all the low-key-not things he's always speaking back against. How I listen to him do this work, all the time, at home. How it's that I know enough, I do. But I don't always know enough to fight back, not to end up losing.

We fall quiet. Even the ukulele stops.

"While leafy greens do help protect your teeth and gums," Hank says slowly, "I really fucking hate kale."

We laugh like this is the funniest thing. I laugh so hard my eyes tear up. Brynn pulls another sleeve of Oreos from her pack. And while the city lights shine bright, I don't find them so ugly anymore. From far away, in fact, they're awfully pretty. They aren't the stars, but they're not trying to compete. From the top of this mountain, they look like they belong as much as the trees do.

Maybe that's a lesson. Of a kind.

Maybe that's worth memorizing.

NOW

Hank

A ITA for wanting to keep the sketchy hiker around because the sketchy hiker is exactly the kind of person that annoys and irritates my sister?

Ugh. I'm not even posting this.

I already know the answer.

MILE 425

Traylor

This stretch sees us descending again. And it's finally hit me. Five days after we meet up with Brynn and sort of adopt her without Molly fighting adding another person to our hiking group. The way she's always been a little unwelcoming, a little protective of what's hers. It finally hit me, the awful burden of carrying myself across these miles.

My feet hurt. Constantly.

In a way that I didn't think they could. And ice skates are not a walk in the park.

But it's not just my feet. It's my calves, my neck, even the skin stretched over my elbows. This isn't the kind of pain you get used to, the way hockey hurt, the way training for this trip hurt, but also felt good.

This is only pain.

I'm not searching for pine cones, for the perfect pine cone. And I'm not thinking about a different life. One where I'm flying first class, or at least charter from one city to the next. Where the puck drops. Where the crowd cheers for the team.

I'm attempting to step differently, more intentionally, while Hank and our new friend talk nonstop.

"Another tree, another step. Anyone else think this is bananas?" Brynn wipes sweat from her face with her shirt. "That we might be bananas for doing this?"

Hank digs his hiking pole into the hard ground, leaning forward so his pack weight shifts off his hot spots. "I'm starting to think nature is homophobic. Or hiking is."

"Hank!" Brynn exclaims.

She's shocked.

Because Hank only makes these kinds of jokes when he's sure he's in safe spaces, I know he's kidding. And while we've talked about our lives in broad strokes, we haven't gotten this specific yet.

"It's okay, I'm gay," my best friend says like it's a revelation.

And maybe it is to Brynn. She doesn't actually know us yet. But like a good song, one that from the first listen you know will stay with you, one you're not trying to take apart to find out how it works, I trust Brynn most of the way without knowing her. The first morning, she asked if I was Native American. I laughed, tensing. But Brynn, instead of being an asshole, instead of telling me whatever she's heard or thought or believes, simply said: *What Nation?* And then, *I don't know anything about the Métis, tell me everything!*

"I'm gay too!" she almost screams, even though she hasn't been hiding where her sympathies lie. "But gay for girls. Exclusively girls and femmes. Okay, maybe not just girls. But not guys, for sure. Definitely not cis guys. They're boring."

She's so charming. I laugh. "Ouch."

"The truth hurts she says," in one breath, mutters "Sorry" in the next.

I bypass her, then Hank, when the trail widens. "No hard feelings."

Hank just keeps the conversation going. "We're gay! But not for each other!"

"Not for each other," Brynn agrees, a smile warming her voice.

And ahead of me, Molly's brightly colored pack sways with each step. I wonder what she thinks, if she's smiling too. These days, she never hikes so far ahead that she's out of sight or out of earshot.

I wonder if I should sing her my song. The one I've been working on. *She's a sharp girl / Her love's not easy to earn / But she's lost herself, lost her laugh / And it's criminal, what she's doing to me.*

Not here, not now. Out of the way, somewhere where I can pretend it's only Molly and me. She'd probably hate that. Before, I'd have wanted to play with her. To tease out that annoyance until it turned warm, melting like honey. I like to rile Mollycakes up. Always have. But today, this is different.

Today, I think I want to argue with her.

Behind me, Hank pauses, then explodes with enthusiasm: "We're the perfect wingmen. Revise that, wingpeople. We're both gay, so we understand each other in a very important way. And we're never going to crush on each other or the same person so we can't become rivals or, worse, bad-romance frenemies. It's perfect."

Somewhere in the subtext is a comment about how I can't get it, not 100 percent. I probably can't. The way Hank can't understand what it's like to be Native in Canada or to be Red River

Métis in particular. But he tries and so do I.

Relationships are about trying. Trying every day.

"Ooooh, I like that. We're going to wingperson each other so hard!"

"Now, Brynny, I just told you I'm gay. Stop flirting with me." Hank pauses. "Tray, she's flirting with me."

"Excuse you! Who is flirting with whom now?"

I turn around. "She's got a point, yeah, buddy."

"I flirt without discrimination." Hank shrugs. "It's a real problem."

I laugh.

"And cuddle with anybody too," my best friend adds.

"Hey, now, I thought I was special," I say.

Hank just rolls his eyes. And then, gently, "Sorry, buddy."

"So cuddle puddle tonight?" Brynn bounces, her shortish hair in stick-up pigtails bouncing too. "You're most definitely invited! Even boring cis guys are invited to the cuddle puddle."

"Thanks, yeah."

These two are hilarious.

I start walking again. We're slowing our pace, now that we're talking, not so focused on the end goal. It's more human, what we're doing now. Still my lungs remain tight.

"One sec," Hank stage-whispers to Brynn, and double-times it to catch up, to make sure I'm okay, like really okay. That I haven't been hurt here, unintentionally. "Tray, you're always invited. Standing invitation. Sitting invitation. Lying-down invitation, buddy. Any which manner. Always, eh."

I smile as if Hank has overdone it and not as if he's made my

137

insides warm. "Now that that's clear . . ."

Hank pats me on the back, slowly. Twice.

Brynn catches up too.

The trail turns into this beach-sand consistency again, where each step forward drags you back. I'm sweating, drenched, miserable.

I've never heard Hank-the-Tank be so loud about being queer. He wasn't in the closet before his accident. I've known Hank was into guys since Grade 8. We've talked about it, yeah. But always at a whisper. Hank used to be reticent. Not ashamed, not that. A little unsure of himself.

Or the people around him.

It's not that nobody is gay in Edmonton. Or across Alberta, even though it's a conservative place in all the worst ways. There were other queer people at our school. We had a fledgling gender-and-sexuality alliance. Not that Hank joined.

Or that I did. Or Molly did.

We thought we didn't need anyone else to complete us.

But home has always been a place where Hank was quiet about who he crushed on. About that fuzzy future in Toronto for dental school. Or unreachable men: straight cis Roughriders with great behinds or Daddy Pedro Pascal. And if they weren't unreachable, Hank's crushes were always hypothetical.

This, it's nice to see.

I wonder if it's Brynn or if it's the trail.

As we push through the sand, the two of them plan their moves for wingpersoning and pinkie swear they'll give it a go the next time we end up in a town that's big enough. Like they can't imagine being queer in a small place. Or they can't imagine a gay person hiking, as if the two of them aren't actual real-life queer humans, walking on this trail. That makes me laugh.

"Let's do it! If, you know, the conditions are right," Hank says, breathing heavy now.

This sand is a beast.

Hank has shifted back into hypothetical territory. Maybe I'm looking for change where there isn't any. His accident has primed me for it. Or Molly has, the way she's assumed her brother is this new person.

But nobody changes all the way. We don't.

Later, when we catch up to Molly, who is moving faster than I can manage today, she's sitting in the middle of the trail, pulling every single snack she's carrying out into the shade. It's the perfect idea. A rest, while the sun is at its peak.

I collapse next to her. Close but not touching.

She hands me a protein bar. "You're there, aren't you? Like I was, a week into this trip."

"That obvious?"

It's the cake-flavored one she refuses to eat, but that I've started to like. The way a thing grows on you after multiple exposures. Molly would know better, but that's how taste buds work, yeah. We don't know what we like, not at first.

She bites into her own protein bar, chews. "It's just that I know you," she says finally.

"Yeah, you do."

And that's why all of this, what's between us, is killing me.

"I need to ask you something," she says.

It could be anything. It could hurt. It could fix things. "Ask away, Mollycakes."

I don't know if I'm using my favorite of her nicknames because it's how I think of her, softer than she is most days, the kind of girl who throws her whole body into it when she gets good news. Or if it's only that we're eating. Because we eat almost all the time, crunch on unsatisfying foods that come from packaging we'll trek out for proper disposal.

She rolls her eyes. Sharp like a knife, but that's Molly being playful. "Your parents really don't care?" she asks. "About what you have planned next? I mean after the summer?"

"Do you mean, they don't care that I don't have everything planned? That I'm not going to university right away?"

I want to love this. To gather it up, revel in it. But I'm feeling bad for myself, which I normally hate. With hockey, you're never in the spotlight alone. With hockey, you don't have to offer up your culture for consumption, you don't have to do anything but play the game.

And this is the thing I didn't realize when I decided to follow the notes, that music would ask me to give more than I'm able.

Molly breaks the quiet. "Either. Both."

Her voice is small.

"They trust me, yeah." I say it, and then realize it might hurt.

"It cannot be that easy," she scoffs, trying to hide that, yes, it hurts. "No, I refuse to believe that's the solve."

Dr. Yaliza has convinced me it's unhealthy thinking, wanting to go backward, as if we could. Here, in the woods, I'm backsliding.

"What if it is?" I ask. "What if it's exactly, one hundred percent that easy."

"So you're saying my parents don't trust me?"

Molly watches as I drink from my canteen. I never told her about the texts her mom sent before we left, the ones that said she was only letting her daughter go because she was with me, or the way when I visited her dad to return a book of music I'd borrowed, how he wasn't as okay with these summer plans as he let on.

"Don't lie to me," she says, and I can tell that what Molly's really saying is *I'm hurting, this hurts.*

"Just because they want to protect you doesn't mean they don't trust you. When it counts."

Molly doesn't believe me. "Okay."

Now that we're out of the sand, the trail is only dirt again. I crush a clump between my fingers. You can't snap out of pain. You need to go through it. It's one of the fundamental things I've learned in eighteen years of being on this land, of breathing on this land.

"I don't think . . . No, I know. I'm not as . . . traditional as you are," she says. "I wasn't raised like you. With two parents who were raised knowing all these things. I can't believe a thing just because someone tells me a nice story."

I react instantly: "Yeah, that's utter bear shit."

I wait for Molly to shut down, to go on the attack.

"It's something I've been thinking about a lot . . . lately," she finishes weakly. "Since . . ."

It would be so easy to say Hank's name.

I know what I need to do. What my therapist would say. This

141

is as much on me as it is on Molly. *It takes two to tango.*

But I chicken out, don't even try to catch this girl's weaksauce pass. Or tell her that the only thing she's got going that I don't is all that colonized thinking.

When Brynn and Hank catch up, the two of them hover over us, unaware of what they've stumbled into. "This is what I love about you all," Brynn says. "You eat when you're hungry."

Molly only turns to Brynn, says, "You don't?"

She drops *our* conversation entirely.

"Oooh, I do." Brynn settles onto the ground. "Did I not tell you I was homeschooled?"

Hank smiles, his chipped front tooth on display. "Brynny, you're withholding."

"I know it feels like we've known each other forever. But, in the real world, this is still the first date," she replies in her sugar-sweet voice.

She's very good at shifting her register. It's something I'm still working on, surprising people with what my voice can do. Asking them to focus on the instrument, not only the familiar lyrics.

"So yeah, I'm fat and I eat when I'm hungry," she says. "I'm not fat because I eat when I'm hungry, but people, back home, that's how they see it. A fat person eating must be fat because of food."

I'm watching Molly carefully. Her body language gets tight before she forces herself to relax. "Yeah. A fat girl can't like cake or cake is why she's fat."

"A fat girl can't go on a little hike without it being in service of shrinking." Brynn bites into her health-food granola bar.

"A fat girl cannot sit comfortably on an airplane."

This from Molly.

Hank and I only watch. The conversation isn't for us.

Brynn nods. "A fat girl can only have a pretty face."

"A fat girl can only get small, make space for others." Molly hugs herself, and I want to comfort her. "She can't expand. Can't be expansive."

"But you're a small fat," Brynn says eventually. "And there are some things a small fat girl will never understand. Some things she can do, like shop for clothes in most stores, like get to call herself midsize and nobody snickers."

Molly nods.

"I've never heard it like that," I say, because Molly is right that the world limits her, and so is Brynn, that Molly's world isn't as limited.

"Oh, it's my favorite way to think about fatness." Brynn picks up her water bottle but doesn't drink. "See, I'm a mid-fat. Yeah, I can usually find clothes, but only at specialty shops. Not all fat people face the same barriers, the same discrimination. When you're a large fat, you can basically only shop online and, even then, you're maxing out sizes, like clothing can't even imagine you. But it's complicated, right?"

"Bodies change," Molly offers.

Hank nods there. Once.

"You know what?" Brynn says, not smiling at all. "I like you. I really do like all of you."

As we pack away our garbage and reclaim our packs, now the three of them are talking. As animated as they are, my friends can't distract me from the reality of the trail. It used to be that my friendship with Molly and Hank could balm over anything.

I didn't stop keeping up with my hockey buddies. They stopped keeping up with me. Not because they wanted to. It was more innocuous than that, yeah. Resentment's sweet voice is painting that other future, the one I could have had if I'd stayed on the ice and given up Hank and his little sister. Then I wouldn't care she's been kissing other people because we wouldn't still be friends.

That hurts. Gnaws at me like another kind of hunger.

When we stop for the night, Molly's watching Brynn put up her canvas A-frame tent, a grimace on her face. "Please can we give that horrible thing away the next time we go into town? It makes me sad."

"It makes me sad too." Brynn keeps working the lead lines that pull the canvas taut.

Hank returns from gathering water, our canteens hanging from his splayed fingers. "Great, let's get rid of the sad thing."

"It's settled," Molly says. "The tent goes in Kennedy Meadows unless we stop sooner."

It's practical, if we've adopted Brynn. We can distribute a little more weight across the group, if she's sharing one of our tents.

It could help, lessen the burden, reduce the pain.

"You're okay with that?" Brynn meets each of our eyes, one by one. "Really okay sharing space with me?"

Hank takes the lead. "Anytime, Brynny."

Molly adds, "I wasn't trying to banish you."

Brynn laughs.

"Same," I say. "I follow their lead on almost anything."

The statement might not be entirely true these days. But it's what Brynn needs to hear.

She laughs again, freer. "Codependent much?"

I've dug myself this deep, so I keep going. "I prefer to think that we are, not one heart, because Molly would tell you that's biologically unsustainable, but that our three hearts beat in a common rhythm. On this and most other things."

"Traylor, buddy, you cinnamon roll," Hank says.

Molly glances my way, and her face, it surprises me. Her eyes, her lips, her chin, they're all soft.

If we were alone, I think I'd kiss her.

I'd risk it.

Even if, still, there's a part of me that can't believe she thinks she's allowed to be angry with me, with her brother.

Brynn shifts, pulls her knees to her chest. "I can bunk with Hank if you two want . . ."

And then there's no softness at all. At the same time, both me and Molly say, "No." When I stop, Molly keeps going, "No, no, no. It's not like that."

The song I'm writing, it isn't a love song.

Today, I realized that.

"And when we finish the summer," Hank says, "we'll leave you with one of our tents."

I'm watching Molly so carefully. She nods but doesn't like the idea at all. Sometimes, this girl can see only one path. It doesn't have to be her tent. With Molly it's all or nothing, which, respectfully, is a hard way to live this life.

"Oh, would you?" Brynn asks. "I'll mail it back when I'm done.

Or, since I'll already be in Canada, maybe I can come for a visit?"

Hank jumps on the idea.

I watch Molly, who stays quiet, until she catches me at it.

I'm thinking that we'll have to leave Brynn a heck of a lot more than a tent, the way the girl was drinking water straight, without filtering it. I'm thinking about my not-love song.

The first chance I get, I'm singing it.

I make this vow to myself, with the trail, all these pine cones, as witness.

MILE 742.4

Molly

We leave the desert behind five days after our first town stop with Brynn in Kennedy Meadows. She needs it bad. It's obvious, this girl is not a planner, not like me. It was a quick overnight. A visit to the general store for resupply and the restaurant for burgers. Brynn spent a lot, emptying out most of the cash she had with her all smiles.

"Ooooh, this could be fun! Buffalo-style chicken mac! And pad Thai with chicken! And yellow curry with chicken and rice!"

"I'm sensing a theme," I offer as she adds her picks to the checkout counter.

Brynn laughs. "They really like their chicken."

"Who doesn't like chicken," the older man behind the counter says, deadpan, standing next to his display of Mountain Beef Jerky.

We camped in a field eating all manner of delicious convenience-store treats, two burgers each, and to balance out all the chicken, we bought a metric shit ton of the local beef jerky. We gather our resupply boxes, including our bear canisters. We load Brynn up with gear from a particularly well-stocked hiker box.

The herd has long passed this point.

"Ooooh, it's orange! Construction-worker orange! Your brother's going to be so jelly." Brynn finds a headlamp to replace her flashlight, the *CAMP HMMNGBRD* stencil mostly faded away. She picks up a compass. "Do you know how to use this? Because even though it's super cool, it seems silly to carry it if I don't."

"I can teach you," I offer, thanking all the gods, each one of you, that you made me a planner. Without my plans, I'd be in the back forty thousand not knowing which way is up. Like Brynn.

I don't leave the hoodie behind.

I tell myself it's because it's cold at night. Not like there's something to trade for. And it would be deeply unsmart to go into the Sierras without a layer for warmth. The day we rejoin the trail, leaving the desert behind, and climbing into this new section of the PCT, Tray still feels like total shit. While my brother and Brynn wander ahead, I fall back.

"It *is* still bad," I say while he hikes next to me.

It's not a question.

Tray's eyes fill with something close to hurt. "Do you want to kick me when I'm down? Is that what this is? This chat. Are you playing with your food, little bear?"

"It's not . . . I'm not . . ."

I'm inarticulate. Wouldn't earn a passing grade.

"Don't lie to yourself, Molly. Lie to everyone else, to me as much as you need to be whole. But not to yourself." Tray stops, his face tight, his dimple hidden. His T-shirt is heavy with sweat at the neckline, under his arms, along where his pack waist buckle sits on his hips. The boy looks miserable. "You wanted to hurt me, and you did. Can you stop now?"

I haven't ever seen Traylor this torn down.

In the hospital, months ago, he stumbled toward me, blood on his shirt. He'd been caught by a piece of metal as he stepped under my brother, as if to catch Hank. Tray pulled me against him, and even that day, the worst day of our lives so far, he hadn't seemed this ruined.

"That's not what I was doing . . . Not here. Not right now." I think of other times where it was intended, where easy anger won out.

"And I don't think it matters." He pauses like he wants to say something else. "We've got another eight miles to slog through. Let's just walk. In the quiet."

A smart girl would let it go.

Filled with shame, overflowing with it, I'm nowhere close to smart. "I'm not a little bear. I'm not a bear at all," I say.

It comes off more defensive than I intended. For once, there isn't any noise. Tray isn't humming some chord. The world is not loudly screaming around me.

"Do you hear yourself?" Tray exhales. "Every sentence out of your mouth is *I* this and *I* that. And so yeah, I don't know what I was thinking. You're not a bear because I wouldn't do that to bears. It would be unkind."

It's the wrong thing to say, hindsight allows me to know this, but even without anger fueling me, I cannot stop: "Tell me how you really feel, Tray."

"Do you actually want to do this? Right here, yeah?"

"Yes."

"Fine," he says. "Molly Lee, I will always love you because in spite of how you've been behaving for months, like a spoiled kid whose favorite plastic toy was swept by the wind over the edge of Niagara Falls, kicking and screaming all over the place even though what happened wasn't your fault and it wasn't mine and it certainly wasn't Hank's. You cannot blame the wind for being windy. In spite of all that, you are still my best friend. I might not be yours anymore. But I can't shake you. So I will always love you, Molly, hear me say that on this incredible, horrible trail." He waits until I meet his eyes. "But, Mols, hear this too. I don't really like you these days."

It's how I imagine being struck by lightning hurts, an instant flash of pain, then a throbbing, everywhere all at once. Traylor called me *Mols*.

That name.

"Ouch."

"Yeah," he agrees. "Um, so you know. I didn't say this to do you harm. I said it because you asked. Though, now I'm thinking *Tell me how you really feel* might have been sarcasm, and so I'm sorry too. For telling you what you asked but didn't really want."

He broke my heart because I consented. Then apologizes. I stash the hurt away, like the bear I'm not gathers berries and other food to survive a long winter. "So, is it still bad?" I ask, making sure it's a question this time.

And this time Tray answers me.

We walk eight more miles, together, in careful-like-surgery conversation.

Six days later, we descend from the trail into Lone Pine. We catch a ride with a hiker who's been out for a week, who's headed home. We agree. We'll spend two consecutive nights sleeping in actual beds.

Turns out, in the real world, it's a Friday.

Brynn and I abandon the boys, who are showering, to go see what's up. "Don't use all the hot water," she hollers as we step out into the motel parking lot.

Leaving the desert was relief in some ways, not in others. Shade is a glorious thing, but even in high summer, navigating the Sierra Nevadas is hard, brutal work. In some ways, now this is a new freaking hike entirely. So it feels almost like we're home, here in Lone Pine, where the desert is alive and well.

Trees are few, the air is dry, dusty, the vista gloriously flattened. The sun is too hot. Without our packs, even that's pleasant.

I could sleep for a year. But it doesn't mean I can sit and patiently wait for my brother to get out of the shower. Once I'm clean and stationary, I'll have to answer my parents' texts.

They are overflowing again.

"Oh, the general store! And look, there's a post office! So cute!" Brynn exclaims as we walk up the main road in this kitschy town, twenty-five miles and a world away from the trailhead. "And is that a Mexican restaurant slash tequila bar slash axe throwing establishment?"

"Oh Jesus, it is."

"I mean tacos are the height of mortal foods." Brynn smiles brighter. "I like this town already."

My trail brain takes more than a minute to catch up with my

town brain. Before I can say anything on topic, my stomach cuts in. "If I don't eat chips and salsa immediately, I might actually die."

Brynn nods. "Big same."

We wander inside, where we're greeted by someone our age wearing an open green-and-brown flannel, a name tag that says *I'm Matteo, they/them*, over a fitted T-shirt. It's a dinosaur with a dialogue bubble that says *Brush Those Chompers!*

I burst out laughing. "I like your shirt."

It's pink, while Hank's is a bright, sunny yellow.

"Hikers?" Matteo asks, unimpressed with my lack of manners. We are unbathed, sunburnt, dressed in sweat-stained clothing.

Brynn smiles. "You got it!"

The girl smiles a lot, I'm noticing.

"That wasn't sarcasm," I offer. "I really do like your shirt. My brother, who I love desperately, has the same one. It's his favorite."

Matteo relaxes, but only barely. Compliments won't get us past this desk.

"So you want a table? You actually want to sit in my family's place of business dressed like that? We do takeout . . ." They fade out hopefully.

"I know, we're gross. We haven't showered. Not for a while if I'm being honest," I say. "Unless you count swimming in a river?"

"I do not," they reply. "I bathe, like, twice a day. I have since I was eight."

Matteo's not kidding.

They are very much clean, styled. Both ears feature big diamond studs, their septum piercing is pretty, delicate. I don't think Matteo would survive a night on the PCT. Not that anyone could drag them out there willingly. And also, I'm trying to be kinder these days. To be careful with other people. Because Tray doesn't like me anymore. And I've been walking and I've been thinking, no, I can't blame him. "How about we do takeout now and come back later when we're clean?"

They finally smile. "We would appreciate that."

I glance at Brynn.

She's distracted, searching her pockets. "Can we maybe get, like, a couple orders of chips and salsa to go? That's not too expensive, right?"

"Four extra-large orders, please, my very clean new friend behind the counter," I say. "I'm not sharing. I'm too hungry."

Matteo rolls their eyes. It's almost friendly.

Brynn counts her money. It's mostly coins, a few one-dollar bills. "Can I pay you back, Molly? I need to find a cash machine."

"It's all good." I hand over a twenty. Though I didn't want to at first, as if it was a habit, a leftover vestigial organ, I know now that we can trust Brynn. While we've been helping her, she shares everything she has too.

"Only people from the mountains come in here with cash these days," Matteo says, judging us again. "And really old folks."

I drop a one-dollar bill and assorted coins into the empty tip jar by the old-school register, missing loonies and toonies, suddenly, sharply. In towns, it's harder to forget how very far away I am from my home. But even far away, my parents' voices are loud.

Mom: Have you had enough adventure yet?

Dad: Back to Batoche is next weekend. I know you never come along but maybe, if I pay, would you fly out?

153

Parents: Oh, that's a good idea. Fly home for a week or two, Molly. Just a little break.

This from my mom, though she's using the shared chat now.

Matteo gestures at the jar. "That's going to get me all the way to university in Seattle."

I laugh because I understand them. This tone. This gentle-not-gentle ribbing. "We'll come back later, ready to eat. Showered and everything. You'll see how we tip when we actually get to sit down for a meal."

"Yeah, yeah." Now they're smiling outright.

Matteo leaves the host stand, taking our order to the kitchen.

The lobby is small, lacking in natural light. A handful of posters are pinned on the long wall. Axe-throwing lessons. Two-for-one Margarita Tuesdays. A sign-up sheet for a songwriters' competition. The poster says: *No covers!* And below the event details someone has scribbled in red pen: *Original music only, Thom! We are sick of Bob Dylan!* And in blue, this note: *Cosigned. For god's sake no more Dylan.*

Having been rescheduled twice, it's finally happening tonight.

My skin prickles. Tray will hate me for this. But I'm trying to be a better friend. Or I want to be a better friend. I'm not sure if the distinction matters, how to quantify it, how to test out this hypothesis.

Brynn collapses onto the bench under the poster wall. She's worn out. An afternoon nap is exactly what I need to have a shot at staying awake past midnight. The show starts at 9:00 p.m., here, in the party room.

"Okay, chips and salsa," Matteo announces. "I threw in extra.

You can have them if you promise to get clean before you come back. Like, use soap, a washcloth, and everything."

I smile. "You like us, you do."

Matteo breaks. "I think I might. And you seem like you need it. There's hiker hunger all over your faces. I mean the extra chips, not the shower. You definitely require that."

Brynn laughs. "We agree. The showers were just occupied earlier."

I stare at the sign-up sheet.

Someone who was looking out for Tray, someone who loved him, wouldn't let him hide the way he does. His voice behind other people's words when he writes his own music. He needs a big shove onto a low-key stage. I grab the pen hanging from the board and I write *Traylor Lambert* right next to number 13.

As we stroll past the general store, I stop. Back home, I don't drink them. Here, they fill a hole in me. "You know, I really want a Snapple."

Tray's drinking them too.

Usually, he's buying, leaving one for me to find.

Brynn points at a yellowed ATM sign in the window. "I can get cash, pay you back. And maybe a lemonade . . . ooooh, no, an Arnold Palmer."

Inside, I wander to the very vintage drink fridges. Tray will fight this. I know he's got stage nerves. But I can't forget how he told me that he loves me but that he doesn't like me. So this is what's best for him and it's okay because I've already messed it up. The risk I'm taking is minor. It's not the big bear in the sky.

It's the smaller one. The one that nobody would miss, if it were to disappear.

I stroll back and forth. He can't like me any less.

But a part of me thinks if I ask, he'll sing. Tray would sing for a minor bear. Maybe that makes me powerful. As strong, as grown, as equal to anyone else, no matter my size, my age, or theirs.

I grab two peach Snapples and a yellow sports drink, the kind Hank has become addicted to, even though I believe that yellow is the worst sports drink flavor.

At the cash register, Brynn is absolutely flirting with the girl behind the counter. "No way! They only stock the thing once a month? Is that a true story? Or are you taking advantage of my newness to tell me tales?"

"Are you from LA? How did you end up here?" The cashier matches Brynn's energy. "I can't quite tell, under all the dirt, if you're a city chick playing at the backcountry, or a backcountry chick who's used to city privileges."

Brynn tucks her short hair behind her ears. "I grew up in Dana Point. The OC."

"I'm sorry," the cashier says all snappy. When she catches me standing there, she smiles my way, friendly and warm. "Are you Brynn's hiking friend?"

I nod.

"Hey, I'm Faith. This is my parents' store. I'll be a senior next year."

"Just graduated," I say. "But I'm seventeen too. I skipped a grade."

"Lucky," Faith says. "If I knew being a smarty-pants would get me out of school faster, maybe I'd have tried it out. Only I'm not that smart."

Brynn cuts in. "Don't say that about yourself! Everyone can put on their smart pants. Whenever they want." Then she shifts tones. "And right? I didn't know there was an early release from hell either."

Faith smiles. "Ugh, it is a prison, isn't it?"

"Several long, endless years," Brynn says, smiling back.

In a lot of ways, I liked school. Or I liked knowing things and having people know I knew them. Which is probably not an attractive quality. I liked being in the same grade as Tray and Hank. So while I only did three years, I would have done another with my brother. With Traylor.

"What are you up to tonight?" I drop my drinks on the counter. "Add whatever Brynny wants too."

"Thank you, Molly!" Brynn screams, dancing over to the fridges.

While she picks out something cold and full of that good, needed sugar, Faith starts ringing me up. "I'm off at eight. Um, I don't really have plans. This place is kinda boring, I hate to break it to you. You seem nice. You don't deserve this."

Brynn adds an Arnold Palmer to the counter. "Come with us to the Mexican restaurant, tequila bar, axe-throwing shop for the local songwriter competition."

While she says this with a straight face, all three of us laugh at the same time. Saying all the things out loud in a row, it's freaking absolutely absurd.

"Don't knock it till you've tried it. Most of my birthdays have happened at the Garcías' place. Sixteen and seventeen were both axe-throwing parties. Because, like I said, this town is pretty boring and I'm not *not* friends with the Garcías' youngest, Matty. They're the axe-throwing coach, in case you were wondering." Faith announces my total. "If I'm still here when I turn twenty-one, it'll be a tequila birthday party. A sad, sad tequila party, which should be a country song if it isn't already. Welcome to Lone Pine. It's only mildly depressing here."

We leave with our drinks and a promise from Faith that she'll come over to the motel after she locks up.

"It's going to be great," I say, wondering if Tray will be more or less likely to freak out if we have a guest in the room when I tell him that I signed him up to perform tonight. If I had a Magic 8 Ball, the answer would be: *It's freaking cloudy*.

I'm living dangerously these days.

Yeah, you know.

LATE JULY
LONE PINE, CA
Traylor

'm sitting on Molly's bed pretending to answer my dad's rambling email when she emerges from the bathroom. Skin sunburnt in places, sun-browned in others, she's clean, smells like the soap here at the motel. Citrusy, with a bite of Old Spice. Since I bought new deodorant at the general store, we smell the same now. That's weird comfort.

I finished the Snapple hours ago, sitting in the late-afternoon sun, while catching up on my mom's texts. It was nice, yeah. A cold and sweet kindness.

It also felt like a bribe.

In our friendship, I'm the gift giver.

"So . . . ," Molly says awkwardly, hesitating.

Her hair drips onto the floor. She crosses her arms in her town dress, this green that's like muddy spring, undertones of yellow and brown. It should be ugly. Instead, all I'm thinking of is that Barenaked Ladies song, the one about having a million dollars, how green dresses are somehow cruel.

"So . . ." I mirror her.

Next door, Brynn and Hank are goofing off. The TV is on. Some cartoon. Because Hank's always watching some cartoon. Molly's wrong. Her brother's core hasn't changed. She's the one who's different.

The fan in the bathroom is struggling. I want to turn it off, but I can't move. Not while this girl who has been my best friend, this girl who has been kissing someone else, this girl I don't recognize one minute and know like she's part of me the next, not when she's looking at me like this: with so much unfiltered intensity.

"Don't hate me, okay?" she says quietly. "And don't like me any less either. I couldn't handle that."

Oh, it's serious.

"I won't."

This girl is going to break my heart again. Damn her and damn me too.

"You say that now . . ." She peers sharply in my direction and then sits on the edge of the bed, close but not touching. Until the cheap motel mattress sinks us toward each other. She throws a hand down to keep from rolling into me. Her fingers are close enough I feel her heat.

"Spit it out, Mollycakes," I say, hating this.

Her hair drips between us, onto my pant leg.

She stares ahead at the big TV. "I signed you up for a competition. Original music only, because I guess one of the locals has been going hard on Dylan covers, and well, it's a songwriter's competition. Those tend to be populated by actual people who write songs, not just sing them, yes? It's, um, tonight, at nine, and I want you to do it, you know for you, and really, you promised not to hate me, so stop looking at me like that. I can see you in the reflection on the TV." She bites her bottom lip hard. "I'm going to ask you to do it, please and thank you. All other pretty polite words are in effect too."

I want to bite her back.

We sit quietly while I think on what it would look like to leave a mark, the imprint of my teeth on Molly's skin, and yeah, I hate myself. But not as much as I expected. I rub at the water on my hand.

"Okay," she says, "now you need to say something. That's how conversations work. I go, then you go."

"Can I ask a follow-up question?" I keep my tone light. I don't want to spook her. "Is that within the bounds of how you think conversations between actual people go down?"

She looks right at me. Finally. "Don't be a dick."

"I'm gonna take that as a yes." I smile. I wait. When I speak, emotion leaks out in my voice. "Do you want me to do it?"

"I said that, right?"

She's purposely missing the point. And maybe that's something I've been misreading, how you can be bright when it comes to many things and completely terrible at many others. I know she's a year younger, but Molly has, since I've known her, seemed so competent at everything.

Only she's not.

We all flail around making decisions, not knowing where they'll end us up, not knowing the smallest thing can change someone's life. Change your own. It's a set of spoons, but they make music. It's a handful of strings on a wooden frame, but the fiddle is also everything.

I try adding as much specificity as I can. It's what we were told made good persuasive essays great in every English class I've ever taken. "No, but do you, Molly Lee Norris-Norquay, want me, Traylor Lambert, to sing for you?"

She nods. "Yes, I really kind of do."

"Kinda?"

"Sorry, this is hard." Her laughter is anxious. "Talking to you."

"I don't know why," I say, but I do. At times, a thing calls for gentleness. It doesn't always have to be a loud note. Or a hat trick. Though both are good when they happen.

"So . . . ?"

She's biting her lip again, and this time, I reach out, brush my finger against her skin, untangle her lip from her teeth.

Molly freezes the way deer do when they sense a predator. Only she's not a deer and I'm not trying to make her my dinner. She might fight against it, but I think she's got more in common with the bear. They drop their body temperature, freeze out the rest of the world as needed, slumber onward.

I brush my finger against her lip until she exhales. "Yeah, Molly. I'll do it. But so you know, I'm only doing this thing because you asked."

She exhales again, a little shaky.

And I love it.

But also, I said I wasn't a predator and here I am behaving like one. "Sorry," I offer. "For touching you. Without permission. Or for touching you at all. I don't know, but I know, I'm sorry."

I push off the bed, leave her there, even though I don't want to leave her, and head next door to watch cartoons. Molly needs to think on this, to wonder how it got so far out of her control, so fast.

I'm gonna throw up.

"Take a load off for a minute or sixty. There's plenty of room," Hank says.

He's flirting with the server, who started out cold but now, halfway through our first town meal in ages, is flirting right back. We're in a sticky red vinyl circular booth, under dim lights.

"I can push Tray over a titch."

Hank actually tries to shove me.

Matteo laughs. "I'm working. This apron didn't give the plot away?"

My best friend only smiles.

"I will hang out with you. Later," Matteo says.

Hank stretches, throws an arm up to rest against the vinyl. "That a promise, eh?"

Matteo looks like they're hurting. "Don't use your Canadian superpowers on me."

"Too much?"

"Too much," they agree, but sit at the end of the booth in the small space next to Hank. "I have to emcee the songwriter's competition . . ."

Hank-the-Tank's face falls.

". . . but I will sit with you and your friends, okay? Save you a table, right up front. And as my personal VIPs, I'll keep your sodas full. On the house."

I push food around my plate. I'm starving, yeah. But also, I can't eat. It's been weeks without those voices, those critiques, all that *Indians this, Indians that* BS. Tonight, it's likely to start up again. If I sing, I'll invite it in.

Next to me, Molly eats her dinner. Brynn smiles, chewing, her wingpersoning entirely unneeded. Right off the trail, in this desert place, Hank's freer.

"Do you do everything in this joint?" he asks as Matteo stands.

"You're only getting that now? Come on, keep up!"

Hank laughs. So do Matteo and Brynn.

"You nervous?" Molly asks me in modulated tones.

Without his distraction, Hank's all aboard too. "Yeah, buddy, you nervous?"

"Oh, is Traylor nervous?" Brynn asks. "Isn't this like your dream?"

"Yeah," Hank answers for me. "But he's a bit scared."

"Ohhhh, Tray." Brynn stares from across the booth. "I'm certain you're amazing."

Molly turns. "Why do you say that?"

It's her science brain. She needs to know the how, the what, but especially the why of things. Before, I would never have thought her questions unkind. Now they're irritating.

"Oh, you know, he sings like every second on the trail. And he sounds a bit like Hozier." She fans herself, rolls her eyes back in her head. "Okay, Hank, you need to know this, if that man ever said, *Hey, Brynny, let's go to church,* I would flip the switch, become one of the straights. Like, flash, bang, done."

Hank claps once. "I witness this statement and will ratify it at

164

the next gay agenda meeting."

Everyone laughs but me.

We still have massive amounts of food in front of us—six different kinds of tacos and aguachiles, queso fundido, carne al carbon, carne zarandeada.

My friends quiet, stare my way, their eyes hot like spotlight.

"I . . ." Jesus H. Christ, I really am going to throw up.

"Ooooh fuck, we broke him," Brynn says slowly.

Under the table, Molly grabs my hand.

"Yeah," I say, "I'm terrified."

"But why? You're so good." This from Brynn.

Molly doesn't let go. She squeezes, rests our hands against her thigh.

"I feel exposed . . . ," I say, holding on to Molly where nobody can see, clinging to her, not caring that my palm is sweaty, overheating.

"Well, Tray, technically you are exposed. Sitting on a stage. Under lights. With people watching." Hank says it all droll.

Like we haven't talked about this before.

"That's not it, though." I tangle my fingers with Molly's harder, the gentle bite of her nails comforting. "It's something I don't think you can understand, Hank, as a white person."

"Well, make me, buddy."

"I'm trying," I say.

Molly moves her thumb against my skin, sinking in, dragging a little, the way earlier I touched her lip.

"When I sing songs I've written myself, yeah, I feel that they're giving settlers something I shouldn't offer them. That I'm

165

commodifying my culture. That to do well in this business, I'm being asked to open up what it means to be Métis, to offer these things that shouldn't be consumed so someone, probably a settler, can make money. And while they're asking in a way, like there'd be a contract, at times I wouldn't be able to say no. It's a zero-zero game and both players in the shoot-out are on the record label's team. I can't win, no matter how I play it."

Though her hand stays soft, her voice is pure Molly. Sharp like a knife. "Well, that's a load of complete bear shit. No offense to bears," she says.

Brynn inhales sharply.

Hank just shrugs, like yeah, she's right, buddy.

"Is William Prince doing harm?" Molly asks.

I love his work. *Reliever* is one of the most perfect albums I've ever heard. "No."

"He's from Peguis First Nation, right?"

I nod.

"What about Jeremy Dutcher?"

Dutcher is Molly's dad's hero. "Of course not."

"Samantha Crain?"

She's fabulous. I shake my head.

"Kalyn Fay?"

Big same.

"Snotty Nose Rez Kids?" Molly continues lightning fast. "Tanya Tagaq? George Leach? The Halluci Nation? Supaman?" She pauses loudly. "Kelly freaking Fraser."

"Rest in peace," Hank says, throwing back the rest of his Coke.

"I get your point." I speak slowly. She doesn't mention it, but there are Native record labels, producers. Indigenous economies too. More than one path.

Molly's left eyebrow spikes. "Respectfully, do you really?"

"Yes." I squeeze her hand.

"Well, then eat up," she orders. "You must be starved."

Next to me, Hank leans back, smiles. "So . . ." He pulls a bottle of tequila out of nowhere like he's a magician. "Do you want?"

Molly passes her glass over. I shrug, send mine too.

"No pressure," Molly says to Brynn, who is hesitating. "Technically, back home, Tray and Hank are legal. You are too. Technically, back in our home. Though that's not true here. But again, no pressure."

"Why the heck not." Brynn rolls her shoulders. "Maybe it will help with Tray's nerves."

"That's what I was thinking," I offer.

And Brynn laughs. "You think my drinking might help your nerves?"

"And you were thinking your drinking would help me out?"

She nods. "I'm powerful like that."

"You know what, you are because it kinda does." Suddenly, I'm hungry. Suddenly, I could eat. Digging in with my nondominant hand is awkward, but I won't let go of Molly first. Under my fingers, her pulse thunders.

"I'm right at least half the time," Brynn says, and tucks her hair behind her ears.

"Winner, winner, chicken dinner!" Hank announces like he's

the big voice calling plays at the game.

"Actually . . ." Brynn furrows her nose. "I'm a little sick of chicken."

We laugh. We drink and we eat. And this, Molly's hand in mine, my hand in Molly's, this is good.

We drink more than we should. Almost the whole bottle. And when I say *we*, I mean the others. I quit after the first one. I'm not holding on to Molly anymore. But she's all soft around me, so different from the last time I saw her drunk.

Your fucking fault.

She's warm like sunshine. She's everything everywhere. She's—

"And number thirteen." Matteo's voice echoes from the stage, where when their parents aren't hosting quinces for the local community, retirement parties, stags and stagettes, they're letting the aspiring songwriters of Inyo County and beyond show off. "A friend from a faraway place. Who showered, I have on good account, just for you! From the Pacific Crest Trail and also Canada, the man, the legend, Traylor Lambert!"

The audience screams. They've been screaming like this for everyone.

It's been a great night.

My friends are safe, happy, a little drunk.

I step onto the low stage, grab a borrowed guitar I've already tuned. "Okay, this is . . . Well, this is for Molly."

I fix my eyes on hers and play, sing on, sing clear, hoping I won't regret this, hoping that whatever fire has started between us, it can heal, and then once it's done that, it can last.

NOW

Hank

AITA for parent trapping my best friend and sister because I wanted to hook up with a perfect-for-me they/them and also get the band back together in one fell swoop?

I'm (18 yo cis gay white man) drunk! That's the first thing! You should please remember this in your assessment.

The second thing? Who sees the bio update? I don't usually talk about it, make it a thing. But hi, I'm Hank and I'm gay.

Third? Yeah, I'm getting to it.

So I met a they/them (18 yo HOT FOR ME not-so-cis Mexican American person). They are funny and gorgeous and their teeth, they have this perfect tiny overbite. It's devastating.

I might have been hanging out with my sister (17 yo cis probably-het-but-I've-never-asked Native woman), my best friend (18 yo cis het Native man), who, yes, has a massive crush on my sister. He wrote her a song! And sang it for her! We were all hanging out with some other cool humans, and I might have, I'll say it fast, ParentTrappedMySisterAndMyBestFriend. Sort of. It's an imperfect metaphor.

We only have two motel rooms.

My they/them and me are claiming one and kicking the best friend out for the night.

So I'm forcing my sister and my bestie to spend time together. Because I don't want the friend group to get a divorce. I want us happy and together, forever and ever and ever. Maybe they'll kiss it out and stop fucking fighting so much.

I await your verdict.

[Edited to say]

It's morning. I'm definitely the asshole this time.

[OpinionatedAardavark]: Have to say it's not very cool to parent trap someone. Especially not without talking to them both and seeing if they want to be parent trapped, you know? Like we need more details. Are there enough beds? Are you putting your sister in a scary position?

[floss-ophy]: Agreed. There's a lot going on here.

[YouBatterBelieveIt]: Gay! Yay! But also, not loving the parent trapping.

[EverybodysGay:] Congrats on being gay! I'm an ally!

[boneappetits]: You can't just leave us like this. It's a rule of the internet. What happened? Finish the story!

LATE JULY
LONE PINE, CA
Molly

I want to blame what happens next on Hank disappearing with Matteo. Blame it on the fact that Brynn and Faith are so cutely tangled up in each other that they don't stop me, like it's their freaking job. I want to blame it on the alcohol.

Should.

Will add tequila to my never-again list as soon as everything settles. Right now, the world is vibrating so fast, it's all noise.

"No, I grew up in a worse town," Brynn says, her words slurring a little, her arms wrapped around Faith like if she lets go, the universe will take the girl away.

Faith is blushing, or this is how she gets when she drinks. "Do you see what we're doing tonight? In Lone Pine?"

"We're listening to a youngish, wannabe Bobby Dylan."

Faith laughs at Brynn. Because we are.

Others have returned to the stage, but not Tray. Not Tray, who sang that song, the one I've been hearing snippets of all along the trail. *She doesn't know how to cry, for / the bison, the hurting world around / her tears they'd fix me, they'd / carry us all / if she could*

172

cry them soft / Oh, sharp girl. Not Tray, who touched my lip like it belonged to him, then apologized. This person, sitting so close, shoulder to shoulder, arm to arm, we're basically leaning into each other.

And I'm thinking about what he'll do if I kiss him.

Because yes, I kissed that sad white boy in the hospital cafeteria near the sandwich vending machine. He asked for it. Needed it. And I needed a moment. Of weakness, or openness, a moment to be vulnerable in the face of everything. A week later, I kissed that girl in the same hospital cafeteria.

Neither kiss had me feeling anything as much as Tray's finger against my lip.

"*Saaaaaraaa, oooh, Saaaaaaraaa,*" the guy onstage croons.

I get why Dylan was outlawed, at least until the room was drunk enough for it. We're all there now. And here in the dark, I tell myself I was heartbroken when I had my first kiss and then my second. Maybe they didn't feel right because I wasn't right. There was something muddying up the slide, so the experiment was fouled from the start. Would never turn out. And I tell myself maybe it didn't feel right because it wasn't Tray.

So I'm a little tipsy and I'm going to kiss this boy. As soon as I get the nerve.

And then, to be certain of my hypothesis, I'll kiss someone else.

Maybe a few someones.

I could do it here. With the lights focused on the stage, it's private enough. We're close enough. But Tray's absorbed by the music, his eyes facing forward. And I'm a freaking chicken.

Not a bear. A chicken.

A bear would just do it. And chickens, they don't do much of anything brave. They chicken about in the yard until someone makes them into a sandwich or a freeze-dried hiker meal.

"Ready?" Tray asks when the set finishes.

"Yeah," I offer back. Then louder to Brynn and Faith, "We're leaving. You coming?"

Brynn tries to stand but promptly sits back down. "Yes, but I think I'm gonna need some assistance." She sways, and Tray and Faith each take a side. "This is nice. You're very nice friends."

Outside in the moonlight, I'm slightly ahead of them, wondering how I'm going to get that kiss now. How I'll test my hypothesis. Then I notice the glow. It's a full moon. That's a bad, bad sign. Things get heavy during a full moon. Animals act differently.

Hank, he fell the afternoon the moon would come up full.

This, it's pure science, not story. Study after study exists on the effects of the moon on wildlife, preterm birth, violent, terrible upswings in fatal car accidents. For months afterward, I read them like they were bedtime stories, trying to make sense of Hank's fall.

The way the phenomenon sounded like fiction but isn't.

Tonight, it takes us half our average mile time to walk a few blocks. I realize I'm not drunk anymore. Haven't had a drink in hours that wasn't plain water, and later after Tray whispered something to Matteo, water with lemon. Neither has Tray.

But Brynny's in rough shape.

I'm only noticing this now.

We stop to let her throw up four, no, five times. It might be the way the moon shifts things, but her skin is edging into blue.

Wiping at her face, Brynn looks right at Tray, eyes vacant.

"Dad, let me go . . . You can't!"

Faith turns to me. "I don't like this. I'm scared."

Brynn's head rises slowly. "Not scary! I-m-erfet."

This is the full moon in action. Brynn was drunk, yes, but okay enough. And now she's not. Now her skin is, yes, blue. Everything I know about the body tells me this is critical.

"Where's the hospital at?" Tray asks.

"Should I call an ambulance or . . . ?" This from Faith.

"Nobulance!" Brynn yells, her legs giving out, knees kissing the pavement in a way I know will hurt for a long time.

"My truck is parked . . . out back the store . . ." Faith runs a hand through Brynn's hair while she whines. "But I can't drive. I'm still too . . . tequila."

"I can," I say.

"No, Molly, I'll do it."

Tray is always trying to protect me. Now I wonder if he does it because he doesn't trust me to protect myself. If my parents have had other conversations with him, asking him to watch over me. If graduation was only the first time I noticed.

What kind of scientist misses these pertinent details?

"I can drive!" I say, louder than I mean to.

There's no one else on the street. This town looks abandoned. But unlike the trail, it isn't comfort. Being out there isn't terrifying like this.

"No, you can't," Tray says patiently. "Your blood alcohol level is still too high. I'd bet on it."

"Yours isn't?"

"No, Molly. I had one drink, hours back. I was gonna keep an eye on all of you. Fuck." He sighs, his shoulders shaking. "Faith, where are your keys?"

She's down on the cement. "In the truck. On the floor mat."

Brynn peers up at me. "Fat girls can drink more," she says, like we've gone back in time and we're exchanging hurtful truths. "Because they're fat."

I check her pulse. It's rapid. Tachy. She doesn't speak again, not even when we drive to the tiny local hospital, and we help her inside, and the overtired nurse at the desk behind the glass is asking us for her last name.

"We only know her as Brynn," Tray says.

"She's eighteen," I add. "I think her birthday's in April?"

"Home is Dana Point. She's hiking the PCT," Faith offers.

This is everything we know. Least it's the things we know about Brynn that a hospital would want.

"She's uninsured?" the woman asks.

"Probably not." I think about the stories of her mother and the marina. How living like that takes money.

The woman calls for a wheelchair. "Okay, we're going to get her help. Have a seat."

Since we aren't family, none of us is allowed back.

In the gray waiting room, Tray's got my hand in his, but as if that's not enough, he's almost hugging my arm. I'm pulled against him. Faith's on the floor, legs anchored to chest, and I want to tell her that in a hospital, the floor's probably not a great choice for sitting. Only the waiting room chairs likely aren't much better and she's already kicking herself for making suspect choices tonight.

"I'm the one who sourced more tequila when your brother ran

out . . . I went over to the store."

"Hey," Tray says. "Brynn's an adult. She can make her own decisions. You didn't force her."

"God, I really hope she'll be okay." Faith is crying now, tears tracking down her face. "That was so terrifying. I've never seen someone that bad off, and Brynn, who is so sunny and happy and great, she was . . . God, my parents are going to murder me."

Now I'm worried.

She catches my face. "Not literally. Oh God, not literally."

I disentangle myself, slip to the floor.

That's when a man in a police uniform emerges from behind the swinging doors. "You kids friends with Noelle Brynn Hensley?"

When we first met, she told us it was Brynn, no last name like Cher or Beyoncé. I knew she had to have a last name. But on the PCT, it's how people sign trail registers, one name, trail name, no name at all.

"We are," Tray says, and stands.

The police officer's tone is much too aggressive. "Sit down, kid."

Tray does. I lean against his legs, pinning him, as if I can protect him. As if I can keep him safe.

"Faith Ann," the police officer says now, staring at the floor.

Faith pushes herself onto a chair, drops her head. "Lieutenant Green."

"Your parents are getting called the second I sort this nonsense out. You almost killed that girl tonight. Letting her drink like a fish."

Faith sobs.

"Hey, now," Tray says. "That's not exactly fair."

"How old are you, boy?"

"Eighteen."

"And you?" Lieutenant Green asks me.

"Seventeen."

"And what is the legal drinking age in these United States?"

Faith cuts in. "It was my alcohol. Not theirs."

Which is only half-true.

"And you got it from the store, did you? Now your parents are on the line too."

"She's lying," I say. "It was all mine."

"Ours," Tray says.

Lieutenant Green shrugs. "You can be held legally responsible if anything happens to that girl. You know that, right?"

It's unclear if he's talking to Faith or to all of us.

"She's sixteen," Lieutenant Green says like that's not a revelation. "And she's a runaway. Did you help her with that too? Because if you did, that's another misdemeanor."

"Is she okay?" Faith asks.

The man's eyes harden. "They've pumped her stomach."

"Can we see her?" I ask.

The nurse watches all this through the window where she first registered us. She stands. She knocks three times on the glass. "For Christ's sake, Green, leave those kids alone. Don't you think they've been through enough tonight? I'm coming out there, and you'd better be done with your posturing at that point."

Lieutenant Green takes her seriously. "I need your IDs. And

don't leave town. This girl's parents have the right to press charges."

"They're at our motel."

He scoffs at me. "Let me guess. The Garcías didn't ID you? They shirk the law like these laws aren't here to keep your friend from dying."

"We didn't buy alcohol from them," I growl back. "Aren't you listening? We told you already."

Lieutenant Green ignores me. "You're hereby ordered to attend the sheriff's office tomorrow morning with proof of identity so I can record this. If that girl's parents want to take you to court, I'll help every step. She was at a camp for the summer, for her health, and what you've done, putting her in danger, will set her back."

I remember each piece of gear Brynn left behind, hiker box by hiker box, as we walked. CAMP HMMNGBRD.

She really did run away.

And then she lied like it wasn't even a thing.

"Enough," the nurse says from behind the cop. "Come with me, kids. I'll let you see your friend and then it's time for you to get to bed, okay? It'll be brighter in the morning," she says, then stops. "That's not true. Not always. But in this case, everything will be okay in the morning. Your friend's already sleeping."

We crowd around Brynn, who looks younger now that I know she's only sixteen, who looks younger because she's unconscious in a hospital bed. It's nothing like Hank's ICU room. This place is older, smaller, the lights yellow. Even the smell is shifted, dry in a way Edmonton isn't, reminding me the desert is outside these doors. But it's also because I'm here again, in a hospital, with someone I care about hurt, that I realize, I can't blame Tray anymore.

Sometimes bad things happen to good people. Bad things happen to everyone, good or bad or neutral. That's not science or story, but it's real. Brynn shouldn't have been drinking. None of us should have been drinking tonight. And yet we made that choice.

But we didn't choose this, a friend hurt. We didn't choose this damage.

It wasn't clear.

What was at stake.

When we went out into the world to have a good night, picked up our glasses. When Tray chose that pink belay device. When Hank decided to go first up the wall. In another universe, it was Tray who fell. It was Hank's fault. It was mine. In another universe, where you gods rule too, maybe rule louder, the fall was worse. In that other universe, one of us dies tonight.

But it wasn't clear, what we were risking, written out like evidence after an experiment. I balk against the unfairness, watching Faith touch Brynn's IV-laced hand. She's on oxygen, is being pumped full of electrolytes. They call it a banana bag, which I've always found funny.

Only this isn't funny at all.

When the nurse tells us to leave, that she'll call if anything happens, we take Faith's truck back to the general sore. She points at a small blue house up the alleyway. "That's mine. You two all right walking?"

Tray nods.

We've walked farther, loaded down with more than this.

We travel in silence.

So different than the first silence.

At the motel, Tray doesn't stop, stalks right up to the room he's sharing with Hank as if he's going to leave me without a word. On the door, he finds a handwritten note: *Please sleep somewhere else, anywhere else. Please. Do it for me, buddy.*

Tray laughs under his breath. "Can I?"

"Sure." I unlock my door. "Glad one of us is having a good night."

"Before," Tray says, "we were too, yeah?"

He's opening himself up. Trusting I won't hurt him anymore. And it's becoming clear that hurting Tray hurts me too. It's ridiculous, against nature, against science, to do damage to your own self. But sometimes, we do it.

"Your song was really amazing. I didn't say it. But it was."

"It's your song, Molly."

"I have a song," I say.

Brynn's backpack sits on the bed closest to the door. Neither of us moves it. I wonder what secrets it holds.

"Sleep?" Tray asks.

"Yeah. It's been . . . a night."

There's nothing romantic about watching your friend throw up so violently she bursts a blood vessel in her eye, nothing kissable about hospitals. I've learned through experiment. I strip, not caring that I'm only wearing a sports bra and underwear. My dress puddled on the floor, I pull back the covers.

When Tray returns from the bathroom, he's not fully himself. "I don't want to sleep alone."

"Me either."

"That an invitation? Or a statement in kind?"

"Why do you think I'm all the way over on this side with the blankets open?"

"Is this an invitation, Molly?" he asks, like he needs to be certain, beyond a doubt.

I pat the bed. "Yes."

"Good."

He turns out the bathroom light. He climbs into bed, lies on his back, his arms holding a pillow, the pillow cradling his head. His hair is loose, wavy.

We're not as close as we've been in the tent before Hank showed up. I turn, facing Tray. Inch over until I'm next to him. The way we like it most days, nearby but not exactly touching. That thing I thought was only friendship. The way gravity's invisible until you don't have it holding you in place.

"Tray?"

"Yeah, Mollycakes?"

"I'm sorry."

"For what?" he says, and he rolls to face me.

Now we're knee to knee, my legs against his.

"For all things lately. But mostly, for the way I was . . . after Hank fell."

"You were incredibly horrible to me."

"I very freaking was."

Tray laughs, cups my shoulder. "I'm not over it yet."

I am disappointed. But it's not fair to expect him to be where I'm at, after what I've done, even if we're in the same space, sharing the same air. The full moon isn't finished with tonight. For now, things will go wrong, even apologies. Maybe, especially apologies, after easy anger runs out its welcome.

"I hate that I'm not over it yet," he says gently. "That *sorry*, even a sincere one, doesn't fix things."

I butt my knee against his. "Are you being stubborn?"

"Maybe some, little bear."

He can't see my blush in the dark. "That's okay. You're kinda a stubborn person."

He laughs, his grip on my shoulder tightening. "Am not."

Like this isn't scientific proof.

"My parents are the stubborn ones," he says.

Now I laugh. "Where do you think you got it from, eh?"

We fall quiet. Parents can do that. Mine flood our text chats with their worries, their demands. It's been happening for weeks now. But it's intensifying. The full moon is helping them along too.

"Do you think we're in legal trouble?" Tray asks just when I'm sure we're going to decide to sleep like this, facing each other.

"You're not avoiding the stubborn thing?"

He runs a hand down my shoulder to my wrist and back again, like I'm cold and he's warming me. "Not only. I really want to know what you think."

"I think . . . ," I say carefully, my parents crowding my mind. "Well, I think that this kind of thing happens all the time. Teens drinking. That the banana bag will get Brynn right. And we don't need to worry about it because it won't come to all that."

My parents would be so upset with me for tonight, like it's proof I'm not grown enough, can't handle myself.

"Should we call my mom?"

"Not yet," I say, and maybe it's me being rigid. Because if we call Tray's mom, she'll tell mine, and then this summer, it will come to a swift end. They made me promise we'd do everything to be as safe as we could, to come back home without new scars. For a second time, I've sincerely promised an impossible thing.

This must be a character flaw.

Tray whispers, "Did you imagine that she was lying to us?"

"No," I whisper back.

"Me either."

"That hurts, doesn't it?"

"Yeah."

"Can I change the subject?" I ask, still all quiet, like this room is one of the magical places left on the planet. Like maybe not all those places are on the land. That magic finds a way. Even though Brynn lied, I want her to be okay. All aftereffects gone. All possible side effects sidestepped.

"Is this part of your requirements for good conversation?"

"If you really want to know, I'm working on my communication skills. Because they've been a bit garbage lately."

Tray doesn't laugh and I love him for it.

"Yeah, subject change consented to."

"Okay," I say, and stop.

"Okay?" he asks.

I say it fast, hoping this place is holding me safe, that I won't fall, won't fall and fall: "Can I kiss you?"

"Yes," he says back just as fast.

And so I do.

It's freaking great.

Like I want to kiss Tray for the rest of my life or at least through the rest of the time the full moon has in the night sky. And that's when I realize the scientific method isn't infallible. That's when I realize I'm kind of in trouble.

Time gets weird.

The room smaller.

It's only this, only us.

But like all things, nothing, even this, can continue forever. The moon only has so much power. Tray pulls his lips from mine, presses them to my neck, my collarbone. This is also great. Different but great.

"We should stop," he says, breathing rough. "Sleep," he says, bringing his fingers to my eyes to coax them closed.

I nod because I can't speak. There isn't a coherent thought left.

Tray pulls me against him. And still, I'm brainless. Basically boneless. All from a kiss. My breathing calms, becomes deep, and sleep arrives gently. The last thing I think is muddy, fuzzy: it wouldn't be this great with anyone else. Kissing, that is. I don't need science to tell me that. Don't need reassurance at all. This is known.

THE CHORUS STAR, REPRISE

It's not the same one, but a twin. A version of what's come before. Unexpected but right. Enter the jaw harp. A flexible tongue, bamboo or metal, held within a key-shaped frame.

Watch how words shift here, in this part of the song. Watch how the design must change.

LATE JULY
LONE PINE, CA
Traylor

The first time I wake, I think I'm dreaming one of those good, good dreams. Molly curls into me, her hair a tangle. Citrus, Old Spice, keys me in, lets me know this is for real. It's easy to say this is better than hockey, sweeter than music.

The second time, it's panic. The clock says it's early. Before dawn. My heart thunders like I've been running. All that's left is the sense of remembering, waking to find that good dream slipping away, then fully gone. But Molly has only flung her body across the bed.

I follow.

This last time, I come out of sleep the way a hymn moves, slow, languid. For the first time in weeks, I don't hurt in unbearable ways. I'm rested. And that's everything. It's revelatory. The clock is turned away, out of reach. I find my phone on the carpeted floor, the battery barely holding on.

It's late. After ten a.m.

The bathroom door's open. But the light and fan are off.

Molly's gone.

It could be as simple as breakfast. But I know, almost immediately, it's not. I roll over, bury my face in her pillow, mumble, "It's never easy, yeah?"

The room doesn't answer me.

I burn off frustration by kicking my way out from under the covers.

In my heart, I don't believe the love lines tied between people, the land, and our nonhuman kin are supposed to be easy. That easy's not a given, shouldn't be. And I'm always happier with Molly than I am without, even after all these miles together. After every long moment since September.

I fix my hair into braids and head outside to track her down.

LATE JULY
LONE PINE, CA
Molly

It's Saturday, 7:50 a.m.

We are tangled together, pressed close, my back to Tray's front. He's mostly edges, muscles honed first playing hockey, then climbing, hiking, adventuring. One of his arms curls around my stomach at the point where it swells out most, his fingers curved against the fat I carry on my hips. He holds me like I'm going to freaking bolt, and even in sleep, he'd rather stop that from happening.

This boy knows me too, too well.

I try not to think about bodies, about how warm Tray is when I slip out of the bed, stumble-stepping toward the bathroom like I'm still drunk. Once I reach the door, I peek. He's asleep. And it hits me that I've been searching for safety too. Like if he wakes while I'm in the bathroom, I'm safe.

If I win the competition, I'm safe.

If I'm safe, I win.

All of that, it's absolute garbage. It's what Hank's been wrapping himself in. It's what Tray's doing, following me out here, refusing to see who he is without me.

"Fuck," I whisper, frantically searching for my dress on the floor. It blends into the carpet.

Unlike my dress, my passport is easy to locate. So is Tray's. I lift Brynn's pack from the bed nobody slept in, grab a key to the motel, and flip the bedside clock around so Tray can't see the hour from the bed. It might buy me some time to get this done. Outside in the morning sun, I don't look back. I'm ready to do this.

Eyes wide, eyes open.

The sheriff's office is sleepy. A coffee machine somewhere in the back is burning what's left in the pot. "Can I help you?" a young man with a serious mustache asks, rising from his desk. He's in uniform. It's familiar but not.

This isn't home.

These aren't the police I know. That doesn't mean they're any different.

Though my shoulders are used to the weight, I drop Brynn's pack on the tile floor. My voice is clear, not muddied with feeling or fear. "Last night, one of your colleagues, he told me to come in this morning."

"Yeah? You need to report something?"

"No."

We stare at each other. He peers over the counter at the sleeping bag in the waterproof stuff sack, at empty water bottles stored in exterior pockets.

"I'm seventeen," I say, but the man interrupts before I can get any further.

He sighs, shaking his head. "Are you making a report, miss? Do you need . . . food? Or something?"

"No." I step back and away. "But thanks."

And though now he seems worried, or thinks he should worry, the man with the mustache doesn't stop me from walking out of the cop shop.

On the street, it's hot and getting hotter. Because somehow, we're back in the desert. We thought we left, but we didn't escape.

I head toward the hospital. It's a hike.

I don't mind.

As I walk, I am not thinking about that kiss. I'm thinking hard about how police are the same all over. It's not like Lieutenant Green will ever see me or Tray again, not like he wasn't trying to scare us straight the only way he knows how, with intimidation and threats. These police don't care about us, not beyond the scope of flexing their power. Brynn won't rat us out to her parents. She wouldn't do that. So we can leave Tray's mom out of this mess. We need to get back on the trail. I need to walk onward.

Brynn isn't alone when I make it to her room, the nurse from last night replaced by a Black woman in pink scrubs who leads me through. "Call if you need anything, honeys," she tells us.

Faith sleeps in the only chair, hunched over a corner of the bed.

"Brought you a change of clothes," I say, lowering the pack from my shoulders.

Brynn's voice is pitched low, like it hurts to talk. "Thanks."

And maybe it does. Pumping a stomach is violent. But her color is back, the oxygen mask gone.

There isn't another chair in the room, so I stand. My legs ache, my shoulders burn. But this is only ordinary now. Like knowing that safety is a bedtime story, a lie told to small children.

"Are they mad at me?" Brynn asks eventually, still entirely too subdued. "The guys?"

They aren't here and she thinks it's personal. Maybe that's something you learn at seventeen, at eighteen. Maybe it's something you never quite gather up, that it doesn't matter how young Brynn is, right now, right here—she's worried her friends are angry with her.

Because anger is easier than grief.

"No, they're asleep."

"Oh. Are you mad?" she asks.

"It bites that you didn't trust us, but I get why. We were strangers. There was no guarantee."

Trust implies a kind of safety.

A promise to be careful with each other.

A promise not to make it hurt.

"Yeah. You were. But it's hard to unravel something like that once it gets going." Brynn readjusts so there isn't so much pressure on her IV line. "It's not like I could have been all, hey, guys, gals, and nonbinary pals, here's the full story: I'm not eighteen, didn't graduate. In fact, I ran away from the fat camp my parents forced me to attend so I won't embarrass them. My name's Noelle, but I hate that name more than a thousand hellish fires. Side note: my parents are really litigious, but will you forgive me? Will you still be my friends?" Brynn exhales, coughs. "It's not like I could have done that either."

"It *is* hard," I offer back. "But, Brynny, you didn't ask us."

I wait longer than I would have after Hank fell for her to decide to try. Longer than I would have before Hank's accident too. I want to offer her grace to do this hard thing. But Brynn never does. And then Faith wakes, and Brynn turns on her sunshiny self, and that girl, she'll never ask.

I'm not willing to do it either, to just tell her. *Yes, I'm your friend. Even though. Even when.*

So after the nurse informs Brynn that her parents are sending a car for her, after Faith offers to drive Hank and Tray and me out to the trail early tomorrow morning, after we don't say goodbye, but know this is goodbye, I walk very slowly a long way back to the motel. I add these bonus miles to my trail count.

I've earned them.

Hank and Matteo sit outside under a pergola in patio chairs, sunglasses on, drinking coffee. "You were up early. Couldn't take Tray's weird mouth-breathing a second longer?" my brother asks.

I don't know where Tray is. And that's for the best. I can't be that girl, the one who drinks underage without consequence, who can have a good, good night, who kisses her best friend. I can't be that girl and also be the girl I need to be.

That as much as anything else is clear under the desert's morning sun.

"I went to the hospital," I say. "To see Brynn."

"She's in the hospital? She okay?" Matteo asks, straightening, pulling their sunglasses off. Their eyes are deep brown, worried.

I sit on the paving stones even though there's another patio chair, cross my legs even though, in this dress, that's awkward.

"She's fine now. Traylor didn't tell you the story?"

"That boy came out of your motel room, half the morning wasted, all shirtless and sleepy, asking where you were." Hank leans toward me. "Like that was the most important thing. Buddy didn't even say good morning. Rude."

"I left a note." I try not to blush. To distract my brother, I fill them in on Brynn. That she's okay. That she lied. That her parents are coming to get her. "No," I correct myself. "They're sending a car."

"Who does that?" Hank asks.

"Rich fuckers," Matteo says.

"Well, duh." My brother smiles. It's warm and private. "Matty, that was rhetorical."

"Let's not hide statements inside questions." Matteo adjusts their septum ring. "Feels insincere."

"It's too close to the is-that-a-regular-everyday-object-or-is-it-cake thing." I nod, agreeing entirely. "Even when it's cake, you're a little less happy to have cake in front of you."

Matteo smiles. "Exactly like that."

"Noted," Hank says, but he's watching me funny.

When Tray emerges, he's freshly showered. His hair needs to air-dry, his T-shirt sticks to his chest. Yesterday, I hated that citrus shampoo was my only option, fantasized about going to the general store to buy something else even though I'd be leaving it behind when we walked on. Now I only want more. He settles on the ground next to me, but I shift away.

He notices. Hank does too. But we don't say anything. We've practiced this, hibernating from each other, these long months past.

194

After all, we're only minor bears.

My brother, his body relaxed though he has been forced to change. Matteo, this homegrown kid who wants to drink coffee in rainy Seattle. Traylor Lambert, who needs to be loved so badly but who protects himself too much to open wide, to take a big risk. Brynny, who lied because she couldn't imagine another way, who makes T-shirts for fat girls, even plain white daisies, shine.

"Here." I extract Tray's passport from my dress pocket.

He's been to the US a lot on this, back when he played hockey. His mom took him to Cuba once, in Grade 10, in February, took him right out of school. That week, I was untethered. Missed Tray like he'd packed a critical piece of me in his suitcase, like whichever bone he borrowed, while it still lived inside me, still held me upright, it was emptied of marrow.

Tray returned, all tanned up. Came over to our house direct from the airport. Let himself in the front door like always and climbed the stairs to push into my room. He hugged me hard. "I missed you so much, Mollycakes. Yeah, I'm never leaving again. Don't make me do it."

He said it like it was my fault he went on an all-inclusive vacation with his mom.

At the time, I thought, this is why friendship matters. How deeply it matters, that you can miss someone even when you're on holiday.

Hank showed up, leaned against my doorframe, his hair overgrown. "And I'm what? Easy to leave behind? I would have killed it on the beach in Cuba."

Tray hesitated. A second too long.

"Wow. I see how it is, buddy." My brother wasn't hurt.

No, it was something else.

Tray released me slowly. He ran to the doorway, picked Hank up, and threw him on my bed, and all three of us landed there laughing, happy to be back in alignment. To be filled up with what we needed, and what we wanted too.

Here, in the sunshine, in Lone Pine, California, Tray says, "Yeah, so it's all good?"

"It's all good," I echo back. "Faith'll get us in the morning, and we can head out."

"You didn't even ask me, eh?" Matteo says, and they look at Hank pointedly. After a beat, both of them devolve into laughter.

"Come along for the ride," Hank says once he can speak. "Also, yeah, I've, uh . . . heard a rumor. There are probably dental programs in Seattle."

Matteo plays with their septum piercing. "You think?"

My brother looks at his best friend. "They have teeth up that way, right, Tray?"

"I've heard that, yeah, buddy." Tray's face is straight, his voice as droll as it freaking can be. "Mollycakes? You think they have teeth up Seattle-way?"

"It's possible." I shrug. "Probably even. Most humans are born with two full sets."

Hank throws his hands up in the air. "Well, now, I'm thinking that's a wild tale. Science fiction. Some big-ass story. X-rays of babies, mouths all full up with teeth. That's Photoshop shit if I ever did—"

"Please for the love of a good afternoon, kindly shut up,"

Matteo says, that warm smile still on their face.

"For you?" Hank laughs. "Yeah."

Tray leans even farther away from me, to rest on his elbows, his hair almost dry. "Well, isn't this cute?"

"This is a rhetorical-question-free zone," Hank volleys back.

"Never liked them anyway," Tray says, not missing a beat.

This, this is good.

So good.

I want to finger-comb Tray's hair. But I curl my hands into fists to stop myself. Because we're warm and we could be mostly happy here, if we weren't leaving, if we didn't have to leave one critical person behind.

Two, when I count Matteo, which I do. And Faith makes three. We're walking, but we're gathering people to us too.

"So, in this friend group," Matteo asks, looking somewhere across the street, "do we talk about when one person sings a really great song for another person in the friend group, or do we cone-of-silence this stuff? And no, this question is not rhetorical."

Hank doesn't say a thing.

All I manage is to shake my head back and forth.

Tray says, "What song?" and that's enough for us all to laugh.

We find a groove, get lunch, sit on a patio eating massive burgers and fatty, golden fries. Later we stock up at the general store, ready ourselves for the trail. And at night, even though Matteo stays over again, Tray seems to understand that I need a room to myself. Lying against pillows embedded with citrus shampoo, and something deeper, like warm boy, or simply Tray, I'm sleepless, melancholy.

I swipe through my text chats again, my phone lighting up the space. This started Friday night, while my phone was in the room, charging, and has continued nonstop. I've paid so little attention to this device since we started walking in the world. I only discovered these after my shower an hour ago.

Mom: I called Calgary. To set up a payment plan. And Molly Lee, I accepted the offer on your behalf. You better have a really good story to tell me. You're incredibly lucky they still want you.

Mom: The very next time you get a cell signal, I'm expecting to hear from you.

Dad: Your brother tells it that you're ignoring us, ma fii. He's worried too. And I'm telling you this so you know it's important: if we don't hear from you soon, your mother's booking us tickets to fly down. We're having this conversation one way or another.

Dad: If you think that's wrong, I'll say it, it's not. We're your parents.

Dad: So call.

It's unkind, but I think about the years when he went away, when his parenting was long-distance, awfully low-key. Every other weekend at its peak. Once every six months at its worst.

Mom: Your dad said he wouldn't let this go, won't go easy on you. Maybe you'll listen to him.

Mom: What is this, Molly? A breakdown? You need to see a therapist. Like I asked months ago. Are you really letting Hank's accident derail your bright future? Because that's what this looks like. Not

accepting the offer! Ignoring them! Did you know
they weren't going to hold it much longer?

I keep reading, grab the pillow Tray used, hug it. It's not safety.
But it is, at least for tonight, needed comfort.

Mom: Or maybe this is a temper tantrum. I love you
Molly, always, but you were good at these as a
toddler. I thought you'd outgrown the habit.

Mom: Answer your phone. I know you're around. Your
brother says you have service.

Under *Recents*, I find a slew of missed calls, time-stamped in
red one after another.

Missed call.

Missed call.

Missed call.

Missed call.

Missed call.

She gave up while I was packing, hanging out with Tray, Hank,
and Matteo. Clicking the screen off, my eyes get tight, heavy, wet.
She accepted on my behalf! I cling to the pillow, wishing it was
the boy instead. And if it wasn't unimaginable, beyond the bounds
of good science, I'd be wishing I could knock quietly on the door
next to mine and, when the door opens, I'd crawl into his bed.
There, I would be loved, exactly as I am.

Loved without restrictions.

For too long I was content to be angry, to blame, to scream,
bite and lash out under the weight of my hurt, and now that I'm
not, I have to return to my place in my parents' constellation:
shining daughter on the premed track at the U of Calgary, her

close-to-perfect GPA, her accelerated graduation, her toxic daisies, and then, as if foregone the way stars are, she'll seek admission to medical school.

I open my parents' joint text chat, select the voice message option.

"Hi, Mom, hi, Dad. I'm okay. I really am. Hank hasn't said a thing to me, so I don't know what he's telling you. I'm better than ever. You should see my calf muscles." I pause, watch the recording count empty seconds. "I messed up," I say finally. "After Hank. I, um, forgot what I wanted. Forgot how to be myself if Hank wasn't there next to me. But this, this is good for me. You need to know that. I need you to hear that. And I love you both. So much."

I can't thank my mom for saying yes, not yet.

I hover over the send button, but delete the recording instead.

When I try again, it's easier, clearer, my voice isn't so strained on the word *need*: "I love you both. I really do. It was a mistake not to accept. I was distracted. But it's fixed now."

I understand what I need to do. Who I need to be.

Maarsi for this, for holding me to it. And maarsi for seeing Brynn through a scary night, for seeing her to the other side of the full moon, only a little scathed. If I try hard enough, it's possible to be happy on the path I need to walk. The one I used to crave the way the girl from the song loved her flowers big, her flowers in unnatural, neon hues.

But I can't let go of this pillow. Not yet.

And you can't make me.

MILE 762.3

Traylor

Walking next to me, his hiking pole thumping against the ground with every step, Hank's moping. Truly sad to leave Matteo behind even if the Sierras are grandiose. Everywhere we turn it's big and bigger views. *Sunshine embellished with magnificent storms.* John Muir. Scottish American conservationist.

A poet too, the way he wrote about the Sierras.

He was a product of his time, yeah. A white man who believed in his own supremacy. We forget that now. All the girlies and mountain bros who post photos and caption it with Muir's *The mountains are calling, and I must go.* Those voices I wanted to get space from have been quiet, but they are still here. John Muir wouldn't want me or Molly hiking in his mountains. Probably not Hank or Brynn either. And yet, John Muir is the reason people care about these mountains so deeply.

It's uncomfortable, yeah, quoting him.

Above the tree line, the vista is all lichen and valiant grasses. Below, where we are now, it's abundant lakes, silver fir, silver pine, giant sequoia.

Today, Hank's off-balance, a little less stable. "They would have been okay out here, right? Like they'd have learned to love this too. What's not to love? An abundance of trees or their complete absence. The way your back hurts from carrying all the things you need to mostly survive."

Two mornings ago, Molly left a note next to my sunglasses on the dresser: *Went to visit that cop. Took your passport too. NO NEED TO CALL YOUR MOM.* And now, after Faith returned us to the trailhead, without Brynn, whose parents sent a car for her, Molly is acting like we didn't take steps to repair things.

She's skittish.

I raise my eyebrows at her brother.

"Yeah, you're right, buddy." Hank sighs. "Matty would hate everything about this."

Ahead of us, Molly stalls. Waits for us to catch up, her head bowed. Then she stretches, makes eye contact. "What are we having for lunch? And can we stop soon?"

This is impersonal. Almost back to how we started, all those miles ago. But something is different after Friday night. She's shifted somehow.

Songs, stories, they're powerful. They might have enough power to change someone's mind. Maybe I had that wrong. Maybe that's exactly what my mom does, day after day in her suits, her beaded earrings.

"Peanut butter will star in the meal," Hank says, forlorn. "You bought us three jars."

"It might sound gross to you, but I'm going to sprinkle chocolate chips on the stuff, wrap it in a tortilla, and go to town."

I laugh at Molly.

She only kicks at the dirt and then, with a huff, tackles the next torturous incline.

For someone who wanted to be better at communication, she's not using any words, but she is, I'll give her this, expressing herself. Saving her energy. The Sierras are incredibly hard work. Now that we're out here, they seem impossible to imagine.

Like a dream of a postcard.

But Mollycakes is incredible at the impossible. She might think she's all for science, that stories have no hold on her. That's her misconception. The impossible, it belongs entirely in story's wheelhouse. Western science doesn't understand the impossible. Refuses to believe in it.

She taught me that in Grade 10 Bio.

I barely got through that class, wouldn't have without her study sessions, her careful attention to our lab reports, to my understanding of what Molly considers basic fact.

Lately, I've been thinking about crickets and care. I've been thinking about telling a cricket story or maybe working it into a song. And I'm thinking if I had been braver, if I'd knocked on her door last night, I wonder if we'd be like this today. Or if she'd be softer. If I'd be softer too.

If that had happened, we'd be better primed to pass soft forward, to soften this world.

If, fucking if.

Every mile is hard won.

Crossing these mountains in early spring would have been that much harder, when even now we still find snow at high altitude. It's as if the time we spent dehydrated in the desert was only an appetizer, only the long intro to this trail song. When we get up high, Molly keeps checking her phone even though it's less than smart. Hank too. We stopped in town, were connected to other people, to the world again, and maybe it was too long. Even I'm stuck there, humming Molly's song under my breath.

Arriving at our campsite, tucked below the tree line of this mountain we've been fighting all day, I'm ready to eat and sleep. To try again tomorrow. But that song, and dwelling on it all day, on the way it felt to be onstage singing those words for that girl, it's got me twisted. My strings are too tight. The comb is missing too many teeth to make music. And I've never gotten the hang of the jaw harp. If Molly was walking next to me, I'd be grounded, okay with my choices, the ones that led me here.

Maybe if Molly was next to me, I could imagine another stage.

Could imagine other songs.

The stage could get larger and I wouldn't notice. I'd just keep singing about a girl and maybe about cricket eggs and how we can be soft, how we should gather softness to our chests and inhale it, bury it in the body, make it part of our code.

Hank checks his phone for the three hundredth time today. "Come on, bars! Let's get to two! You can do it!"

Near a pile of deadfall, Molly collapses on the ground, pack and all. She's sweaty and I should have noticed it sooner: she's hurting bad. The sound she makes guts me. Half groan, half whine, like she couldn't hold it in any longer.

Her brother doesn't even glance away from his phone. "Mols,

put the tents up, and I'll go get us water. Tray can start on food."

She's still lying on the ground. "No, thank you."

I freeze. The words themselves aren't anything to note.

But fuck, her tone, it's a knife already bloodied.

"No, I don't think I will," she says, struggling out of her pack. "I'm not doing you any favors today, Hank. You don't deserve them."

"That time of the month, eh?"

Molly's face crumples when he blames this on her body, like that's how you talk to a person who menstruates when they're hurting. Like his sister is not intentional about so many things.

Can I change the subject?

Can I kiss you?

"Hank," I admonish.

"Course you're on her side!"

"What side?" I say.

"Is this what I have to look forward to when you two finally get over yourselves and couple up?"

Now Molly is livid, her cheeks gone red, her eyes emptied of tender things.

She pushes herself up with a pained sigh, then steps right up to her brother's gear, which Hank has dumped in the middle of the trail. Molly picks up his discarded hiking pole. "This," she says slowly, "is not safety. Not in the hands of someone so freaking irresponsible!"

Hank smirks. "In what way am I being irresponsible, using a tool to help me do this really hard thing? It's not like you don't have one too. Right there, strapped to your pack."

It's the wrong move, that smirk.

"To answer that question, let's go back to the beginning." She holds the hiking pole in her hand so tightly. "It's what you learn, the very first thing, the first day, to check your equipment. Not to place implicit trust in it. And did you do it, Hank? That Saturday, did you run the equipment checks, or did you just assume someone else would do it for you?"

Hank shrugs.

"I've . . . Jesus, I've been angry at the wrong person, at myself, for months. And what have you done? What have you said?" She stops, catches her breath. "Yeah, not a thing. You kept your mouth shut. Until you freaking didn't."

I've never asked him that straight up. Have never been brave enough. Or angry enough to do it. *Hank, before we started to climb, did you do a safety check?* Because outside of hockey, where aggression has its place, I crave softness like it's the music, the end goal.

"You know, Hank, I've never told Mom or my dad anything that they'd hear and be hurting over. Not when you sold your bus pass to help pay for that rare Pokémon card and then told Mom you lost the pass. Or even after you crashed my dad's truck because you were on your phone! But I'm really done now," she says, her voice breaking open.

Molly doesn't cry often. She toughs through. Or maybe this girl only cries when she's alone. Because her cheeks are wet. She picks up her half-empty canteen and stalks past the deadfall and into the healthy trees.

When his sister's gone far enough and she won't hear him, Hanks speaks: "What was that?"

It bothers me that I don't know. That she's not telling me what hurts. Without Brynn here to keep us steady, Molly has, in so many ways, gone back to the start of the trail. I feel Brynn missing from us viscerally. By the time I made it to the hospital yesterday, she'd been discharged already.

There's only one thing I can think of, the way a song returns to the chorus again and again. How that's intentional, the repetition. "Have you talked with your sister? You know, since?"

"She barely left my side. Mols knows everything already."

"Hank."

"Traylor."

"Now there's a load of bear shit."

"Well, at least it's not another pretty pine cone!"

"Jesus, Hank." I exhale my words. "Your sister loves you."

He grimaces, then crumples, shoulders falling in, head low. He bites out his words. "And I love her. But—"

"It's like in the *I love you* playbook to never follow that statement with *but*," I say, and wonder how much it hurt when I did the same thing. Only a couple dozen miles ago.

I love you. But I don't really like you these days.

"Haven't you noticed? My sister has given up on so much since the accident. Did she tell you she only applied to one university? And she didn't accept the offer. She lied to my parents about it all. Or did some fancy fucking footwork not to say her lies out loud." Hank swallows. "So I had to tell them."

I shake my head. I assumed she wasn't sharing her good news with me. How school after school was begging her to attend their program. Which one she picked and why. And at graduation it

207

hurt viscerally, knowing she'd made this big decision without asking where I'd be. If I'd be along for the adventure.

"Did she tell you she's not coming home with us?" Hank continues. "That she plans to finish the trail, even though she's not prepared? Goddamn, nobody should be out here alone. And Mols yells at me about irresponsibility."

I look off in her direction. She left her pack, wouldn't go forward without. Wouldn't leave us here.

"She's the one gone off the deep end. The only reason I'm out here. I should be in summer school, making up credits. So don't tell me that I need to talk to my sister. I know her better than you ever will. No matter what."

He could be right about that.

But Hank-the-Tank is wrong too. He owes Molly a conversation. The way he's made sure I'm okay with what happened to him, to us. Hank's done that over and over. Offered that to me but doesn't think his sister deserves the same level of care.

"I'm going to check up on her," I say, frustrated he's kept this from me. When I asked why he changed his mind. And all this time, he's what? Been watching over Molly for their parents?

"You're always running after this girl, buddy." Hank spits out rough laughter. "Aren't you tired yet? When she never runs toward you?"

There's a band drawing tight and tighter across my forehead. I don't answer Hank. I follow a small path through the trees. It's probably human-made, but it reminds me of the trails that deer, moose, even bears carve through the backwoods. Paths they walk again and again, until the earth is scored. That just like

208

people, animals crave routine.

I duck under a dense branch.

Where the trees open up, the vista is sharp, perfect. Molly, sitting on top of a massive gray boulder, dressed mostly in pink, her hair caught up in a knotted red bandanna. The sky is blue, cloudless. The mountains loom in every direction, still green, for now.

It's hot during the day, but at night, it's chilly. The snow is coming.

"You okay?" I ask from the ground looking up.

Molly shrugs, doesn't turn in my direction. So I find my way up to the top as easy as she did with years of climbing and bouldering behind us, sit next to her. The rock is warm from the sun. If I closed my eyes, I could imagine us a beach. But this place feels the way I've been told holy places do for those who believe. Alive, shimmering.

"I don't recognize him anymore," she says eventually.

I play back the highlight reel, what just happened. "We're all changing," I say. Because Hank is not a different person, but like everyone else, he's growing, becoming.

"Are you? Changing?"

"I hope so."

"I'm not." She laughs, dejected. "I have to stay exactly the same."

"Jesus H. Christ, what is it with the Norris-Norquay siblings today and all the very bad, no-good takes?"

"Tray," she says like she truly believes herself, "I'm not allowed to grow beyond what my parents can imagine for me. It's something I get now. It's science or nothing. Because I'm supposed to be Molly the doctor. You get to keep your future, all possibilities open. Your alternate endings remain in play until you decide which you want. Hank, too, he gets that. Now that he's . . . okay again." She pulls her knees to her chest. "But I don't."

I want to hug her. To make her understand she's wrong through touch. That she's changed too. In good ways, and in ones that hurt her, don't serve her heart.

"Can I tell you something? It's a story, but it's a story about some science." I'm thinking of the graduation gift I was too chicken to give her back in June. A signed edition of *Braiding Sweetgrass*, one my mom helped me track down.

"I am not in the mood."

"Humor me. Please, Mollycakes."

She nods, once.

"So there's this cricket. Grandmother cricket. And she lives her life. And it's a good one, yeah. She gets everything she needs and more. Has movie dates and hot-tub dates with good gentleman crickets who treat her well, who respect her, know she's all-powerful and that to spend time with her is a gift. Never doubts herself, always finds herself in good spirits. Later, she has babies and later still they have babies of their own. Here's what you'll like," I say, taking a pause. "It's scientifically proven, in a study, by a Kaw scientist, that her babies and her babies' babies do well. They have a good life too, enough of enough. Can survive conditions that another cricket's third generation can't."

We both stare at the mountains. Below us there's an alpine lake, its water clear.

"And you know this. It's not a story, yet, not until there's another grandmother cricket. So . . ." I pause again, wishing she'd look my way, that I could compete with this view for her prickly affection. "There's this other grandmother cricket, yeah. Her young life is struggle for food, for shelter in the bad weather, for enough. She doesn't know what it means to be sated. And yeah, she has babies too. Some. And some of her babies have babies eventually. It's not that she fails as a grandmother because this isn't her fault. But those babies, the third generation, they carry something passed down from her, through their mother, and that thing makes their lives harder."

Molly's hand flattens on the boulder next to mine.

"Here's what the scientist found when they went looking. The second grandmother's descendants don't do as well when faced with the same challenges as the first grandmother cricket's progeny."

Molly scoffs, just like her brother does when he's sure he's right. "Yeah, congratulations, you've discovered epigenetics."

She doesn't get it.

Still thinks it's one or the other. That it's all or nothing. Western science or Indigenous storytelling. She can't join the parts of herself together.

"No, Mollycakes, this is story. Real experiments don't happen in a vacuum. Maybe they did in BIO10. But your science needs story. It's not this thing without narrative. Not empirical in the absolute. Pure, like that's possible in this world. It's a story you have, a story you search for evidence to support, like our people have been doing forever. With controlled burns to care for forests, with agriculture and the Three Sisters, who need each other to all grow well. It's life and it's all story, all of it. But it's all science too."

"I want to believe you," she says carefully. "But that's not my experience of the universe."

"And that's the story you're telling yourself. Don't you see?"

"No," she says, "that's what the evidence proves. When I line it up piece by piece, it's so obvious. Hank falls and our parents can't let me fall next. Hank falls and now the world is unstable. At its core, it's so utterly unsafe!"

"That's a different way of saying the same thing, Mols."

She recoils. "Stop calling me that! I'm so fucking tired of this. Of being called *Mols*, like it isn't a slap in the face! Tired of wanting things I can't have! Freaking done with my brother ratting me out to our parents . . . reporting on me, without talking to me first. Without checking to make sure I was . . . okay."

If I had perfect recall, I'd know. Instead, I wonder if every time Hank's been uncareful with her name, whether she's flinched like that. The way you do when you realize what comes after free fall is impact.

"I didn't know that hurt, Molly. You have to tell Hank. He wouldn't . . . I won't call you that again. Not now that I know."

"Do you forgive me yet?" she asks fast, the way she used to jump on a teacher's questions in class, like if she didn't get to the front of the line, there would be nothing left.

I swallow. "Not quite."

"It all hurts," she says. "All of it."

"I'm sorry for that." The alpine lake, we could climb down to it, if we tried. But then we'd have to climb up again. "When

Hank's accident happened, the world didn't change. It's always been this way. But, Molly, not to harp the same point too hard, you've been buying into this narrative."

She shakes her head but doesn't speak.

"You buy into this thing that hurts us all. It's a story, a story that the Western world is built on, one that says disability is what's wrong and not all the systems around it, the ones that make it hard to live in a disabled body."

"I am the first person to show up, to stand up for Hank," she says. "You know this."

"Yeah, you are. But also, you can do that and still carry around this completely toxic worldview." I say it again for her. "*Stand up. Do you get how that's a problem too? Saying it like that, framing it like that?"

"It's not that simple!" she hollers, and then pauses. "I don't know why it's so easy for you. Why you rely so much on stories! Why you can jazz up someone's science to prove your point and call it objective."

I want the disharmony to stop. To go back to before I told her about cricket eggs. "Okay, Molly. Whatever you say. That must be right. Because you know it all."

"Whatever you say."

When she echoes it back, in the same register, I hear myself. Yeah, I don't forgive her. I stand, looking out at the mountains, that lake, for a minute. They're out here, I know it. It's why we're carrying bear-proof canisters for our foodstuffs. And I wish we could see one. Wish for a minute, that one would amble by, for Molly and me to witness. Because maybe, that would fix this.

A bear could fix this.

"Would you go now?" Molly's closed off, her whole body shut down to protect itself. "Let me sit alone for a while?"

"Yeah. I can do that."

Back at camp I find Hank's put up both tents, and that he's finished making dinner, that he's eaten and gone to bed. The cell phone glow from inside our tent means he's not sleeping yet, but he's done for the day.

Sitting out there with Molly, it didn't feel that long.

I've always been thankful she wasn't with us that day. And that's fucked up. Being happy it was Hank and not his sister. She would have run for it, the pink metallic belay device. Maybe we're beyond the help a bear could offer.

Maybe I'm falling too, falling into my dad's low-key paranoia, the way he clings to his language camp like it could save us all.

MILE 780.8

Molly

When I wake, a text is waiting for me from my mom: That's not enough. It's too little too late. Instead of starting my day the way I have for weeks now, by awkwardly peeing in the woods, I lie on the ground, exchanging increasingly upsetting messages.

I can't unclench my jaw. Too-easy anger inhabits my muscles, all my extra fat.

And because Hank is on his phone too, sullen, refusing to leave the tent, we have a late start. The day is hot and the ibuprofen Tray slips me with breakfast won't help much, but I swallow it anyway.

"Thanks," I say.

He just nods, begins breaking down camp. First mine, then the tent he shares with my brother, while I eat. Hank's off somewhere in the woods.

As the day burns onward, it doesn't matter if I'm halfway up the mountainside or taking a break in the shade, I'm still messaging with my mom. It's a twisting conversation, cut off when I need to stash my phone in the waistband of my stretchy bike shorts to concentrate on the trail, on my steps. My left knee is bloodied.

I've tripped more than once.

I'm hiking a mountain range, part of a continuous chain, like the trail is a spine, each mountain a vertebra, traveling up into Canada, as if daring the universe to hurt me.

My mom's stuck on the concept of waste. Like what I'm doing now is wasteful. She thinks I played weekends away in the Rockies, another part of this mountainous spine, when I ought to have been reading, studying, memorizing.

Mom: It could have been a whole lost year! You're flailing around, throwing the baby out with the bathwater!

Me: What does that even mean?

Mom: It's a saying, Molly.

Me: What I'm doing here is . . .

Me: Important.

Me: To me.

Mom: Isn't the plan important? Where you're supposed to be by the time you're 25?

I freeze. Stop in the middle of the trail. Covered in a sheen of sweat, my dry-fast shirt is unable to dry. I type carefully, with intent: You know how much I wanted this.

I mean the hike. This time with my brother and Tray. Because graduation was an ending, where Hank would go to Toronto, Tray would head north or off to school somewhere else, and I'd have to follow the plan alone.

They're ahead of me for once.

Like he knows I need it, Tray peers over his shoulder, checking up on me. But he's afraid of doing any more than that. And my brother, who I have always loved beyond measure, even though we have different fathers, even though I'm Native and he's not, I always believed that we were the same. Carved from the same bone. That if it were needed, if one of us required a transplant, we'd find we were a perfect match. It would shock doctors, defy science.

But it would be true.

Hank is ignoring me, absolutely. Texting with someone, probably Matteo. But if it's our mom, if he's still reporting to her from the trail like a bad spy, I think I might unravel.

I consider hurling my phone into the trees. Overhand, with heft.

My mom types. Three floating dots appear and disappear. When her text arrives, it's a big block.

Mom: It's not that it's out of character, it's that you're
not being honest about what you're planning.
Hank told us about the notes in your room, on your
laptop. I checked your credit card statement, talked
to Andrew at MEC. You bought an ice axe when
you didn't plan to be out in the snow! You're due at
school, hear me on that. And you are not allowed to
do this hike alone. That's my line, Molly Lee. You're
seventeen, a child still!

I inhale roughly.

Don't believe in that butterfly effect BS.

Don't believe that because I stayed home that Saturday, because I did that, Hank had to fall. The butterfly effect is only an idea, not a practice that can be studied, organized, known to behave in regular, notable ways.

I'm furious with my brother, my mom, with myself, but all I type is: Okay, mom. Okay.

I ache.

The maple protein bar I'm eating is chalky. No one wants to talk. If Hank tries, I'll only yell at him again. That's certainty. If Tray does . . . I worry I'll break open, beg him to help me find another way, a way out. Tell him about the promises I've made. Ask him what he knows, how much total bear shit I've gotten myself into. No offense to the bears.

I can't stop saying this. None of us can. Tray's up in my head, and Hank always picks up what Tray puts down.

We're connected.

Tied together in invisible ways, even now.

It comes down to math, to fractions. I'm not enough. Too big, too much, yes. But not Métis enough to know the stories. To know how to get out of these promises.

My dad's always been so disappointed that every year I skip Back to Batoche for science camp.

I start walking again, push forward up the next hill.

I'm in my own head the whole time, overheating, but knowing that if I strip down to my sports bra, I'll end up with worse pressure sores across my shoulders. There will be more blood. I can't see a way out of this, can't imagine myself out of the problem. My mother expects one thing from me, to get back on track. And while my dad is quiet today, he's on my mom's team. And you all, none of you creatures of power, you lumbering animal kin, you birds of prey, seem to want to help me. Because I promised it and, in the moment, I meant it.

I would have done anything for Hank to wake up, *stand up*.

I cringe. Tray's right.

But what if I was wrong about something fundamental too? Because while I pretend I'm talking to the old gods, to the ones in textbooks, with shrines on roadsides and up mountainsides, the ones who inhabit the sweet spots all around the world, to them and to Creator, but also to all tricksters, nobody answers.

All this time, I've been talking to myself. Relying on this voice, as if she were my chance. As if I could imagine I didn't make that covenant, that I was only doing what everyone else does and talking shit in my own head.

There wasn't an official test. Nobody scored my attempt. But I didn't pass, couldn't make rank.

We camp early, nowhere near meeting our daily goal. Decide without much more than a nod when one of us stumbles to a stop. Tents up, our meal cooking over the tiny stove, we're not talking when another group of hikers comes upon us.

We know these people.

Though I never wanted to see them again, this is the way of the world.

"Hot Sauce, girlie," the dark-haired guy who goes by Lucky Strike says, like he's thoroughly unimpressed. "We were wondering when we'd catch up to you and your grumbling bodyguards."

His friends, Fresno and Doublecross, step into the small pocket off the trail, sweaty, reeking of weed. Before I can wonder where the others are, behind them, taking up the rear, is Noelle Brynn Hensley. She's wearing her plain white daisy shirt, the front hem tucked into her sports bra.

"Hi," she says, but hangs back.

The loud, dramatic one puts his hands all over her, like he's marking out territory. She doesn't dislodge him. It makes me low-key sick.

"Brynny!" Hank says excitedly at first, and then he flattens.

Caught up in his own stuff, my brother shrugged, didn't even try to go see her in the hospital. Tray did. I might not have said the words. But there was a goodbye between us.

"You know these three?" Lucky Strike asks. "'Cause we stumbled on them once before. Had a grand ole time."

Brynn smiles. It's not as bright as she normally would. "I walked with them for a while. But I stayed back to rest up when they carried on."

That's a lie.

Tray's not having any of it. "Thought your parents were sending a car for you, yeah?"

Brynn only shrugs.

"Come on, Brynny," the guy next to her, the one with his hands all over her, says. He goes by Fresno out here, but it worries me that we don't know his real name. "We've got miles to go before we slip into sleep. And while you're a fun fat chick, you're slow."

I want to deck him.

So does Hank.

Even Tray looks like he'd use that hockey brawn of his for good. Or, finally, break out and behave like the rock star he wants to be. The kind who'd jump off the stage into the crowd, the kind who gets caught.

Brynn rolls her eyes as if that comment doesn't hurt. "You don't need to keep saying it. We both know I'm fat. And, my dude, it was only a little funny the first half dozen times."

He giggles, like this is only a joke. "Maybe you need a trail name?"

Hank's gone all red. "If you say another word . . ."

"Let's go, Brynn. Right now like," Lucky Strike says. "Frez is being a jerk-off. But he'll quit that."

Brynn glances at us for a second, and it's like she doesn't get what she's seeking. She adjusts her T-shirt, so that the triangle of skin she's exposing is smaller. "Okay."

"This is ridiculous. You're not going with them," I say loudly. "Nohow, no freaking way."

"You can come too, Hot Sauce," Doublecross says with a smile. "If Brynny's going to be keeping those guys warm in their tent, I'll freeze alone in mine."

Tray comes up next to me like I need backup. And maybe I do.

"Brynn," Tray says. "Don't go off with them."

She takes a step forward, stalls. It's all noise. Overwhelming noise, growing louder and louder.

"No, no, no," Lucky Strike says, grabbing her by the wrist.

"This isn't funny." Brynn pulls against his grip. "Now you're being the jerk-off."

"Am I laughing?" Lucky Strike speaks and then he laughs.

Hank shifts his upper body my way, talks low. "I mean, I'm gay but I can probably fight? I've got those climbing muscles and my

221

legs are ripped from all this walking."

I roll my eyes at my brother.

"Nobody's fighting," Tray says. "Jesus H., what is this? Brynn, we're your friends."

And that's what snaps her out of it. The air around us goes slack. The noise dissipates.

She pulls hard on her hand, and this time, Lucky Strike releases. "Sorry, my dudes. I didn't tell you earlier, when you were all, like, come hike with us, we're friendly guys who don't seem threatening at all. But I'm only sixteen. And soooo probably . . . ," she says. "Like, for legal reasons, it's best if you take off without me, you know? Also, I'm not into dudes, and I bet none of you are cousins with the golden-voiced Hozier and want to arrange our marriage."

Hank laughs.

"Your loss." Lucky Strike seems bored all of a sudden. He lights a cigarette with one, two flicks of a barbecue lighter extracted from his cargo shorts. As they take off farther down the trail, one of them begins a song. It's a children's song.

"Old MacDonald Had a Farm."

The others make animal noises.

I curl over, feeling sick. Wonder where Joey is, where Russ, the other guy, went. If they got smart and left. If something worse happened. An accident they couldn't escape from.

As soon as we can't hear the other hikers anymore, Tray reprimands me. "That was dangerous, Molly."

"Yeah, fuck," Hank adds. "I almost had a heart attack. And I'm too young and my teeth are far too pretty for death, Mols."

Maybe I'm hurt enough now. There isn't room for more.

Because for once this, being called *Mols*, only aches quietly, like a fading bruise.

Tray's shaking his head as if he's a disappointed dad.

I bristle. I have one of those already and don't need another. Even if Tray is right about some things.

Brynn only laughs because maybe she doesn't know. How close my brother came to dying in September. "Anyone else starved?" she asks.

We all nod. And so we eat.

Tonight, we prove we are bad actors. We pretend Brynn didn't run away again, escaping from the hospital before the car her parents ordered arrived. I pretend my brother hasn't broken my heart. That I'm not drowning. That I can't hear the ocean, angry, throwing water, all this against the pull of the moon, when I'm up well over ten thousand feet.

Brynn's asleep in her dream world like she never left us, but I can't make it to mine. In the green tent, the boys are talking. Not even at a whisper.

"Can you imagine how that would have gone down if my sister were out here alone?"

"I don't want to. Don't make me." This from Tray, like I hurt him, like being around me hurts him.

They must believe I'm out cold.

Because if not, I'm wondering if they ever trusted me at all. If I've always been too young to do these things with them. That when we graduated from bikes in the cul-de-sac, I became a liability. But since I'm Hank's little sister, because blood is strongest, because my dad was gone, they had to include me. I wonder if the boys have always felt I was a chore, some unasked-for responsibility.

If I'm nothing but extra weight to them.

"Without us, she'd . . . They could have . . . Fuck, I can't even say it."

"Don't say it, please. Just don't, Hank."

I push out of my sleeping bag and crawl to the zipper. Outside, it's chilly enough that I grab my hoodie, slip into it before finding my camp sandals. I walk over to the boys' tent, crouch down.

"It's rude to talk about someone like they're not right next to you, eh?" I sound confident, exactly like I used to before. When I knew what I wanted. When I believed I wanted it. Without waiting for a response, I push up to standing, my legs screaming.

"Jesus," Tray says. "Don't go off anywhere, Molly! It's fucking dark."

"Don't you trust me?"

"That's not it." Tray scrambles out of the tent. He's wearing his wool pants, a T-shirt. It's full of holes, needs to be thrown out. *You Are on Native Land.*

He was in this shirt when we almost missed our flight. Back then, I wanted to hate him so badly, as if that would stop the world from spinning madly around me. "What is it, then? Because you both were loud enough. I get the message now. Unless you want to repeat it to my face. For, I don't know, shits and giggles." I brush hair from my face, tuck it behind my ears. "I might not have gotten it before. But now I understand."

"You understand nothing, Mols," Hank says, crawling to the door of the tent.

"Do not call me *Mols*."

"Your brother doesn't mean it that way," Tray says, all soft.

"Quit teaming up on me!"

"We're not, Molly," Tray insists.

I don't scream. I talk very slow, very calm. "So what was all that? Can you imagine how it would've gone down if poor Molly were out here all alone? Because Molly can't handle herself. No she needs the boys or her mom to make all her decisions."

"Those guys were unhinged," Hank says. "And the one you liked wasn't even with them."

"This has nothing to do with those guys, and you know it."

"Do I?" Hank asks, and then he laughs. "Well, you'd know, wouldn't you? Because Miss Molly, she knows everything. Thinks she can go off on her own, hiking on her own, that she won't end up lonely or hurt or something much worse."

"Safety isn't a guarantee," I say. "You ought to understand this by now."

We fall quiet.

Brynn sleeps, dreams onward.

And maybe it's not the problem I thought I was facing. In an ableist world, safety seems like protection against this thing worse than death, worse than dying. Because in an ableist world, the worst thing would be to live with a disability. I've been raging against this, how after my brother fell, this world didn't fit him anymore.

Doesn't fit any of us anymore.

But no, like everything else, it never fit, never welcomed us.

I just couldn't see it yet.

"It's a bad idea, Mollycakes," Tray says carefully a minute later. "You going forward alone. This is something you shouldn't do by yourself."

If I look up to the sky, I'm afraid all the stars will have shifted. That the minor bear will have been replaced by something else.

I exhale shakily. "The two of you are only a year older than me. There are thirteen months, Hank, between you and me. And it's only science, you know. Girls mature faster than boys. My brain will be fully formed long before yours. My decisions will be steadier than yours, faster than yours."

I'm still raging. Even now that I get it.

My brother is exasperated. "Will be. Those are the key words, Mols."

"Hank, she asked you to stop," Tray says, peacekeeping.

And maybe, too, he's protecting me.

"Yeah." Hank scratches at his scars. "Fuck."

"It's not the first time," I say, even though I probably shouldn't. It's completely unsmart. But I can't help myself. "I've asked you not to call me *Mols* three times now."

Hank stares at the ground. In the dark, it's hard to see much. But he looks anyway. "Yeah, well, that's part of the problem, eh. Because I don't fucking remember that."

NOW

Hank

AITA for following my sister to the mountains?

AITA for snooping in her bedroom, digging through her secrets?

AITA for telling our parents, not when I found out, but when it served me most?

For downplaying the memory loss? For marking it minor on a list of side effects?

AITA for wishing I was anywhere but here?

For wanting Matteo here with me?

Wanting a hot tub just over that way, tucked under the trees, a hot tub more than anything right now?

Unpublished.

MILE 780.8

Traylor

Molly goes from pissed off, and rightly so, yeah, to worried in a flash. Her eyebrows tighten. She stands, paces left, then right. "Do you want to explain that statement? Unpack it. Do some fucking context work!"

"You know what? I'm done," Hank says, like he can't see his sister is upset. "I don't want to do this anymore. I'm going home."

Maybe he doesn't care.

"Hank," she says. "You don't give up just because something gets hard. You don't do that."

"That's not what this is."

"It is."

"Mollycakes, let the man say his piece, yeah?" I offer this softly, trying to make space for them to talk.

She nods.

Hank is sitting half inside our tent, his knees drawn into his chest. Molly sits. She's wearing that hoodie I loaned her years back. The one I got at a show in Edmonton, wore once. By lunch, she'd borrowed it. Seeing her in it, still after all that's between us,

228

makes me warm. I sit close to Molly, close, but not touching.

"But so it's clear. I really don't need you, Traylor," she says, "to keep taking his side."

"Yeah," Hank agrees.

"You two." I laugh suddenly, here in the dark. "You're too much alike not to see that I'm always on both of your sides."

"That's bear shit," Molly says.

"No offense to bears," Hank quips.

It breaks us down.

Forces us to back away from the hurt enough to see it.

If I imagine the future, there's one where Hank lives next door, maybe with Matteo, maybe not. And in our big backyard, the one where in winter the skating rink is the very best place, one day, one of those future kids is finally going to be grown enough to ask us what's up with the bear. How much of this story will we tell them? How much will we hold on to? Or will we forget the words' origin, forget how on this night they saved us?

I sink here for a long time.

The Norris-Norquay siblings are quiet too, thinking their own thoughts.

"How are we going to help Brynn?" Molly sits up straighter. "Because quitting, that doesn't help her. At all."

"Fuck," Hank agrees. "We could take her home with us."

His sister shakes her head. "It's not a good fix. Minors can't cross the border without their parents' permission."

I have this feeling.

It's a bad one.

All pending disaster, soured, flat.

"Maybe my mom can help?"

She's not in family and child law, but she's connected like that. We're all invested in breaking down harmful systems, keeping kids out of foster care.

Hank sighs. "We should call."

In her sharp voice, Molly volleys out: "We should ask Brynn what *she* needs."

"Settle, yeah, little bear," I say because I can't help myself. I'm tired all of a sudden. My lungs won't fully open. "In the morning, okay?"

"I wasn't suggesting we wake her."

Hank laughs at Molly, who looks at me like she's going to make a point with her teeth. Like she's going to bite.

Her brother, my best friend, Hank-the-Tank, he can't stop himself either. He thinks we've let it go, what he said. About remembering.

"You let him call you that? Little bear?" Hank asks, and then screws up his face. "Are the straights okay?"

"Shut up, Hank," I offer.

"Yeah, Hank, shut it," Molly says, her cheeks red.

Hank-the-Tank shrugs. "Okay, okay, fine. But I would just like to point out that we're doing the same thing to Brynny that you came after us for."

Molly pulls her body into the too-big hoodie, tucking it over her knees. "I realize that."

"Soooooo? What do you have to say to me?"

"I'm not apologizing. You two were being dicks."

Maybe so. But that wasn't our intent. "We were only looking out for you, Mollycakes."

Hank smirks.

Molly hugs herself. "How bad is it exactly, Hank? Your memory? What are you not remembering? Because you saying that scares me."

Hank falls backward into the tent, rolls over. Now only his feet stick out into the night. His voice is muffled, like he's buried in his sleeping bag. "I might have . . . underplayed the memory-loss thing. A smidge. I might have needed to keep something to myself."

There's a night bird in one of the trees nearby. It's screeching.

Molly puts a hand, palm down, on the ground between us. "Can I ask a question, Hank?"

"Yeah. You were going to anyway."

"How is this different than what I did? Making plans to finish the hike. And not telling you."

I stare at Molly's fingers, all her pink polish from day one of this trip worn away, wanting to twist my fingers up with hers. To make this easier on her. On me.

"Maybe it's not," Molly concludes when her brother doesn't answer.

Hank shakes his head now. "It's dangerous. What you're doing."

"Hi, pot, I'd like you to meet the freaking kettle," his sister says.

"It's not you that I don't trust in this situation."

"So what? Other hikers?"

I'm staying out of their conversation.

"You made this point yourself, just the other day. Don't you remember?" Hank pauses a second. "It's not safe. None of it is."

"Oh."

"Yeah, fucking oh, Molly."

"So what should any of us do? In this world?"

"Why are you asking me?" Hank says without bite. "It's obvious I have no idea which way's up these days. Can't remember shit."

Molly taps my knee. "You're awfully quiet."

I get her intent. If Hank won't talk to her, maybe he'll warm for me. But all I say is "Yeah. I'm . . . exhausted, yeah."

Molly laughs. "Me too."

"Me three."

"Look at us," I say to my two best friends. "We're a mess."

"Nothing sleep can't fix," Molly says. "I've read all the studies."

During the weeks when Hank wouldn't wake, I found her, in the hospital at all hours, studying scientific reports on brain injuries, comas, on what it meant to be stuck in sleep.

"I think we'd have to rack for about a year." Hank fakes nonchalance, all airy and droll. "Because three weeks and what, four days? That didn't fix me."

"Not funny," Molly says.

"Kinda is," Hank offers.

I clear my throat. It's heavy, thick, like my body wants to stop my voice from ringing out. This, I've only felt it before when I think about stepping onto a stage and performing my songs. "You're going to hate this, Mollycakes. But I think Hank is right . . . It's time for us to go home."

She opens her mouth as if to say something. To argue.

"Give me a minute, yeah."

She nods, quick and sharp.

"Once we help Brynn in a real way. With something that she wants, that's not more running off, and that's not going back to her parents, something right, once we do that, my heart is saying it's time we go home. All three of us."

We can't continue this way.

I think it, but I can't say it.

"I want to help Brynn." Molly shudders, like she's cold. "But I don't want to go back yet. I want to finish this. To walk farther."

"You can't always get what you want, Mols—I mean Molly," Hank corrects himself fast.

"What if it's not a want?" she asks quietly. "What if it's a need?"

The song I wrote for Molly comes to me now. *She's neon daisies, yeah / She's scissors against the guitar strings / Yeah, yeah, yeah.*

It's not a love song, but it's filled with notes of care.

While I was writing it, I missed this. That she needs this walk. Believes she does.

But Hank isn't there yet.

"There's nothing about your life that's so bad that you can't go home," Hank says. "Our parents, they support everything you do. We have enough money, enough love. Nobody is hurting you. You're smart, too smart sometimes. If you'd just accept the offer, the one that's waiting for you at seventeen years old from one of Canada's top universities, you've got everything set up all shining, golden. I don't get how all that leads to need."

"Do you *need* to get it to support me in this?" Molly asks roughly. "I didn't understand what you were going through. But I was there. For you."

Hank sighs.

It's not fair, but I get where he's coming from. "We talked about this, earlier, when you were getting water. If you keep walking, so do we, Molly."

She crumples inward. "I am not asking you to do that. I'm not asking you to drop out of high school, Hank, my god. And, Tray, you have plans. Your trip up north. Music or school or whatever."

"It's simple like that." Hank speaks like this is final. "If you keep going, so do we. And you've already pointed out all the ways that's fucked."

"This is manipulative," Molly says, directly to me.

"Yeah, I guess it is." She's not wrong, I know it. "But also, I can't let you stay on the trail on your own. I can't do that."

Nobody speaks. Behind the forest's night sounds, and Brynn's gentle snoring, that flat, sour note rings out. The fiddle cowers.

Molly's careful, planning her next move, the way she always has, methodically, from one rock to another. "I won't forgive you for this."

"Mollycakes, I still don't forgive you either."

Hank laughs at us. "It's incredibly late. We have a long day tomorrow. And my head's killing me. Can we continue this fight in the morning?"

He didn't used to get headaches, not before the accident. "Yeah, buddy."

Molly pushes up from the ground. "Fine, okay. But so you know, I'm starting to think forgiveness might be overrated."

"Night," I offer as she kicks her sandals off, climbs back into her tent.

Hank snickers. "Oooooh, she's mad at you!"

"Hank."

"Tray."

"Respectfully, go the fuck to sleep."

"You too, buddy," he says, lying back, curling over. "Respectfully."

But before he drifts off, Hank whispers, so his sister can't hear, "She'll get over herself. Eventually. But I still don't think this girl is ever going to run toward you. And that's what you want. What you need. I run after her because she's my family, my best friend. You run after her because you want her to run after you." He goes softer, quieter.

I'm leaning close.

"And, Tray, my sister, she doesn't need anyone. Not really."

"Do you believe that?"

"I have to, buddy."

Hank falls asleep fast.

And I'm thinking my mom might be right. But not in the way she thought. The other day, perched on that boulder, looking out at the world, I didn't lie when I said I was changing, growing too. I used to think I was in love with Molly. Madly, the way songwriters always are in the music. And now, I'm thinking, this isn't love. This isn't how you love another person. That if I was in love with Molly, I'd forgive her.

When the fiddle agrees, I feel sick.

But it's a sickness I have to learn to live with. Maybe this is another song. After all, the songwriters, they don't sing about a love that never ends. They sing love songs and then they sing their heartbreak. That's how the story goes.

THE BRIDGE

The movement that creates harmony out of discordant parts. The section of the design that brings cohesion. It might be another star, another chord or key, but it's integral.

MILE 793.8

Molly

We wake too freaking early. Before the sun. Brynn insists we'll talk, that she'll tell us everything so long as we keep on walking. She seems fragile, like she'd run again, this time from us, if we don't do it. So without question we break camp as dawn greets the day. When we're done, when I look back one last time, I can't imagine Tray, Hank, and me sitting in the dirt, arguing.

Because I don't fucking remember that.

Hank, half in, half out of the green tent. My brother acting wrong, so different from before the accident, when he would never have brought our parents in to referee. Tray next to me. The way he always seems to end up, close without actually touching. And me, in that hoodie.

I might have . . . underplayed the memory-loss thing.

Can't remember shit.

The ground is disturbed a little. Small divots remain from where our tent guy lines were staked into the earth.

But there's nothing else. And so we leave.

From her place on the trail sandwiched between the boys and

me, Brynn speaks: "Soooooo. In Lone Pine. Not sure if it was obvious . . . but that was the first time I've ever had alcohol."

We're not willing to leave her unprotected, it seems. Or she's a flight risk. Could be both.

"And I didn't realize how much, you know," she says. "How fast. And I'm sorry that you . . . had to basically carry me to the emergency room."

Hank doesn't let her statement sit. He pounces. "My first time . . . I threw up all over my mom's flower planters. She'd just gotten them. Was big proud. Had filled them with these pretty pink blooms. She'd gone back and forth on whether she'd plant petunias like everyone else on our block or if she'd get what she wanted. I was fourteen, and I don't think I've ever seen her so . . . disappointed."

I hated those flowers.

Ranunculus. Too sweet, like blushing girls.

For a few days, Hank tiptoed through the house, and Mom, she grumbled *Boys will be boys* under her breath. What my brother doesn't get is that when he decided to throw me to my parents, that, yes, Mom, this time, because it was me, she was more disappointed.

Ruined flowers could never compete.

I win, Hank.

I win.

And it freaking sucks.

"Oh yeah, but that has nothing on me." I hear the smile in Tray's voice. And while I know this story, I like the way he tells it. "I was up at the language camp with my dad. It was winter. Like

238

deep winter. Cold as a witch's tits."

Hank smirks. "No offense to witches."

"So not only did I get sick all over the place," Tray continues, "but my dad laughed at me the whole time. Like pointing his finger, laughing so hard he cried. Since the only way in and out in the winter is by snowmobile, I was stuck. There's a stain on his deck to this day. I'll never live it down."

"Molly?" Brynn turns back. "Do you have a story?"

I stumble.

We haven't been going long enough, but Hank takes advantage of a level ridge, slips out of his pack, and distributes snacks.

"Not the kind you're looking for," I say, accepting a handful of nuts. I pass the Brazil nut to Tray because I can't stand them.

I chew and think.

I shouldn't do this, tell Brynn this story when there are others around. But because of last night, because maybe I'm ready for it, I start where you're supposed to, with the beginning. "One night when I was really sad, my heart broken into such tiny fragments I didn't think I'd ever find a way to make it beat regularly again, the way a heart should. I went downstairs to my parents' liquor cabinet and took a bottle of my dad's rye. An unopened bottle. Like my heart was failing so badly, I didn't think to attempt to avoid detection. And there was an open bottle. Funny thing was, in the end, my parents never noticed." I'm trying to keep my voice flat. "I knew I wasn't alone in the house, but I didn't care. I drank and drank. It burned my throat, my stomach, and still I didn't stop."

I refuse to look at Tray. Or my brother.

So I stare at my bright pink hiking boots. How they're filthy, worn. At MEC we have this policy. If gear doesn't perform to your satisfaction, whatever it is, bring it back for a full refund. I saw some awfully trashed things come in. But over the two years I worked at MEC, I never saw a pair of shoes in as bad a shape as mine cross the returns counter. Because, after everything, the blackened nails and the toe pain, these boots have done their job. The evidence is in how filthy they are, how worn. How they've carried me a long ways.

There's a prickling sensation running down my spine, bone by bone. I look up. Everyone is waiting on me.

I swallow water, clear my throat. "Remember when I said I wasn't alone. Well, I told the person who was in the house with me all the ways I was hurt. Yes, I was drunk. But in return, they said nothing. And they haven't said a thing since. Can you imagine it?"

No one has the guts to answer.

I pass Tray another Brazil nut.

His hand shakes.

"So yeah, that night sucked. Totally." I stand, force them to join me, start walking. "The only part that didn't," I say, louder now, my voice sharp, clear, "was, that unlike the rest of you, I managed not to vomit. And in the morning, I woke encased in this pillow fort, like surrounded by so many fucking pillows. Because even if you were hurting me, Tray, you didn't want me to hurt myself, yeah?"

All he does is stop, face me, nod.

"That's the drinking story you get from me. Hope it helped."

I'm being flippant. Because I can't not be.

Brynn stops, pulls me into a hug. Holds on hard, whispers, "I care about you, you know that?"

I nod shakily.

The top section of Brynn's hair is in space buns. They move gently, back and forth, side to side. I'm trying to let the motion calm me.

"I'm pretty sure you all get this now," she says, "but my parents forced me to go to fat camp. A weight-reduction summer program for obese children and teens. That's what was in the brochure our family doctor handed us. Camp Hummingbird, where your critically obese child or teen will learn to value their vessel and treat it with the respect a healthy, developing body deserves. Be slim like the hummingbird."

"Jesus," Tray says.

"They weren't going to let me go back to school, in person, unless I agreed. And you can't imagine how upsetting it was hardly leaving the house, the way I spent hours in the basement on the treadmill or strapped into the rowing machine when I was homeschooled. The way I didn't have any friends." Brynn pauses thoughtfully. "Well, any in-person friends."

"That's . . . fucking cruel," Hank says.

I have my brother.

And I have Tray.

I thought that was enough. That the three of us didn't need anyone else. That if we let other friends in, we'd dilute what we had. We'd lose something, lose each other.

"Homeschooling was fine when I was little, small. I kind of liked it," Brynn says. "All that time with my mom. But the year I turned ten, it was obvious I was only getting bigger. I had boobs and rounded hips and this belly. It didn't matter what I ate, what diet my parents implemented. Atkins, even after that one was proven to be low-key bad for your heart. Ugh, keto. Weight Watchers. Intermittent fasting was their favorite because, yeah, it produced results. Until they let me eat again."

"They starved you?" Hank asks, shocked, sickened.

In our house, there are no rules around food, no restrictions on eating.

And my brother has always been a soft human. Hasn't wanted to look too hard at the painful things that happen every day, all around us. Doesn't use social media to keep up with the news. Hates the news. He only knew life was hard in this cerebral way. Nobody bullied him at school for being gay. Even coming out to our parents was easy. At least, this was true before one of the things that happen in this world happened to him.

Brynn keeps walking, shrugs. "Soooooo, it was a fight to get to go to high school in person anyhow. And once I was there, even if I was the fattest person in my grade by a lot, I had friends. And got to eat lunch regularly."

Things flatten out. Open up. We've reached Muir Pass. We're crossing Goddard Divide, Mount Solomons on one side, Mount Warlow on the other.

There's snow in the distance. Not much, but enough.

At the Muir hut, Hank refills our water from a nearby alpine lake. I grab tortillas, peanut butter, chocolate chips, more nuts, and the last of the beef jerky we bought in Kennedy Meadows.

"Brynn," Tray says once we're all sitting. "You ran away again."

She finishes chewing. "I very much did. Couldn't wait there in that hospital for the car my parents sent. Because I know it wasn't taking me home. They'd just return me to camp. And at that camp, we walked the same stretch of trail every day. Every damn day, we'd wake up and go at it, like a forced march up some biggish hills would be the thing to get the stubborn weight to come off our bodies. There were seven-year-olds at camp."

"Fuck them and fuck that," I say, thinking of growing bones under incredible strain. I'm furious, this different-from-easy anger.

Hank adds in his two cents. "Cosigned."

"Thirded." This from Tray.

"So one day, before the march, I liberated some gear and said, you know what, I'm going to walk this trail the way it's supposed to be walked. As a personal challenge, not a weight-loss program. And so I did. We were barely supervised because the rule was to check in at the top and get back to camp before dinner or . . . well, you didn't eat."

Tray puts his lunch down. "Jesus."

"A friend gave me their emergency Oreo stash, and I took, like, all the apples, the health-food bars, from the canteen, figuring I'd stop and buy real hiking meals when I got far enough away. Two days later, I ran into all of you. From that point on, it's important to note, I've been having a really awesome time."

Tray cleans up methodically, making sure we're not leaving anything unwanted behind. "I am so glad you're not there anymore. Like so glad. Only we still have a problem, yeah."

"What are we going to do?" Hank asks.

"Well, finish this hike?" Brynn says it like a question, as if she's not sure. "At home, they restrict my calories. Sometimes only eight hundred a day, when the number on the scale gets really upsetting. At least at the camp, they let us eat twelve hundred most days. So that was better."

Hank makes an ugly noise.

"But out here," Brynn says, ignoring my brother, "I eat when I'm hungry. My body is fat and strong. And well, I have you all around me."

"That's abuse," Tray says. "What they're doing to you, it's abuse."

Someone had to speak it.

Brynn shakes her head rapidly, her space buns spinning as if they're caught in a violent storm. "My parents have never hit me. I swear it. They aren't bad people. They buy me birthday presents, and my dad and I do these movie nights with popcorn and my mom taught me how to do makeup, buys me as many books as I want, even romance novels. They're not bad people. That's not it."

She's still caught up in either-or. How it's not as clear-cut as a fire lane, those wide slashes down mountainsides, when it comes to people. How people hurt each other and can still love each other. How that doesn't always mean the hurt is forgivable. That the hurt is okay just because there is love too.

My brother exhales hard. "They starved you, Brynny. That's fucking textbook. You're their child. Parents are supposed to help you grow, feed you, love you, not starve you because you're bigger than they imagined you would be."

Hank knows. His father was hurting our mom, in so many ways. For years, up until I was six or seven, Hank's father would come around and claim he still loved my mom.

Muir Pass feels like the top of the world. Nothing grows. It's all sharp gray stone and snow. But even here, in this place, it's like people couldn't help themselves. That drive to mark the land, they carried it this far. Someone built this hut, someone put up a plaque.

The Range of Light.

I'm thankful. Thankful we made it this far.

Whatever comes next.

"Say I believe you," Brynn hedges. "Let's do a hypothetical. Because, in the hospital, as many times as I thought it over, all I knew was getting into that car wasn't safe. That getting back on the trail was the best thing, not only for my body, but for my . . . heart or soul or whatever makes us all people. That part of me is dying with them. So, I want to keep walking."

I finish off my last bite of lunch, brush my hands against my bike shorts. I hoist my pack onto bruised shoulders. "All right, let's go."

It's not a perfect solution.

Hank throws me a look, like he thinks I'm being selfish, doing this for me, when that couldn't be further from the truth. Brynn needs this. She's just told us so.

I throw my brother a look back.

We don't have time for words, for what's broken between us. This is triage.

We make it to our goal for the day, only a little farther down the mountain. It's dusk, and while we haven't seen snow since lunch, it's chilly too, like it might rain. Tray's humming something, in muted tones. Hank's hiking pole hits the earth in a regular, steady beat. Brynn's breathing is labored.

So is mine.

I've been thinking on what my brother said last night. That he wants to go home, that he doesn't remember these important and not-so-important things. I know my mom won't be okay with Brynn as my person. Even if my mom is a feminist, she's only ever let me do these exciting things because I had boys along with me. I know this about my mom.

I forgive her for being limited in her thinking.

And Brynn can't be my person. Even if she doesn't recognize it yet, she has to deal with her life. It took me almost eight hundred miles. We can offer our friend a few more days. But Brynn needs to know that the boys have changed their minds.

Hank's mouth is stuffed with tonight's dinner, yellow curry with chicken and rice, and not realizing I'm taking a misstep, the kind that might send a person over the edge of a mountain, I say: "They want to go home."

My brother makes a muffled sound around his spork.

Fast as fucking lightning, Tray shows up in defense. "You know," he says, "every once in a while, you could play nicely, Molly. It doesn't always have to be a puck whipped full force across the ice."

I cross my arms, my hoodie tucked over my bike shorts, because even though it's chilly, it's not cold enough to pull out all my other gear.

Brynn looks across our circle at the three of us, wary.

Tray puts his dinner down next to our tiny stove. He's barely eaten. "You know what, yeah? I'm gonna . . . take a walk."

And he leaves.

Hank finally speaks. "Look what you did."

He sounds like our mother. I clench my jaw because it will piss him off. "I didn't make that boy do anything. He's absolutely his own person. And he makes all his own decisions."

My brother's smile is brittle. "Keep telling yourself that."

"What does that mean?"

Hank stares at me like this is a dare. And like every other dare he's been given since we were old enough to know what the word meant, he takes it. "All right, then, plain talk. Traylor Lambert has been in love with you since Grade 7. Like absolutely obsessed with every little thing about you. In his storybook narrative, you can do no wrong, and even when you fuck it up, it's one more thing to love about you, how you're only human. How cute, eh. And because he's all deep end over you, he makes his decisions thinking about what you want. It's something I've known for a long time, Molly. Something I forgot until I made it out here."

"Big Bear," I say.

Hank nods. "As soon as he was, I like the way she smells, all dopey and lovey, it came back to me."

"Oh."

"Oooooh," Brynn says.

Hank laughs now. "You never noticed?"

I get warm, uncomfortable under their gazes. "I thought that was . . . friendship. Big, all-consuming."

"The song?" Brynn leans forward, resting against her drawn knees.

The evidence stacks up. We're listening to music together in the back room of Matteo's family restaurant. There are lemons in my ice water. Later, at the motel, we kiss. Tray holds on to me in sleep.

I'm nowhere near a dictionary. To check the meaning of the word. And yes, this *is* friendship. Maybe even when you're in love with someone, you should be their best friend too.

I exhale, my skin buzzing, itchy.

"It's important for me to know this," I say. "It . . . changes things. So I need you to stop brushing me off, Hank. What else have you forgotten?"

My brother shrugs. "For a long time, that whole day. Waking up, getting dressed, the bus to the climbing gym. What I had for breakfast. Whether you were there, on belay, whether you witnessed my fall. Later when they told me it was Tray, that Tray tried to catch me, whether you told me you weren't coming or not. Whether we argued."

Brynn is quiet, watchful. She hugs her stuffy.

"For sure the whole day, the accident itself. I still don't remember the hospital. Or the weeks after. I know I existed for you during those weeks, Molly, but I . . . I didn't exist for myself. I might as well have been . . . It was so empty there. In that place."

I was with him, but he was going through this alone too.

My brother clears his throat. "And then, when everything got bright again, heavy again, turns out, there were other pieces I'd forgotten. *Saved!*," he says, putting his bowl aside. "I forgot that was your favorite movie until Tray said something a few days after your seventeenth. I, ugh, forgot your birthday too. So then I was bowled over with guilt, not having access to things that mattered to you. Um, my dad's name. That's still fuzzy. How could I ask

Mom for that, the way he treated her? It's like there are gaps, where instead of the things I've gathered in my life lined up, ready to be accessed, it's all missing, emptied out."

"John," I say. "His name is John."

Hank shrugs like this is all a joke. "Kinda forgettable, eh?"

Brynn laughs. "No, no, not laughing at you. My father's name is John too."

"Ugh," Hank says. "A cursed name. Let's lose it again. Someone hit me over the head."

Brynn fakes like she's going to clobber my brother with the stuffed pony.

They both laugh for a minute.

I eat slow. Try to savor each bite.

When Hank gets control of himself again, it's clear he's not done. That the joke wasn't the end of the story. "And I'm only starting to remember that day while hiking these mountains. I was in a rush. For what? Still don't know. But I was hurrying . . . I . . . Mollycakes, I didn't run the safety checks. I set up, started to climb as soon as Tray got on belay. It's coming back to me, mile after mile, like the closer I get to home, the closer I am to exposing everything about that day."

No wonder he wants to quit the hike.

I finish my meal, stow my hot sauce. There's another bottle waiting in my next bounce box. If we ever pick it up. "Why didn't you tell me? About your memories?"

My brother rolls his eyes playfully. "How could I? You needed me to be okay."

"Hey, don't blame this on your sister!" Brynn orders, shaking her finger at him as menacingly as a person can while cuddling a blue pony.

Hank laughs again. "It's nice to know when Tray's off in the woods sulking that someone will step in and keep my sister safe from me."

"That's not what he's doing."

"That's exactly what he's at, Molly-moo. That boy loves you way beyond friendship. Or maybe that boy loves you exactly right as a friend but wants to add kissing and shit in too."

"I mean . . ." Brynn hesitates, nods.

My face is hot, my lips burn. "Why hasn't he ever said anything?"

"He's a chicken?" Brynn offers, and when she sees my face, laughs.

Hank smiles. "Still want to hear it how it is?"

He's returning us to the dare. Offering me an out. If I take it, he's the winner. "Yes, I do."

"That boy's terrified of you. Literally, you terrify him. Can you imagine, Brynny, if she shuts him down? How will he continue along this mortal coil after he has to come back down to earth with the rest of us?"

"This is all sooooo Shakespearean!"

I protest. "Those plays never end well!"

"I mean, the tragedies don't." Brynn shrugs. "It's sorta in the name."

"My life is not a comedy."

Nobody argues with me. That's not reassuring. Still, I pick up Tray's bowl. His eating utensil is stuck in the curry. There are maybe two bites gone. Not enough. I turn in the direction he took off, then stop myself.

I miss when I was sure.

I used to be so sure about everything. That friendship with Tray was exactly perfect, all I wanted. The noise comes for me. Brynn's breathing, Hank's teeth chewing, the trees shaking against the wind. I exhale, trying to find my heartbeat.

My brother's voice is gentle. "Go after him, eh? Once in a while, a guy needs that."

"Oooooh, yes." Brynn passes me her stuffy.

My skin heats again. "Yeah, fine. I'll do it."

And as I walk into the woods, a blue pony under my arm, it's like there's a tether between me and this boy—our connection, this friendship, whatever it is—I'll find him without really knowing where he's gone. Even after everything, that's something I'm still sure about.

He's uphill a ways, in a circle of tall trees, sitting on the ground, legs stretched out, his back against a sheared-off rock face. It seems on this trip Tray's got all the good luck when it comes to sitting places. This boulder is almost flat, with just enough recline that it probably feels awfully good to lean on.

"Hey," I say.

"Hey back," he offers.

And that's it.

"Can I . . . ?" I gesture at the ground, the rock.

"It doesn't belong to me or anything."

"Dick," I say without bite, and Tray smiles a little.

It's a start.

"You have such a guy mouth," he says.

"I spend all my time with a former hockey player and my brother. You're my only friends. You both happen to be boys. It was bound to go down. You know, exposure therapy and all that."

I offer him his bowl but keep the stuffy.

"I'm not hungry, Molly."

"Okay, that's okay," I say, balancing the bowl on my knees. "So, I want to say it again. That I'm sorry. And that you do not have to forgive me. You don't. But even if you can't now or can't ever manage it, I want to say it again."

Tray nods.

"I'm sorry, Traylor. That I blamed you because I couldn't blame my brother. Because the world didn't make sense if I put all this on my brother." My lungs heave, overfull, like I've been running. It's the altitude, I rationalize. "And . . . I knew you were strong enough to handle it. That you . . . cared enough for me, and because you did, well, you'd carry it."

"Mollycakes," he says, but doesn't say anything else.

"So I'm sorry for that too. For making you shoulder something heavy. Because the world didn't make sense when I put it on you either."

I smell myself, and then, over the pine forest, I smell Tray. We both need showers desperately. But it's not bad, my smell or his. Only very real, very human.

I pass him the stuffy.

He accepts it.

"You know." He leans against the rock and then into me. "If

you'd asked me to help you out, I would have said yes in a heart-beat."

Now he's combing his fingers through the rainbow tail.

"I know that." I do not want him to doubt himself. "Some-times I don't think I deserve . . . well, you."

"Molly. That's bear shit," he says, slow, word by word.

"No offense to the bears," I say, because I can't not say it.

It's become a kind of prayer. It's not sweetgrass, the braid Tray carries around in the top of his pack, next to his other essentials. But maybe it's like that too. A kind of medicine.

His kind.

Mine, if I want it. Sweetgrass is a plant. It grows like any other thing.

"It's not about deserving someone," he says finally. "At least I think that's the wrong word." He sets Brynn's pony on his lap, picks a stray pine cone from the ground.

It's small. None of the sharp, deadly spikes that we've seen along the trail. This one looks as if it came from the trees in my backyard, an absolute world away from here.

"It's care, I think," he says.

"Well, I wanted to say I'm sorry, and I've done that. So, I'll . . ." I move his bowl to one hand so I can use the other to push myself up. "I'll leave you be."

He lets me start walking away before he stops me. "Why don't you stay? I mean would you, ah, stay?"

I bargain with him. "If you'll eat."

"Jesus H.," he says, leaning against the stone, his eyes closed. "You're vicious."

"Yeah, well. Nobody's perfect."

"Too damn smart for your own good, sharp the way a knife is sharp, too sharp sometimes," he continues.

It's what I already know.

I'm too much.

I refuse to cry when all Tray is providing is confirmation. Like he's finally seen the end of the experiment, and now he knows, Molly Lee Norris-Norquay is too much, she's too freaking big.

"You're overwhelming, and absolutely, sometimes you go way hard on science, like Western science will fix everything, like that kind of science isn't making problems for us all, yeah. But, Molly," Tray says, pausing, like he needs to be heard. He opens his eyes. "I am obsessed with you."

"I'm sorry," I say.

I want to offer up something that will fix this for him.

"I fucking love you so much," he says, and then he guts me. "But I am not in love with you, yeah. There's a difference, I'm learning. That my love for you as, like, my future person has always been more fairy story than anything. Because it's been my story of us. Not a shared one. Not one we tell together."

"I'm sorry," I repeat the words again, my cheeks wet. "I am so, so sorry."

Tray stands. "Oh, Mollycakes. Don't cry. When you cry, it's like you're stabbing me in the stomach with a screwdriver."

"I'm—"

"Don't say it again."

I nod.

Tray gets closer. Takes the bowl I've been clutching like it's going to save me, places it on the ground next to the blue pony.

"I forgive you," he says. "You were right. I was being stubborn. It's something I've inherited—that's obvious. From both parents, probably all the way down the line, ancestor after ancestor, stubborn to the core."

I keep nodding, keep crying.

"Hug?" he asks.

"Yes, please."

Tray pulls me hard against him. His arms grip me tight. I sob into his shirt. He loves me but isn't in love with me. His love for me is only a story. It's almost as bad as him loving me but not liking me.

It all hurts.

When I can do more than cry, I hug him hard too. Because a hug needs at least two people. A hug should always be a force met with an equal counterforce. It should balance out, become weightless.

"What did I say that made you cry?"

"All of it," I mutter against his shirt.

"All of it, yeah?"

"Yes."

"That's a lot of things, Molly. Want to name them one by one? Be specific?"

"Do I have to?"

"No, never," Tray says. "That being said, it would be nice. To know so I can make sure you're not hearing something I didn't say. Words are slippery like that."

It's why I distrust stories. But that's not what Tray wants to hear. I have to push away from him to say this. So I do.

I sink back down next to the big rock. Press myself into it. Tray sits next to me, close, close, but he refuses to touch me now.

"I'm too much," I say at a whisper, then get louder. "And not enough."

"Molly."

"No, don't dismiss me. You just said it. I'm too, too smart. Overwhelming."

"That's not how I mean it."

"I'm too much, Tray. Too big, and don't make that face, you know I'm too big for the world, that if I were smaller, things could be different."

It sounds like it pains him to ask. "Is that it? Or is there more?"

"There's always more!"

"So, tell it to me."

"I don't know enough about some things. Like . . . Métis things. My mom *is* white, her grandparents are Scottish and Irish, and my dad was gone for a long time, and when he was gone, we didn't do or learn or . . . and so . . . like mathematically, I'm less too, not Native enough."

"Blood quantum is complete bear shit." Tray pauses. "What, you're not going to say it? I don't make the rules, but it's the rules. Someone needs to say it."

I huff. "Zero offense meant to actual bears. I'm pretty sure we're saying this out of some kind of . . . care, dear bears of the world. We aren't disparaging you. Or your shit."

"It's for sure care," Tray says, as if he, too, is talking to the bears we cannot see.

The population here in the Sierras is growing, healthy. I know this. And so, statistically speaking, we should have run into one by now. It would be almost beyond the possible to finish this part of the hike, to leave the Range of Light, without seeing at least one bear up close.

But I feel stronger now, reminded that you're out here some-where.

"You're saying you're less, but it's not true. You know that being Métis is about kin, not blood quantum. About care and reciproc-ity," Tray says. "It's culture, not math."

I nod. "But I don't know basic stuff. And it's embarrassing to ask when I'm not a kid, when I should already know this. Like why your sash is made up of different colors than my dad's or my uncle's. Like stories. Even what a Métis scientist should care about."

"That's fixable, yeah?"

"What if it isn't? What if I've already totally dicked myself by memorizing all the wrong stuff?"

Tray laughs. "God, I love your mouth."

Even though I don't feel like it, don't get the joke entirely, it's second nature to laugh around Tray. Or it used to be. We used to laugh so much.

"I think I made a promise to the gods, or Creator, or some trickster. When Hank was in the hospital, I wanted him to wake up so badly. And I swore to become a doctor. To save the kids. You know? Balance the scales. No, overbalance them. And then . . . Hank was awake. So, I'm worried I'm stuck, that I can't get out of this promise, that they won't let me now, that I don't know the stories, so I can't find a loophole or a neon fucking flashing exit sign."

"Oh," Tray says.

"It's bad, right?"

Tray laughs again. "Sorry, no. I'm pretty sure that whatever you promised, you only promised it to yourself. Hank woke up when the swelling receded enough, when he'd done enough healing to come out of it and keep healing in another way. That's all."

"That's all?" I sound incredulous, like Tray's just told me the earth is flat.

It's not, by the way.

I can tell you the science some other time.

"I mean, tricksters are good trouble, yeah," Tray says, barreling onward, refusing to let me get stuck here. "But the stories aren't about how if you make a promise, you're bound to it. They've got more in common with science, in a lot of ways. Like I was trying to tell you with the crickets. Stories explain the how and why of things, the same way the big bang theory is a story."

My eyebrows spike.

He refuses to stop, keeps speaking. "Or you tell stories on the trapline to keep everyone in a good mood, to impart knowledge. Sometimes they're a warning, a pointed lesson. Like trickster stories, for the Métis, but for lots of other Peoples too. There are multiple tricksters, many stories, because those ones are about looking inward, seeing your faults reflected back at you. Tricksters show us what it means to be human. Rougarou stories, the black dog, those are warnings. Some stories we only tell during the right season because that's when it's safe to tell them, when the stories are most powerful, most needed. You didn't bind yourself to something . . . more than natural. So stop worrying." Tray pauses. "You did the exact same thing I was doing, making promises to yourself, what you'd give up, what you'd offer. All that to demonstrate how much you love Hank."

It makes sense. I've already assumed that mostly, I've been talking to myself. But I couldn't close the door on the other possibility, without knowing for certain. "My dad," I say, "as much as he cares about people, he's not much of a storyteller. He's more into music—"

"Music."

We speak at the same time.

I laugh, suddenly lighter, freer. But I'm not out of these woods yet, not done with this yet. "Tray?"

"Yeah, Mollycakes?"

"My parents won't let it go. That future. The plan. Like I promised it to them, crossed my heart and hoped to die. And as much as it sounds like death is on the table, you know it's not even an option. So . . ."

"Oh, Molly."

"It hurts," I say.

Tray takes my hand. "What can I do to make it better? Anything?"

I think for a minute. All I wanted when I first came over here was for Tray to finish his meal. "You can eat."

He laughs abruptly. "That's it?"

"Please. I don't like . . . the idea of you not having enough."

Tray drops my hand to gather his bowl, brings the stuffy with him. He presses it into my arms. His dinner is cold, but he eats. And I feel better, so I sit against this rock and breathe.

It's enough, I think, exhaling.

And then, a minute later, another minute of watching Tray fuel his body, it comes to me, in the quiet. I'm probably enough too. Even without a plan, I'm still probably just enough. Because I'm only human. And I'm seventeen, shouldn't lock myself into one future, not if I don't want to. Even if my mom's already said yes.

It's a relief.

Freaking relief.

Now I only have to convince my parents this is okay, possible. I might be a scientist, this might be my disposition, what I'm best at, but I think I'm going to have to learn to rewrite a story that's become important to people who are important to me too, if I have any hope of getting free.

MILE 793.8

Traylor

We sit next to each other a long time. But it gets cold. Too cold for Molly to be wearing only that hoodie and a pair of trail-faded pink bike shorts. Gooseflesh pebbles her legs. I'm feeling it too. How summer in the high places is short.

I force a shiver back. While there's no snow, it's going to be a cold, wet night. "Let's head to bed, yeah?"

"Okay," she agrees quietly.

I help her up, refuse to let her hand go, and she doesn't make me.

Back at camp, everything's tidy, the food and other smellables stored in our bear canister. Hank and Brynn have gone to sleep. I don't know what time it is, but I know I'm tired. I release Molly's hand, finally, and step toward my tent. "Mollycakes?"

She turns, the stuffed toy under her arm.

"I love you, yeah. You are my best friend."

She nods, looks behind me at the trees. "I love you too, Tray. And, obviously, same."

My heart beats double time. She's never told me this, in our long history. My voice sticks in my throat. "The rest of it doesn't matter, yeah."

"Good night."

"Night."

I unzip my tent to find it occupied. Hank bundled in his sleeping bag, with Brynn next to him. They're both out, dreaming. Or they're both pretending. I swallow a laugh. Hank-the-Tank would not.

"They're having a sleepover, I guess?" Molly says, sitting, her legs crisscrossed, my gear stacked side by side with hers.

"Something like that."

She pulls clothing from her pack, goes about her nighttime routine like this is normal.

"I'll cowboy camp, if you'll pass me—"

"Please, you were the one shivering out there."

"My sleeping bag is rated for negative forty. I'll survive."

She still doesn't pass me my gear. She finds her toothbrush. "Stay," she says. "Because it's going to rain and you don't need that and, frankly, neither do I."

"Okay. Yeah." I climb into the tent, riffle through my kit.

And with me sitting there, her back turned, Molly changes out of the hoodie into merino-wool pants and a long-sleeved shirt. She ditches her sports bra. I grab my toothbrush quick, escape.

Suddenly, I welcome the rain.

"Hold up. I'm not scared of bears, but . . ."

I laugh, wait for her. We brush our teeth quickly. It really is cold tonight. Inside our sleeping bags, Molly faces the middle of the tent, lies on her side.

I mirror her, all of a sudden wide awake. "Not sleepy yet?"

"Now that I'm warm, no."

Under her head, she's bundled my Electric Pow Wow hoodie like a pillow.

"That sweatshirt . . . I enjoy seeing you in it. I know I asked for it back—"

"Like, twenty-five times."

"I never wanted it, not really. I like that you have it. That it's yours."

"Yeah?"

"Yeah."

"I'll tell you a secret, then," she whispers.

"Will you, now?" I whisper back.

Her nod is a tiny movement. "In the early days out here, I thought about giving it away. I couldn't wear the thing without thinking about you, without remembering that it's yours. But, you know, I couldn't give it away. Because it's yours."

"I'm glad you didn't."

Eyes closed, she presses her face into her makeshift pillow. "Me too."

"Are we okay, Molly?"

She hesitates, and that should tell me everything. "Yeah, of course."

I don't believe her, not really. But Molly is methodical about so much. She takes her time. And I have to let her.

"Hank must have gone through my things at home," she says eventually. "Like, the minute we left for the airport. I had the whole trip planned, all the extra gear ordered, bounce boxes prepped. And because it's, like, part of my process, I left the written evidence where a basic snoop could discover it."

"He told me."

"I guess I needed to say it out loud. Because my parents, they trust me less now. Over the past few years, they've both gotten rigid, like university is the only path forward. And for me, that's a premed degree. A double major in biology and chemistry, with a minor in English, if I can swing it. And I don't know how to fight them. It feels wrong to fight my parents."

Finally, Molly is talking to me. Even though what she's going through sucks, it's awfully good to be part of her circle.

"Like Brynn. But not, yeah?"

Molly nods.

"My parents put pressure on me too. Maybe not in the same way. But they do. Might be a parent thing." I stop, wonder if this will help her. Ultimately, I decide, yeah, it could. "I never told you how hard my mom, my coaches, a few of my teammates were going after me when I was thinking about leaving hockey. It was . . . a lot. And while they mostly supported me in the end, it wasn't easy for my mom to watch her kid walk a different path."

Jaime, the only other Native guy on the team, our goalie, took it hardest.

"They can't imagine another one for me!" Molly says, all wound up. "My parents can't do it."

"Can you? Like, on my side, it was clear that I was making a choice. I was stepping away from hockey, from a shot at the NHL, for something I wanted harder, more."

We used to text.

Used to meet up.

But Jaime got too busy. And maybe so did I.

"Music," Molly says.

"Music, yeah," I say, because she's right. Yet, at the same time, she's wrong. "And Hank. And you."

"Tray."

"It's true. Not going to hide it anymore. Our friendship was going to fade out if I kept playing, and I knew I wanted to have you both in my life in a real way, more than I wanted to chase the puck."

Molly is quiet. Now that we're in the tent, there's not enough light. Still, I know her eyes are flecked with green, that she carries the northern lights inside her. "Back to my question. What are you imagining for yourself?"

"You should have seen my childhood finger painting. I suck at imagination. And imagination's not a necessary skill. Not in the sciences."

"Bear shit."

"No offense, dear bears," Molly utters, as if it's rote. As if this isn't an integral part of our song now. "But real talk, Tray, I can't imagine it."

"So you need practice. Molly Lee, also known as Guacamolly, Mermolly, Mollycakes, and Molly-moo, if she doesn't become a doctor, she could be . . . an astronaut."

Beside me, she laughs.

It starts to rain, gentle at first and then all out.

I speak louder. "If she doesn't become a doctor, our Molly could be . . . a high school science teacher, a hot one, but yeah, she cares about her students deeply. Wants them to know science, to take science with them when they go out into the world."

Another small laugh, but nothing else.

I keep going, fighting against the deluge of water coming down. "Molly, she could be this long-distance hiker, who takes care of the land as she hikes. She has all these partnerships, sponsorships, and she's a model for other plus-size girls, other Native girls. They'll see themselves in her and know they can do anything. Because of you, they'd be welcome to imagine themselves anywhere, doing any hard thing, and doing it well. You'd invite them along."

Molly inhales fast. "Is that how you see me?"

"Of course. You're powerful, Mollycakes."

"Oh. Wow. Okay." A beat. "Um, I need you to kiss me."

It comes out of nowhere, and since we've been practicing imagination, I need to make sure I didn't imagine this too. "Yeah?"

"Now. Please."

And because this is a gift, and when you're given a gift, you're supposed to honor it, I go slow. Press of lips. Careful exchange of breath. But also, this is a gift, and I want to tear the paper open, the way I've always opened presents.

So I do.

I don't think about this until much later, after we stop kissing and Molly pulls my arm over her sleeping bag and around her stomach. The rain continues. Later, when she's asleep, I think that Hank-the-Tank is vicious too, in his own way. He's playing the puppet master. Brynn, yeah, she'd be all up in this, helping Hank in his machinations. Forcing Molly and me to have it out, to share a small space, to have to sleep next to each other.

But before I stop kissing Molly, and she stops kissing me back, before that happens, Molly breaks away.

"You should have told me," she says.

I'm not following. I'm happily lost in the rain.

"It's hard to think . . . Right now . . . When you're so close," I say. "But also, I know that thinking in *should*s doesn't lead anywhere useful."

"You should have told me," she says again, sharper. "How you felt. About me. Because we could have been doing this all this time."

I laugh. "Solid point."

"I'm good at science," she says. "You're good at stories. But, Tray, we're both really good at this, together."

She's still thinking they're two different things. But that's okay.

We aren't finished becoming.

None of us.

Not yet.

And maybe humans should never stop changing, growing. Maybe, when that happens, we've died even if our bodies keep living. This is a little bit of truth born on this trail that I know I'll carry along for the rest of my life.

We kiss carefully, hard, fast, and then slow again.

When it becomes too much, in the way even good things become too much, too powerful, we stop. Molly sleeps, and I hold her close to me, and I think about my best friend, about how I've been wrong too. That there's growing ahead of me, on my path, yet, and it could lead me anywhere.

In the morning, Molly's still next to me. The sun is up, but a wet chill bites in the air. I can almost see my breath. It's July. Late in the month, yeah, if I check my phone, which I do and find a new rambling email from my dad. I'll answer tonight. We have another month left, and already it's cold in the Sierras. In the next tent, Hank and Brynn talk. Inconsequential things. What's for breakfast, how much longer until the next town stop, if Brynn's toes look okay.

Molly rolls against me, sleep warm, puts a finger to her lips like shhhhh. But she means *play along*. "Tray, oh my god! That's so good."

It's absolutely the worst. Laughable. A terrible actor in a bad movie. But I don't break. I match her enthusiasm. "Molly," I say, like she's everything, staring at the way her eyes are full of mischief. Of payback. "Oh, Molly!"

"Don't stop!" she yells like in this movie, it's a slasher film and she's being chased by the bad guy, but also, she likes it.

We are desperately trying not to laugh, playacting too large for this to get read as realism, but Hank eventually cracks.

"Please if you care about me at all, quit that! I'm grinding my jaw so hard I'm going to snap something. And frankly, the chip I already have in my smile is all the oral defect I can handle."

Molly laughs against me. "Serves you right, Hank."

Now her brother is all innocence. "I don't know what you're talking about. Brynny and me wanted to have a sleepover. While you two were off in the forest doing who knows what, we made an executive decision."

Brynn laughs now. "Don't drag me into this. This was your plan, my dude."

"You enabled me!" my brother argues.

"And I'd do it again," she says. "Their weird make-out play doesn't bother me."

"So I'm the only one of us who is super uncomfortable right now?" Hank asks.

The three of us agree, at the same time:

"Yup."

"Yes."

"Yeah, buddy."

Molly sits, pulls the hoodie on over her sleep shirt, then lies back down, cuddles against my arm. She whispers so only I can hear her, "That was fun."

"Mmm, fun," I agree.

She's brighter today. We all are.

After a few more minutes, I leave the tent so Molly can get dressed in peace. When I come back from the woods, she's wearing her town dress, bike shorts layered underneath to save her thighs. Molly's hair is longer than when we started, and today it's up in a high ponytail. Her bandanna is tied in a bow, like a fancy headband.

She's gorgeous.

I stare long enough that Molly laughs, brushes fake lint off her shoulders. "That good, eh?"

"The best."

Brynn agrees. "You look hot. Like fully edible!"

Hank shakes his head. "I'm going to pretend I didn't hear that."

There's a beat, a pause.

This is the moment in the song where the music stops. Where it could go anywhere, could rage, or, in a softer world, could offer up sweet melody.

"Well then, why don't you forget it?" Molly says, sharp, pointedly, digging into her breakfast like she didn't just go that hard. On purpose.

I freeze.

But Hank laughs, exactly the way he would have before his accident when faced with his sister's sharp words. "Ouch."

"Too soon?" Molly asks.

"No," Hank replies levelly. "Probably, it's a bit late coming."

Molly puts her breakfast down, stalks toward her brother. She gives him just enough time. He readies his stance. She takes a short run and jumps. Hank catches her, wraps her in a hug.

It's relief.

And it's bringing me back to that Saturday. How what was missing that day was Molly, the way she'd do this before every big climb. Her good-luck offering. Without it, Hank was frantic, too eager to scale the wall.

I was off too.

The music was wrong. Someone had thrown on their early 2000s mix. Mariah Carey, Madonna, late Backstreet Boys. But Hank was into it.

Amy Winehouse came on. "Rehab."

Hank sang along.

Climbed, climbed fast.

Brynn's voice filters in from behind me. She's shoving her

things into her pack. "Sooooo, when this adorable hug is complete, can we talk about the other thing. How I need help and how I don't know what to do? But after a night's good sleep I know I can't just walk away from it." She stands, holds her phone face out so we can all see. "I'm not sure if your devices got enough signal, but mine did. My parents are fighting back."

AMBER ALERT: NOELLE BRYNN HENSLEY, SIXTEEN YEARS OLD. MULTIPLE COUNTIES. REFER TO LOCAL MEDIA.

"Shit," I say.

"Bear shit," Hank corrects me.

Molly stays quiet.

"Oooooh. I get to do it this time?" Brynn's laugh is brittle, a little panicky. "No offense to any bears, including panda bears even though they aren't real bears, you know, technically. We don't care about that stuff. No offense to any creature who identifies as a bear."

Molly steps away from Hank, retrieves her breakfast, chews for a while. "When you get reliable service, Brynn, call Faith. See where she can pick us up. It's complicated in this section, I know. But find a point where we can meet. Hank, you're going to get Matteo to book us rooms at the motel, but under his name, understand?" She turns to me. "Can you get your mom on board? We need to know how to fight this. Legally."

We look at Molly, just stare.

She stares back. "Does anyone have questions? Comments? Concerns?"

Brynn starts: "How are you so proficient at emergencies? I mean, damn, girl."

Hank chimes in next: "Did they cover this in Wilderness and Remote First Aid the day I was sick? I knew I missed something."

I only say, "Molly's good at so many things."

"Awwww," Brynn squeaks.

"One of those things is organizing complicated problems. She's a planner, someone who can break a difficult task into its parts."

Molly smiles, bright, but intimate, like this smile is mine. "Maybe that's how I ought to look at it? Not imagine careers, but start with skills?"

"Look at what?" Hank asks.

"Oh, Molly's thinking about making some changes."

"Hank," she says seriously. "I do not want to be a doctor anymore. I really, really don't."

Her brother pauses for one, two seconds. "Well, duh! You literally burned that plan down and ran away to the woods."

"Yep," she says. "That's exactly what I did."

"I mean, it had style." Hank twirls, strikes a pose, doesn't lose his balance, doesn't waver. "But you know Mom hated it, and because Mom hated it, Dad does too."

"That's obvious," she says sarcastically.

"I'm a little sorry about that, eh?"

"Only a little?"

Hank refuses to cower. "Only a little, Guacamolly. Because you went about this in the wrong way too. And I was missing important bits. Like that's not how we are with each other. But respectfully, you would have made a kick-ass doctor. Like you know that? You'd have been real good and capable and shit at the job."

"Fair." Molly shrugs. "But respectfully, my future can wait. Let's find a way down this mountain and to a road."

"Let's!" Brynn says, a little subdued, loading her canteens into her pack.

Her parents filed an AMBER Alert.

That's gotta sting.

Now that the government is involved, we can't keep walking. It's no longer an option. Even if Molly sorted it with the cop, there's a record that we were with Brynn. If they find us together, I worry what it will do to the possibilities Molly wants for herself. It's not fair to close them down until she can do the imagining, until she can tell herself her new story.

The fiddle has been quiet lately. But now its song is present, mournful.

I'm the last to leave our campsite. I scroll through my contacts, through the names of hockey friends I used to know too, too well. I scroll down to the *J*s, pause, hovering. I stash my phone in my pack, take a minute, offer thanks to the land, thanks for caring for us, for holding us. We needed a place where we could be safe. We didn't need the bear, not in the way I assumed.

This must take longer than I think, that, yeah, Molly doubles back looking for me.

"You coming?" she asks, like she doesn't care at all.

But this girl cares so much, in big ways, until she doesn't know where she stands, where her borders are, and so her love drags her under. It doesn't happen for her note by note but in a deluge of song.

"Right beside you," I say, knowing that, yeah, Hank's wrong about his sister. At least in this. She returns for what she wants. She might not run after me, but she won't leave me behind either. I pick up the pace, catch up to Molly, and we hike off the path and down the mountain.

THE CHORUS, YET AGAIN

We're back to familiar ground. In revisiting this, now that we're almost finished, these lyrics, this glow should hit different.

Does it?

EARLY AUGUST
LONE PINE, CA
Molly

Three brutal days later, just after lunch, Faith picks us up in her old Ford truck. Matteo comes along, still as polished as ever, even after driving for two hours with the windows down. We let Brynn and Hank squish into the cab, while Tray and me, we settle into the truck bed, surrounded by everyone's gear.

This time, we're sitting on the same side.

Tray isn't singing, making noise at all.

This time, I'm no longer filled with easy anger.

Tray throws an arm around my shoulders to cushion me from the impact. And while the highway isn't as bad as the overgrown jeep access road Faith used to meet up with us, riding in the truck bed is always bumpy. This time, my body is bruised, worn from walking more than eight hundred miles.

At the beginning, we didn't know what we were getting into.

I'm texting with my parents in our group chat. Since Tray already called his mom, I know mine will find out sooner or later, and I've learned they need to hear things like this from me. That if I want trust, it helps if I'm the one bringing them breaking news.

I'm still not okay with what Hank did. Following me out here and then, later, telling my parents what he found. But I understand the why of it.

    Me: I know you accepted on my behalf. And I know I
        told you I was fine with it. But I'm not.

    Mom answers immediately: Call us!

I wasn't done. I had more to say. Wanted to get these feelings out. To be clear, to be persuasive. But my mom is impatient, always trying to save the world.

So all I type is that I can't: We're in a truck, driving to town. It's too loud.

She video-calls anyway. I text again.

    Me: I told you, it's way too loud. I'll call tonight. Once
        we're settled.

She tries once more.

I send her to voicemail.

Finally, she stops.

But she texts again: This is not open to discussion. You're going to university, Molly.

    Me: I'll call later. Promise.

Tray's watching. I lean into him. Even though I've practiced a little, I'm still not an imagination person. If I close my eyes, what I find is a great big nothing. No images form. No stories come to life. Faced with my mom's plan for me, I can't imagine a Molly who leaves this place without sacrificing herself.

When we started this walk, I was full up on questions. They plagued me. It might be a failure of imagination again, but right now I have only one: "Do you think we can manage this, make sure Brynn doesn't have to go back to that horrid place? To her parents?"

Yesterday, at our makeshift camp, on the phone with Tray's mom, Brynn insisted that her parents loved her, that they weren't abusive. Even Tray's mom couldn't get Brynn to see that when someone starves their child, they're committing an act of abuse. That the violence overshadows any love present before or after the act.

The truck slows as we turn off the secondary highway and into town.

"My mom sent that list of names. Said she made calls, introductions on our behalf. To get ahead of this, we need one of these lawyers to take the case even though none of us have much money. Add the fact is that Brynn isn't set to do what she needs to, then, yeah, Molly, the series is stacked against us."

"Not a sport metaphor," I say, and smile so he knows I'm kidding.

"Sorry."

"Forgiven."

Tray covers my hand with his.

As the truck stops, I muster as much enthusiasm as I can. "Okay, let's crush this."

It's too early to check in to our motel, and we really do have to stay under the radar. We try the first lawyer's office because it's closest, open. It's a lone building with its own parking lot. The asphalt is cracked but recently sealed.

While Matteo holds the door, we file into the air-conditioned, heavy-dark-wood-paneled-with-brass-accents office. We're in the desert again, but this decor screams something else. Money, competence. Like the bookshelves, the secretary's desk, and the leather couches were chosen to suggest trust.

It hits me wrong.

Hard as we try, we can't escape the freaking desert. When we planned this hike, we broke it into five sections: the Desert, the Sierra Nevadas, the Klamaths, and Cascades—the first three all in California. Then in Oregon, the Southern Cascades, and lastly, in Washington State, the Northern Cascades. We researched, planned, and when Hank fell, once we could plan again, we dropped the last two. At night, after Hank was asleep, after Tray went home, I added those mountain ranges back into my plan.

We've made it to the Sierras. Yet, we keep returning to the desert. Like we're drawn here. Like we haven't learned the desert's lesson yet.

Tray takes the lead. "Hi, good day. How are you?"

The secretary raises her eyebrows, gestures for him to hurry up.

Her rudeness sets Tray off course. "Okay. So, um, Michella Lambert called. That's my mom. We were told that your boss . . ." He looks around for the lawyer's name.

"Mr. Rexalli," I say.

"Yeah, that Mr. Rexalli had been briefed, that he might talk with us. About a legal problem we're having."

The secretary raises her too-perfect eyebrow. "This is a group legal problem?"

Tray glances about and shrugs. "Yeah, sort of is."

In the small lobby, Matteo paces. Faith is clinging to Brynn.

Brynn holds Hank's hand. I'm standing next to Tray now, for moral support.

"Sort of," the secretary repeats, bored.

But she calls into the back office on her landline.

When Mr. Rexalli spots us, he sighs, wordlessly ushering us into his inner sanctum. This room is worse. More dark paneled wood, heavy green-glass-topped lamps, not enough natural light. He's wearing a suit, and we're in hiking clothes, street clothes. Four of us smell like we haven't showered in weeks. None of us sit in the chairs placed around the long coffee table.

Before he even hears what we have to say, Mr. Rexalli speaks. He nods at Tray, guessing he's the son of the Native lawyer up in Canada. "The short of it is that I can't help you. I did your mother a favor, seeing you, when I'm quite busy. And it's . . . well . . . parents have every right to decide how to feed their child. She's not . . ." He stares at Brynn. "You're obviously not . . . starving."

My nails bite into my palms. "Stop right there. You're only seeing what you want, only making freaking assumptions. Let's go," I say to my friends.

"Yeah, fuck this guy," Hank says.

The lawyer bows his head. "I can offer you twenty-four hours, as a courtesy to Ms. Lambert. To get ahead of this. Afterward, my secretary will report your appearance to the police. It's expensive to run an AMBER Alert. Noelle should turn herself in. And frankly, the rest of you are not in a good place, legally, harboring a runaway. This could ruin your futures."

Maybe not being able to imagine things is okay. When what we need to do might change what we're allowed to imagine. In some ways, my body is protecting me.

"Why do you think we're looking for help?" Hank asks, but my brother doesn't want an answer to his question.

The lawyer shrugs. "That's as much as I can do."

"Want to do," Tray says. "It's different."

The lawyer hovers near his desk. Hank yanks the door open. The secretary, she doesn't even look up from her computer as we exit the building.

Outside, the sun is bright, hot. It's the kind of day you want to spend by a pool. With full-sugar Cokes, slices of lime, and endless bags of ketchup chips. Good music, something low-key, summery, in the background. Not too loud, not too quiet.

Tray and I climb into the truck bed.

I shut my eyes a second.

"The other nearby place is closed today." Faith stands on the back tire, leans toward me. She's staring at her phone, where the next location is pulled up on her GPS. "But I've made an appointment in the morning, first thing."

"So, we should . . . ?" Brynn leaves it hanging.

"Hide out," I say. "Lay low."

"We're on the lam!" Brynn announces in her brightest voice, like this is a normal day.

At the motel, Matteo and Faith check us into adjoining rooms while everyone else decides who gets dibs on the showers. I let Brynn and Hank start because I'm not sure that once I make it to the water, I'll want to come out.

Faith leaves us, reluctantly. "I have to get to the store. But I'll be back at eight with snacks."

"So, sleepover?" Matteo asks, sitting on one of the queen-size beds.

Tray is sprawled on the carpet, sorting dirty clothing into a pile. Clean things would be nice. But we can't be caught doing laundry and it's too much to ask our friends. Already, we're pushing our luck, returning here. Already, we're asking for so many favors.

I nod. "Yeah, let's."

"I'll bring takeout," Matteo offers. "There's nothing sus about me going into my parents' place."

"Lots of chips, please," I say, pulling my hair from its ponytail. My scalp aches, itches. Like now that I'm this close to a shower, my body remembers how good it feels to be proper clean.

"Dirty, hungry hikers in my restaurant are my worst nightmare." They laugh, heading out the door. "But you all are officially my favorite dirty hikers. I'll bring the goods . . . as long as you both bathe next."

Tray is caught up in his own thing. He only nods.

I smile. "Deal, you clean freak."

The bed would be more comfortable, but I sit on the carpet too. "Well, today sucked . . . really freaking sucked."

"Completely."

"I can't see a way out of this." I keep my voice tempered so Brynn, who sings off-key in the shower, won't overhear us. "We can't fight all these people, her parents, the police, without somebody on our side."

"I don't see a way out either," Tray says slowly. "That does not mean it doesn't exist."

"That traditional knowledge, yeah?" I tease, because I need Tray to smile or laugh, to pull me against him.

"You know what, Molly? I'm out of stories. I don't know what to say to make you feel better here."

For the first time, I think I get what he's been trying to tell me. How stories and science are closer than I've given them credit. Because even if experiments in high school have beginnings and middles, ends and grades, science in the real world doesn't wrap up so nicely. When you finish an experiment, the last step is to iterate. To use your results to drive another hypothesis. And while that's a fancy word, all it means is that you make future predictions.

Predictions aren't science all by themselves. If they were, fortune tellers would be scientists.

Predictions, they are what-ifs.

And what-ifs are the basis for story.

And so, when designing an experiment, you become a storyteller. Or you're testing out a story, seeking results that will lead you to the story you've been telling. I've been so hard focused on experiments, like they don't start with a freaking question, don't, in the natural world, lead to more questions.

And if that's true, there's no cap on stories, no limit. Running out isn't possible. Questions, they are constant.

"Tray," I say carefully. "That's a load."

He smiles now, revealing his lone dimple. "Is it, now?"

"Pure shit, of the bear variety."

He's still smiling at me when Brynn emerges from the bathroom, fully dressed, her hair wrapped in a too-small towel.

"Oooooh, can I do it again?"

He nods.

"Dear bears, we love you and your shit. Signed, us."

I laugh and so does Tray.

Hank enters the room through the connecting door, also wearing a towel on his head. "What did I miss? I missed something. I can tell."

Brynn points at him, laughs.

It's a good moment. And I decide, we deserve a good night. Tomorrow might bring us hard things, but tonight, we're going to be very clean, fully bathed, and we are with people we love. So we're taking it. Claiming it. One good night.

Get ready.

We eat family-style, have just enough. Matteo brings heavy take-out bags, refuses cash when we offer it. At exactly eight, Faith shows up loaded down, and we eat well again. We laugh. We talk. It is a good night. Even if Tray isn't quite himself. Laughing a second late. The ukulele sitting in a corner, next to dirty clothes, forgotten.

It's late. The boys have gone to their beds. Closest to the door, Brynn talks quietly with Faith under the covers, like they're in a tent.

"It's not fair."

Faith replies immediately. "No, it's not."

"That doesn't change anything. Right?"

Faith laughs. "My parents are on my case these days. Lieutenant Green, do you remember him? From the hospital? Well, he definitely told. Because for the first time in my life, my parents are enforcing a curfew. And I'm already ten minutes late."

"What's ten more?"

"Okay, ten more."

They fall to a whisper, and I'm recognizing the good night is already gone. It's lonely in this bed. Lonely without the stars above me.

And as much as I'm not ready to go home, I miss Edmonton. MEC, yeah. The energy, the way it was close to that Christmas feeling. Unpacking new stock with care, savoring the anticipation. I never thought this was possible after what happened to Hank, but I miss chalked hands too. The stretch, the jump from one hold to the next. Even, yes, I miss the fall. The sharp catch of the belay device, that whole-body thud into the pads.

They teach you how, in the first bouldering class you take. In most sports, they teach you how to fall. How to operate the equipment, its limits and your own. And still, knowing what I know, I miss the moment when you trust you'll be okay but you don't know if it's certain.

After a flurry of goodbyes, Faith leaves for home.

The door falls closed.

I want to go outside, strike my tent, sleep in a field. But since I can't, because it's not safe, because in the middle of town in my pink tent, I'd be noticed, I want it more. A tent. In a field. The stars, so I can find the minor bear in the sky.

"Move over," Brynn says.

She's standing next to my bed.

I do.

"This okay?" she asks once she's settled under the covers.

"Really very much okay."

"Oooooh, you're feeling it, aren't you?" She sighs when I nod. "Thought I could spot a kindred spirit one bed over."

"It's too big," I say, even though that's not exactly it. "The bed . . . everything."

Sometimes, words aren't enough.

Brynn points at the alarm clock. "I hate that one's glowing red face."

"Same."

She yanks the cord from the wall.

"The TV too," I say. "Please."

Brynn unplugs every electrical thing in the room, even our phones. "Better?"

"No."

She laughs. "Least we tried."

I didn't call my parents. I made that choice. While I'm sure it's a mistake, even though the good turned sour, I can't regret spending tonight with my friends.

The mattress shifts as Brynn gets comfortable. "Molly?"

"Yeah, Brynny?"

"Will it help, do you think, if when we see the next lawyer, I tell them about the time my mom, while my dad was away for work . . . locked me in my room for three nights without food so I'd fit into a dress for a family thing we had coming up?"

I lay my head on Brynn's warm shoulder. "How many more of these stories do you have?"

"Enough."

"I don't know why anyone should need more. To me, what you're offering, it's plenty. More than. But also, yes, I think a lawyer will want that story. Maybe some others."

"When you all first told me it was . . . abusive . . . I'd blocked some things. After they let me register at school in person, it got better. I think . . . well, my mom, she gave up on having a perfect daughter." Brynn pauses, plays with my hair. "She started taking my cousin with her. My cousin who's fifteen and so skinny I worry that girl's not eating either. They go to the marina, the garden center, all the places my mom likes to be seen. And they leave me at home."

I'm not sure it's going to hit right. But I'm willing to take the chance. "A fat girl can do anything she wants. Freaking absolutely anything."

"A fat girl can walk . . . What is it now for you, like, nine hundred miles?"

I nod in the dark. "A fat girl can wear whatever she wants."

"A fat girl can eat, should eat, as much as she needs."

"A fat girl can fall in love."

"A fat girl can take up space, metaphorically, literally, in all the ways."

I exhale.

"Fall in love? You have something to tell me?" Brynn asks.

I laugh, get warm. "No, nothing. Or yes, I love you, Brynn."

"Love you too, Molly-friend." In the dark, it must be easier to say these things. Because she couldn't do this at the hospital, and she hasn't done this any other day we've been together on the trail. "Thank you for letting me be part of your adventure.

For forgiving me. For letting me sleep in your bed"—she speeds up—"because it's way too scary and lonely in that one."

"Anytime."

I hear impact against carpet. Tray slips into the connecting doorway, holding a pillow against his chest. "What she said." He walks over to my side.

I say, "Shimmy over, Brynn."

Tray crawls next to me. He comes close, really close, pulls me into him. I throw an arm around Brynny. We cuddle.

"Everyone all right with this?" Tray asks a minute later.

Brynn and I both nod.

"Maybe we can get some sleep now?" he wonders out loud, then sighs, like he, too, regrets how good nights sour so easy.

Brynn fidgets with the duvet cover. "Sing us a lullaby, music man?"

Tray laughs softly into my hair. "Any requests?"

I know it before Brynn speaks. She's obsessed.

"Hozier, please."

"Not the sexy ones," I say, and both my friends laugh. Because I'm between them, it's like I'm laughing too. A little bit of the good returns.

"That's basically impossible. Don't ask for the impossible."

"Yeah, Brynn's right, Mollycakes. I call no can do."

"Well, I guess I can compromise," Brynn says, a smile in her voice. "How about Molly's song."

"No, no, no, please." I groan. "Bring on Hozier."

Tray's grip on me tightens. "What if I tell a story instead?"

More feet stumbling across the carpet in the connecting room.

They shuffle closer. "What's this?" my brother asks. "You're doing story time without us?"

"Well, hurry up, buddy," Tray says.

Hank and Matteo flop onto the bed, like children, all elbows and knees.

"Over again, Brynn," I say.

And we shift, making a little more room. Now the bed is full. Now we're together. Instead of sleeping, we tell each other stories. Some are funny, and some, like the one Brynn tells about her thirteenth birthday, are sad. A few are only dreams about rainy cities, good coffee, about cities where it's no big thing to be gay, nonbinary, and at some point, everyone but Tray and I fall asleep.

We're stuck in the middle.

I'm overwarm and Tray keeps sighing. He's been pretending, but something's off, something's not right in his world.

"Should we try?" I ask.

"Try what?"

"To escape? This is great. I'm not complaining. But also, I will never fall asleep like this. And I don't think you can either."

"I'll steady you."

While attempting to get up, I knee Brynn. She stirs but doesn't wake. My legs are shaking, weak, overtired. Tray's holding my hips, practically my butt. It's awkward. Still, instead of taking to the floor, the easy way from one bed to the next, I stand tall, prepare myself, and then I leap.

There's a little thud of springs, of a cheap bed frame, when I land. I'm grinning. "Your turn."

Tray stands awkwardly, the mattress shifting under him. "Count me down."

"One. Two. And . . . three."

We hold on to each other, falling, laughing quietly.

Both of us on top of the covers, my head on Tray's shoulder, his on the only pillow left in this bed, he says, "I'm going to tell you a story. One I got from my dad, who got it from his grandmere, who got it from her grandmere, who got it from her papa. I don't know where he got it. Okay?"

"I'm listening."

And then Tray in a whisper-quiet voice tells me stories, the ones I've been missing. He tells them one after another, offering up their lineage first. Who told it, who heard it from whom. Eventually, even though I don't want to, I fall into sleep where I dream of a mountaintop, of sharpened rocks, massive boulders, of summer's snow in the high places.

EARLY AUGUST
LONE PINE, CA
Traylor

When Faith lets herself inside with the room key, I crawl from the bed, shower quickly to wake up. But I can't shake this heaviness, how my body doesn't respond as fast as I'd like. I scan through my contacts again like it's as easy as that. Sending a text. I hover over the *J*s. Pause when I see Jaime's name. But reaching out after a long while isn't easy. Instead, I check in with my mom.

She's already in court for the day.

None of my clothes are clean. My *You Are on Native Land* tee might be covered in tiny holes, but it's the best option. Again, for a minute, I wish I'd brought my graduation outfit along. It would have been extra weight, yeah. But I'd be clothed the way the Western world expects you to when you walk into a lawyer's office. At my mom's place, you're as likely to see ribbon skirts and shirts as a suit. But even there, trail-wrecked tees aren't to code.

When I'm dressed, teeth brushed, Hank is already outside in the truck with most everyone else. None of us likes being locked indoors. Other than Matteo, and maybe Faith, the rest of us, we're happiest out in the world.

I don't blame them for hurrying.

Sitting on the bed, Molly waits for me. She pulls her hair into a messy ponytail, struggles with the elastic.

"I got it," I offer.

That citrus smell again. It's infused in both of us.

Whatever happens, whatever future is ahead, I'll always match this smell to this girl in this place. It's usually music for me. Not this time. Or with my Mollycakes, it's not only music.

She's tied up in every good memory I have across all my senses.

"Thanks," she says while I finger-comb her hair smooth.

I could do this all day, yeah. Stay right here. Like this.

We both jump when Hank's voice thunders: "Hurry up, lazy bones! Or we're leaving without you."

Now I don't want to step out of this motel. I've been . . . wrong, off, since we came down from the mountain. It's not only the AMBER Alert. It's that even if Molly is letting me close, I haven't asked if there's more between us.

The kisses, this touch, it could mean anything to Molly. I don't want to keep telling a one-sided story.

But I won't know. Until I ask. I'm right back where I was the night after this girl told me how she felt—*your fucking fault*—I'm right back there, too chicken to say anything.

Because if I speak up, I'm inviting change into our lives.

And not all change is good.

"We're going to be late!" Hank hollers again.

I yell back. "Yeah, yeah, we're coming!"

Molly scrunches her nose. "Let's do this?"

Her confidence is wobbly. I realize that's been true for months. That I watched it crumble as she ran into the hospital. While I hugged her, she got smaller. For the first time in her life, Molly doubted herself.

She drops her sunglasses in place. She steps into the bright day. I follow right behind. But instead of looking toward the truck and our impatient friends, I glance left, and that's when I see him: the police officer from that night, Lieutenant Green, without his uniform, exiting the motel office.

"Stop!" he orders when he spots us.

I help Molly into the truck bed. Instead of joining her, I heft the tailgate closed. It's an action without forethought. It's my body moving, conditioned, my muscles responding on a long push across the ice.

"Don't you dare leave this lot," the cop says, getting closer.

"Go."

Molly looks furious, but nods, taps twice on the glass.

"Shit, shit," Faith says, yelling out her open window as she checks the blind spot.

And I can't help but smile when Hank, who seems to be happily rolling with the punches on the bench seat, hollers too: "In this friend group, it's bear shit or there's no shit."

"No offense to bears!" Brynn adds, right on the beat.

The truck takes off.

Now the cop has a choice, and I already know which one he's going to take. It's work, chasing after a vehicle. And I'm standing here. Waiting for him, my hands visible. Because even though he's not in uniform, he's got a gun in a holster.

He spits on the ground near my camp sandal. "You're gonna regret that."

I probably will, yeah. But I don't give him the pleasure. Refusing to speak, to appear a threat, I raise both my hands higher, palms out.

"Come on," he says, grabbing my forearm. "We're going down to the station."

Green hasn't arrested me, but he's got me set up in the back half of the building, on a steel bench, next to a lockable room. The drunk tank. My mom will hate everything about this. Top to bottom. We have a call-anytime-for-any-reason relationship. She might work a lot, but if I need her, she'll buy a plane ticket, fly down, and rage on these people.

"The longer you refuse to talk, the more trouble you'll be in, Traylor."

"That so?" I ask, my throat dry. I push off the bench and walk to the water fountain next to the men's washroom. "I can't quite see what I've done wrong."

At a young age, my mom taught me how to handle the police. And while it's always best to say nothing, to offer nothing at all, I know what this man wants, what gets him off. He wants to argue with someone younger, someone with less power than him.

He doesn't actually care about Brynn. His loyalties lie with her parents, with government, no matter who gets hurt when the letter of the law is held as more important than people, than community.

Lieutenant Green laughs at me. "The runaway didn't tell you her parents are pressing charges, did she? You and your little girlfriend left town after I expressly ordered you not to. I thought, there's not much I can do. My jurisdiction is limited. Then last night, I find the García boy and Faith Ann carrying large quantities of food into the motel. You kids aren't as smart as you think."

"Maybe we aren't," I say, thinking of Molly.

How she said she had this handled.

How I didn't question her.

Because my Molly is smart, wouldn't tell me she handled it when she didn't. She'd take care of things, take care of me, no matter how angry she was in the moment. I believe this. And then I think about how it doesn't matter what she did. My future, it probably only gets a certain shine if I pick up a record here. This is a song writing itself. But for Molly, this could stop her from getting into medical school. I know that's not what her heart wants anymore, yeah. But I want to protect all her futures.

"Tell me if the Hensley girl was in the truck."

"No, don't think I will."

Lieutenant Green runs a hand through his hair. "Okay, then sit pretty. I'm going to check on the radio to see if anyone up or down the highway has spotted Faith Ann's vehicle. I hate to do it, to drag that sweet girl into this. But you're not giving me a choice."

"Can I call my mom? She's a lawyer, yeah."

"You're eighteen, according to your ID. So you're an adult. And until I decide to book you, you've got no rights," Lieutenant Green says, glancing at his scuffed boots. "It's as easy as calling up my

Homeland Security buddies, having you removed from the country. That kind of mark lasts. Makes it awfully hard to travel across my border."

His border.

It's laughable.

The way he claims this line that for Native nations doesn't exist. This line he's protecting like it's critical when it's only ink on a map.

For fifteen minutes, I'm pissed that he won't let me make a call. My phone is on his desk, along with my ID, my bank card. Then I think it through, past the frustration. Yeah, I laugh out loud, and the cop, he glares at me. When he heads farther into the building, I stand, pocket my things, and walk back to the front.

The younger man leaning against the counter has a hipster mustache. "You heading out now?"

I nod. "Yeah, that I am."

"I wondered when you'd figure it out. Green's an asshole," he says, and shrugs.

And if it weren't pressing my luck further than I think it stretches, I'd tell this one that he's a bit of an asshole too. Watching his colleague behaving badly and doing nothing.

It's just as toxic.

But for once, I don't have to say it. I can walk away.

In the parking lot, it's bright. I left my sunglasses in my pack but shouldn't have. Light catches on a metal door as it swings wide. I blink hard.

Molly comes running toward me. "Jesus, Tray, I was so scared! Are you okay?"

"I'm fine, yeah," I say, hugging her.

The others get close too.

"Well, buddy, that was dramatic," Hank offers.

"Just saving the day, buddy."

Hank snorts. "Respectfully, it was a team effort."

"Well, as long as it's done respectfully." I try to elbow Hank.

He ducks behind Matteo for safety.

A black sedan pulls into the parking lot, parks beside the truck. A white woman with pink hair wearing a cream blouse and a red pencil skirt steps out. "This your friend?" she asks everyone.

I don't know how long I've been held up. An hour or more. Long enough that my team has brought in reinforcements.

"Hi, I'm Tray."

"I talked to your mom the other day. She's a cool lady," the woman says all animated and then sobers. "You all right? They didn't violate your civil rights in there, did they?"

"Probably not. Lieutenant Green, he had me thinking I had to come with him, had to wait it out. But I got smart, figured things."

"I really hate that guy." The lawyer sighs. "I was going to do this anyhow, you know, after your mom called and I sat down and took a look at the case law. But knowing Green's messed up in this, I'm going to do my job with extra pep in my step."

"Tray," Molly says, still standing close. "Meet Ms. Zates."

At some point, I'm going to have to ask Molly a handful of important things. But right now, it's back burner.

"Kayla Zates," the lawyer says, offering me her hand. "Family law. I do the rounds this way once a week, but I'm based out of Bakersfield."

We shake.

And I immediately like her. She's not once looked down at us because we're young or because Molly and me are Native. She took the time to check the case law. She's offering us respect. Plus, her pink hair is all kinds of powerful.

"So," Kayla Zates says. "Who wants to go inside and watch me do fancy legal stuff? I can't promise tears, but I bet Green will sweat. I'll make the AMBER Alert go away and get Brynn somewhere safe. As my final act, the proverbial nail in this legal coffin, I'll see what we can do to make sure that Mr. and Mrs. Hensley are reprimanded for using that tool incorrectly. Who the fuck sends a car for their injured daughter? What kind of smarmy BS is that?"

Hank cheers. "Bear shit!"

"No offense to the bears!" everyone but me and Molly announce together, like it's our motto.

While our friends file inside, Molly grabs my hand, stalling me. "Don't ever do that again, okay?"

"What now?"

"Don't play like you don't know."

I shrug. It's a bit mean, but part of me is still not okay. I've forgiven her—I have. Whatever answers she has to offer, I've already forgiven her if they hurt me. But I'm not sure I've offered the same grace to myself. So I pretend everything is fine. That nothing between us has changed. That we are the people we were before Hank's accident, before this summer on the trail.

"We're a team, you dick," Molly says, sharp like a knife, exactly the way I love her. "And, like, I don't know if they taught you this at hockey camp or whatever, but you don't take one for the team like that. You don't sacrifice yourself for the greater good. That is not okay."

"Actually," I say, holding on tighter to her hand, "that's the point of most sports. That you'll sacrifice for the team's success."

"You know I've never been into . . . that," she says. "I like individual challenges."

"Obviously. But in hockey . . . ," I say, teasing her.

"Oh, are you going to tell me a story?"

I laugh my way out of my mood. "Yeah, Mollycakes, you game?"

She smiles up at me. "I'm starting to like stories. But don't tell anyone."

"It would crush your reputation, yeah?"

"Destroy it."

I could push things, could keep teasing her. But the fiddle is saying be happy with what I have. That like Molly I've been too caught up in futures. And even now that I'm away from the trail again, even now that I'm not sure we'll make it back, I'm still learning the trail's lessons.

I'll ask my questions. Eventually.

But right this moment, in the present, the now, we're missing a show.

"Should we go help our friends?"

It's not what I want her to ask me. It's not enough, but I'm pretending so hard that it is. And for now, this is the right thing. One step at a time. That's how you walk a really long ways. "Let's, yeah."

NOW

Hank

Is Aunt Sheila the Asshole?

I know, I know. I'm using this wrong, relying on a tool to get me through life, when this tool isn't infallible. But as much as I needed it, as much fun as it's been, I can't AITA my way through life.

Though it helps, writing things down.

So yeah, Aunt Sheila, Brynn's mom's younger sister, didn't know that Brynny existed. And Brynn had no idea her mom has a sister.

The conversation was funny.

Lawyer Kayla Zates was all like: BUT WHAT ABOUT YOUR MOM'S SISTER? SHE LIVES IN LOS ANGELES. OWNS A HOME. WITH A YARD.

And Brynny was like: WHO?!

And The Kayla Zates was like: YOUR AUNT SHEILA. GOD, BRYNNY, DO YOU WANT TO END UP IN FOSTER CARE?

And then Tray was like: YEAH, BRYNNY. FOSTER CARE IS THE COLONIZER'S TOOL. IT CAUSES INTERGENERATIONAL TRAUMA. DO YOU WANT INTERGENERATIONAL TRAUMA, BRYNNY?

And then Brynn was like: WAIT. BACK IT UP. I'LL TAKE THE SECRET AUNT. THAT SOUNDS LIKE IT'S GOING TO BE EASY AND FUN, NOT LIKE FOSTER CARE!

I'm ad-libbing here. They were much more eloquent.

It seems Aunt Sheila lives with a dermatologist.

Yes, I am holding this against her.

All it takes is one phone call, and Aunt Sheila is making a plan to retrieve Brynn from Superlawyer Kayla Zates's office very late this afternoon.

My sister, she doesn't say a thing. The whole conversation. Maybe I'm holding that against her too. It's not dermatologist-level ass-holery, but it stinks. Because I worry she's planning something, that *hell or high water*, as our mom would say, Molly's heading back to the trail.

EARLY AUGUST
LONE PINE, CA
Molly

I t's late afternoon. Almost evening, but not quite. I'm sitting on
the bed closest to the bathroom, Tray beside me, his legs stretched
out. Like mine, they're scratched up, covered in bug bites. At least
one of his scratches will scar. A handful of mine will too. We
look as if we got lost and stumbled through the woods, searching,
searching for weeks.

In a way, we did.

My parents must be furious, just on fire with how I've left them
hanging. Some of it is want, some of it that absolute dick need. To
have this space away from them and all that pressure, that noise. I
know they know I'm okay. Hank's telling me that he's talking to
them. Playing a little defense on my behalf.

While Tray's here, hanging out with me, very much choosing
to do it, there's something off. Between us, maybe. We haven't
said the things we need, even if we've said more to each other than
we have in months. Part of me believes it's something other than
that. That inside my best friend, there's a thing that hurts him.
Beyond me.

I want to ask, to listen if he needs that.

But all my needs are in competition with each other and this one wins out: handling my parents. I've made my decision. I need to support it.

I owe Hank a reckoning too. He owes me words. More than a half-rotten apology offered because he's thirteen months older and that must mean he knows what's best for me. Like Tray, something deeper is rotted out.

It's beyond the why of the accident.

I want to develop a hypothesis, tell myself a story. But not yet.

Kayla Zates let us have the early afternoon, while she finished at her office. But two hours ago, she picked up Brynn to drive her to her auntie.

Our goodbye-for-now was tearful.

Brynn hugged each of us really hard, promised she'd get her driver's license as soon as possible. That she'd drive to meet us, wherever we were. Along the trail, even all the way to Canada.

I laughed through the tears. "And that's different from running away how, exactly?"

"Okay, so it might take a while." Brynn shrugged. "But I'm coming for you all. That is one hundred percent a threat."

Hank was crying too. "Threaten me anytime, okay, Brynny. Any which way, any fucking how. Okay?"

"Ooooh, I love that offer."

"Accept it, then."

"Accepted. Ratified. Inserted into the meeting minutes."

A few more hugs, and that was it. Zates's sedan drove away. We watched in the parking lot, the cement burning our bare feet. But

I couldn't watch it disappear all the way. Knew my heart wouldn't be okay if I had to stare for that long.

Now the door to the motel is open, the lights and AC are off. I haven't plugged the TV, the alarm clock, or the lamps back in.

Hank is napping next door.

Matteo and Faith are at work. Faith cried until she threw up. We were all happy Brynn didn't witness that.

This summer, this hike, these people, it's as if we're falling to pieces. Our bodies, our hearts. I finally quit snapping my phone in and out of its disaster-proof case. Tray hasn't said a thing about that. It must be aggravating. I force myself to plug in my phone, turn it back on. It takes a minute, loads emails and texts, missed calls, the red notification numbers high.

It's an indication of exactly how worked up my parents have spun themselves. In their story, this is me being inconsistent. Not caring about their feelings. I tap the screen a few times. When the video call connects, my mom says: "Maurice, come over here. We've got Molly."

My dad joins the frame. They're both at the kitchen table. My dad's in the process of restringing one of his fiddles. "Good of you to call, ma fii."

"Hi, Traylor," my mom says, absolutely ignoring me.

Tray waves.

I pull the phone closer, everything but Tray's fingers resting on my left shoulder disappearing from the frame.

"Tell me you've been out of cell reception," my mom says.

"I can't."

"We know," she says, harder. "Hank's been keeping us up to date."

It's only been a day and a half since I said I'd call. They know the trail is full of places where cell phones are basically expensive cameras, where signal doesn't get in the way of living. And they know here in town we've been busy with something important.

"I needed space to think before I could make this call."

Now my parents appear worried. But they stay silent.

"I know you want me to be a doctor. That's not enough anymore. And no matter what you say, you can't make me want it. And you won't try, because you love me. I know that's not what you want to hear. But I can't keep trying to be the perfect daughter, the daughter you've imagined."

My mom's face falls. "We just want you to be successful, Molly."

"Happy." My dad makes a critical adjustment. "We want her to be happy, Lisa."

Mom, she nods fast. And I hate that after this, she's going to cry. Hate that today has been brimming with tears. For so many people I love.

Tray squeezes my shoulder, nothing but quiet comfort.

I can't not say it. Now that it's obvious to me.

So, I travel onward. "There are other ways to be happy. It's not one path. If I don't become a doctor, I'm not throwing out my one chance. And it's facts. The life of a doctor is a freaking lot. Maybe it's good and needed and important, but maybe that would limit my happiness. I want to explore lots of possible paths, to figure it out on my own, and I don't want to do it on some randomly imposed timeline. And I don't want to go to school in Calgary."

My parents don't say anything.

I keep going. "I'm seventeen. Maybe I needed to skip a grade, to work with more challenging material. But when you made that decision—and yes, I know I agreed back then. Back then I wanted it. Only I didn't realize how important a year could be. How much growing I could do in that year. And maybe that's what I need now, one year. Maybe I'll need more later. For now, I want to take the gap year I planned for. Long before Hank's accident. I want to explore, challenge myself over and over again. And those challenges might not look like what you want for me."

My dad nods.

My mom sighs. Untold objections live in that sigh. "Okay, that's . . . fair," she finishes weakly. "I can live with that. But you'll stop shutting us out? Call more often?"

"If we return to the trail—I'm not saying we will—but if we do, it's not like I can call whenever you want. You'll have to understand too."

"We can," Dad says. "Tell Hank we love him."

My mom leans into my dad. "God, I miss my kids."

My dad comforts her.

"Be safe," Mom adds, and while I don't tell her how that's something I can't promise, because then she'll never hang up, I nod, once.

I shove my phone, still connected to the charging cord, under the pillow behind me. I exhale. For a minute, I'm empty. Then a rush floods through me. My heart is doing her job. Eventually, this relief will seep into my bones. When it reaches my bones, I hope I'll be certain again.

That the world will make sense again.

"Better?" Tray asks.

"They listened. That's a start." I rest against the headboard, and I want to sink into a hot tub or into the bath. Part of me could spend the rest of this summer floating in water. "My mom's normal strategy is to regroup, and usually my dad is all about supporting her. But maybe this time, things could go differently."

"It's possible. Want me to send smoke up?"

"If you want."

He hums.

"So are you going to tell me what's with you?" I ask. "Do you need a nap too?"

"Yeah, I do." He laughs. "But it's not only that."

"Well, stop being all mysterious and tell me."

"I mean, I think I have already told you, yeah. And you're treating me to some kind of revenge. The way I couldn't, didn't, speak that night at your house . . . after all the rye."

Oh, we're finally going to talk about it.

"I'm pretty sure I'd know if I was planning some terrible revenge against you?" I say breezily.

He only shrugs.

"Tray."

"I love you, Molly."

"Yeah, you've said."

"Also, and this is important. I get it now. I'm not in love with you."

"Again, you've said this already." I'm only a little frustrated.

307

Only a little hurt. But it's small. I keep telling myself this is minor.

The universe is big, endless, according to science and just as endless in stories.

"Yeah, but Molly, that's the problem. I want to be in love with you more than just in my head where I'm dreaming up a long future, and I want you to be in love with me, and when time gets long between us, I want backyard skating rinks, and a house, where Hank lives next door. And more than anything, I want you to do whatever it is you want. I want that for you." He stops, struggles, but then he says it: "But I want what I want too."

"Oh." My skin is tingly. "I mean, I'm not quite on board with the skating rink. I think I'd rather have a pool, maybe? But . . . Traylor."

He looks at me all hopeful, his forehead creased, his brown eyes waiting.

"I think that I might want to be in love with you. Someday."

"Might?" he says.

"Maybe," I offer.

"You're killing me, Mollycakes."

"Well, that sucks. You can't be my boyfriend if you're dead."

He sits up straight. "Don't play with me."

"But I like playing with you."

"Okay, play with me but say it again. Mean it now. Whatever's in the future, that's all the way down the line. I'm okay with that. But for now, mean it, want it as much as I do."

"Tray . . . Be my freaking boyfriend?"

He nods. "Yes, very much, yeah, please."

"Okay." I stretch, trying to relieve the tightness in my neck.

Fail, sink down into the pillows. "Now that's settled, want to take a nap?"

"Yeah," he says. "My heart is happy, real happy right now. But also, I could sleep for a season."

"Well, we can manage an early night. That will have to be enough. Because tomorrow, we have to check out of here by eleven. And before that, we need to make some decisions."

"Tomorrow," he says. "That's ages away."

"So very far."

"Molly?" Tray asks, his eyes fluttering closed.

We're facing each other.

"Yeah?"

He opens his eyes. "Would it bother you, if when we get home, whenever that is, if I record your song? If I sang it in public? Because I'm going to do that. Well, not unless you're okay with it. But when I go home, I want to give it a real shot. Maybe go to university, maybe not, yeah. But that song is yours and it's important to me to have your permission to share it."

"It's yours. You can do what you want with it."

"No, Molly. Stories belong to the people who tell them, yeah, but also to the people who listen to them. To the people who hand them down. So what I'm trying to say is that this song, it's pieces of you, and pieces of me, and do you consent to me passing those pieces onward? Will you be okay if this song plays on the radio? If it's the song someone plays when they're sad? Are you okay if this song has a life of its own? Beyond you, me, this town? Because it doesn't have to."

I give it a minute. Try to imagine this.

Where I end up is with a girl on a trail. Her hair's in two stubby shoulder-length braids. She's sunburnt, and because she's tired of being in her own head, she starts singing a song that she loves, one that makes her feel that happy-sad, possible-impossible thrill. She's not alone: there are crows in the trees, sharp pine cones scattered everywhere, snakes sleeping on tree branches, in crevices, and somewhere deeper in the mountains there are bears. She sings off-key, and it's loud, not perfect. Instead, it's achingly real.

"Yeah, I do. Consent." And while we're both exhausted, I spend a minute or two telling Tray about that girl, about his music making it farther along the trail than we have. Through the Sierras and into the next mountain range.

"I like that story," he says.

And then we fall quiet, close our eyes.

I sleep for an hour. When I wake, cartoons blare from the connecting room. Hank laughs. I don't hear Matteo or Faith.

My brother is alone.

I walk into the room. Sit on the other bed, face him, cross my legs.

"Tray still sleeping?"

"Yeah," I say.

"Well, that's good."

"We don't need him here, for this," I say.

Because Tray's pulled between us, from one best friend to the other. And since now I'm his girlfriend, and that means he's always on my team, it wouldn't be kind to have this conversation with him around.

He'd be torn between us. And that's not fair to Tray.

And maybe this is what I need. A conversation where my brother and I, we're alone. I don't think we've been alone, properly, since the accident. One of our parents, if not both. Nurses, doctors, PTs. And when that bunch was elsewhere, Tray, always Tray, was sitting next to the hospital bed, or was in our house, watching TV, or in the yard helping rake leaves.

And until this moment, I didn't realize it was intentional.

That my only sibling was keeping bodies between us.

"I'm your big brother," Hank says, on the offensive. "It's my job to look out for you."

"I'm not mad about that. It was a dick thing to do, but I'm mostly over it." I shrug. "I needed space. Just because I needed it that doesn't mean your needs or our parents' matched up."

"Sleep, it's a miracle," he says, like this wasn't real hard work, like I'm not working so hard to understand myself, the people around me.

I ignore him. "It's obvious our needs don't match anymore. That you need something new, different between us. And I don't. Maybe."

Hank rubs at his hair. Like mine, it's growing. But I know when he does this, he's feeling his surgery scars. That they're still raised, still healing. Hank doesn't recognize his body with these scars, not yet.

"Why is it so easy for you to talk with everyone else? Our parents. Tray. Brynn. Even Matteo, who you've known for, like, a minute and a half, they all get to hear what you're thinking."

The cartoons are loud. We're talking over them. The remote is right next to Hank's hand. He could change this.

If he wanted to.

But he doesn't. And he doesn't speak. He stares at the screen.

I wait and wait and wait. My body is starving. But I wait through my hunger. The cartoon goes to commercial, comes back.

And still Hank says nothing.

I uncross my legs, slip off the bed. I'm through the connecting door before my brother calls my name. "What?"

"It's that it's . . . hard . . . to talk to you. Now."

Hank's still staring at the TV.

"Why?"

I am full of one-word questions. The kind that form the backbone to any experiment, any story.

Hank finally turns. He's all red, not crying, but close. "Because, Molly, you aren't good with the surface stuff. You're always digging for more. Like you're this person who's only happy once you've dug deep enough that you've hollowed someone out. You're not happy with pieces. No, you go big." He pauses. "And that's too hard for me right now."

"Explain."

"See?" he says, and then he sighs. "When you ask *How are you today, Hank?* you really want to know. It's not this empty greeting with you, the way it is with others."

I asked that question a lot. I know I did.

After Hank fell.

"When you wanted to know what happened that day, you went so hard. Non-fucking-stop. I'd fake sleep to get away from you. Daily. Because I couldn't walk out of the room."

I never knew he felt trapped. I try to swallow, can't.

"And when I managed to get myself home, you wanted to jump into planning this trip, like if we returned to normal, everything that had changed for me wouldn't matter."

"I—I . . . I love you, Hank."

My brother meets my eyes. "I need you to love me a little less."

"That's impossible!" I'm crying now. Full out.

My brother gets up, heads to the washroom, comes back with a clumsy wad of toilet paper, grabs my shoulders, steers me so I'm sitting again.

He perches across from me. "I'm going through a really hard time. And I'm almost on the other side. But here, this summer, please, can you stop needing things from me? Impossible fucking things? Because what's happened to me, it's not about you, Molly. It's not."

He's right and he's wrong.

I'm right and I'm wrong.

The world is unsafe.

But also, the world holds us.

"I know I didn't fall." I speak carefully because words are slippery things. Because I can see it different now, I have to be careful here not to enact violence on him. "And I know you did. That falling literally changed your body and your brain in ways I will never understand in my own."

"Yes, exactly. Now maybe you can back the fuck off me."

My brother's words are hurtful, carelessly thrown for the biggest impact. I don't let this stop me. I don't let the way he's lashing out, all claws, reach my heart. "I didn't fall," I say again. "But,

Hank, you're my family. So when you fell, when you were in a coma for three weeks and four days, all that time, I was falling too. Our parents were falling. Tray was inconsolable."

He doubles down. "I fell. They didn't."

"That experience, we can't share. But we shared in the after-effects. It might be selfish, I don't know, but we're still sharing in how the fall changed our lives. It changed yours most radically. But because you're a part of us, we had to change too. That we would keep living in this world, the one that said you're the problem, that falling is the problem, or we could change too."

Hank scoffs. "Say I buy this . . ."

"Okay."

"Say I do, but at the same time, it doesn't alter the fact that I need you to stop needing so much from me."

"I can do better." I shrug, like it's immaterial when it's very much a solid, living thing. "But, Hank, you need to tell me when I'm overstepping. And be honest. I didn't need you to chase after me. You did that. I didn't do that to you. So you can stop acting all sanctimonious."

"I told myself I was doing it because you needed me. But real story? It was too fucking . . . quiet in our house with you and Tray gone. And maybe there's something you ought to read. Maybe it would help." Hank grabs his phone, sends me a text. "But also, the internet is anonymous for a reason, so please do not read it in front of me, and please, can we not talk about it?"

"I can do that." My stomach grumbles. It's loud, unmistakable.

"You hungry?" my brother asks, offhand.

"Ravenous."

"Should we get a bite?"

From the other room, Tray's voice is sleep-rumbled. "Can I come?"

"Of course, buddy," Hank says. "Unsurprisingly, I vote for tacos."

"Someone text Faith, invite her along," I say, still sitting on the bed.

Tray says, "Got it."

Hank stands, walks toward me. "We good?"

I know that this isn't the end. That everything is changing, changing onward. For now, this is enough. "We're good."

"Let's eat, eh?"

The walk to Matteo's family's restaurant is something we've only done together once, but tonight, under the stars, it echoes all the other times my brother, our best friend, and I have walked somewhere together in the days before the accident. We're freer than we have been. We're joking, laughing. Even Faith falls into it when she catches up with us.

After a bone breaks, it might never be the same again.

But it can heal. Most bones do.

The world remakes itself every season, sleeps and then emerges abundant with new growth. That's only science. But I'm learning that it's story too, that questions are important, necessary even, but sometimes a person needs to exist in the present, sometimes you need to build your story.

So that's what I do.

The rest of the night is story in the making. Later, when I return to my bed, to my fully charged phone, I follow the link

Hank texted and I read. Jesus H., it's hard, some of this, but also, I laugh.

Tomorrow is coming when tomorrow comes.

The bones, they'll keep healing in the background.

THE LAST STAR

Now the design is finished. This is the final piece, the last part of the song.

    Can you see the minor bear?

    Does it speak to you now?

    Its heart fluttering in sleep in the spoons. Its dream, in the movements of the fiddle, the jaw harp. Know its mind when the accordion sings out.

THE LAST WEEK OF AUGUST
LONE PINE, CA
Traylor

Faith has gone all out today, arranged things so Molly and me aren't needed at the general store, that Matteo and Hank-the-Tank are free from the restaurant. And because we live in two tents in her dusty backyard, she refuses to take any chances, hollers at us from her bedroom window as soon as her alarm sounds off.

Last night was cold in a new way. But the day's warming already. I'm stretched out on my back next to Molly. Her hair, an imperfect, glorious mess, is the only thing sticking out from her sleeping bag.

"It is really morning?" Her voice is muffled. "Please, if you like me, say no."

That's easy. "No."

She makes a happy sound, cuddles into my shoulder.

I check my phone. A few texts from my mom and a new email from my dad. They're waiting to find out what's next. But so am I.

"We have twenty minutes to get dressed and brush our teeth before we have to meet Faith at the truck," Hank says from the other tent. "And don't forget to floss."

Faith won't tell any of us what's up, just that we need an adventure. And one thing I've learned about Faith over the past few weeks is that she's serious about punctuality. It's the least likeable thing about her, which should say everything.

Faith and her parents are kind, welcoming.

"Want the bathroom first?" I ask Molly.

"Yes, please." She shimmies out of her sleeping bag, kisses my cheek. "It's yours in five."

"Love you, Mollycakes."

Even this early, she's sharp. "But are you in love with me?"

"Getting there," I say, like I'm playing too, and then I can't pretend any longer. I have to tell her. "Yeah, no, that's not it. I'm one hundred percent there."

She slips out of the tent. Turning back, she smiles with teeth. "Respectfully, I fully understand."

I laugh. It took the whole summer, but playful Molly is back. Even Hank has relaxed into himself. He still has headaches, sometimes bad ones, and his balance is worse in the evenings or when he's tired. But he's growing out his hair, yeah, and Hank, for the first time in a long time, acts comfortable in his skin.

When Faith, who turns out is an absolute homebody, said we needed an adventure, I didn't argue. Not returning to the trail was the right choice. For me, but for the Norris-Norquay siblings too. That doesn't mean I'm not ready for change, yeah. For a day trip.

A small adventure.

The first time we walked through, I didn't give the desert enough credit. These days, it's my favorite place. Stories blossom here. Storytellers live here. It might be a little magic, the desert. I've run into more storytellers here—some Native, some not—than I have anywhere else. At night, constellations people the sky. At night, yeah, I tell Molly star stories.

And every night, she finds Ursa Minor. And she says this: "There is nothing wrong with being a minor bear. I'm not sure anyone has freaking told you this. So, I'm saying it."

The bear again.

We cannot escape the bear. Not even in the desert.

The fiddle and the spoons love it here, are thriving here, so very far from their home. I've written more songs living and working in a desert world than I have in my life.

They might even be good.

Songwriter's night has become a weekly thing. And yeah, there are more Bob Dylan covers than you might expect, but even Dylan is growing on me.

It's Saturday. Now that we're living off the trail, Western time has reasserted itself. We've been driving over an hour. We're squished into the cab. Molly's hanging half out the window, my arm around her shoulders.

Now that it's welcome, I can't stop touching her.

But she's all touch too.

And not often, but sometimes, Molly comes chasing after me.

We all agree I have taste, so the music is from my phone. To connect to this old truck, I had to order a cable from a shop in San Diego. Today, Matteo is in charge. They've put together a road-trip playlist. And it's the bear's absolute shit—no offense to any bears.

William Prince for those folk-gospel vibes. Little Mix because how could we not. Kesha, Kate Bush, and yes, Carly Rae Jepsen. Lizzy McAlpine's "To the Mountains" because, ironically, it's Matteo's, this absolute indoor kid's, favorite song. Some oldies and some *real* oldies, round it out.

A text lights up my phone.

Jaime.

In some ways, it was that simple. To select his contact, to write him a message. He's in New Hampshire, about to start his first year at Dartmouth College, playing on their Division I team. He decided to put off the draft, for at least four years. To play a little. To learn a little more.

"Are we there yet?" Hank asks, like he's been asking for the past forty minutes.

Faith's hands are at nine and three. "No, buddy."

That used to be my thing with Hank. I love how it's spread. Now everyone does it. Even Faith's parents. Who don't care we're showering in their guest bathroom, who remind us weekly to call home, who pay us under the table for the work we're doing.

Sometimes, it's minding the register. But also, we've sanded the wooden exterior of the store, stained it. We've planted a native desert garden along one side, installed a hiker box and benches along the other. The garden's mostly rocks, yeah. But we've got a variety of cactus, brittlebrush, sand sagebrush, and desert spoon too. The Paiute couple who own the local nursery have been teaching me about desert medicine. I try to stop by, help out around their place, a few hours a week.

It's not what I planned for this summer.

In ways, it's radically different.

But it's good.

Hank-the-Tank's going home soon to start his Grade 12 year over. Molly and me haven't rescheduled our plane tickets yet. We can stay until our tourist visas expire. I don't think we'll stick around the entire six months, but I don't think we'll leave this place when Hank does either.

The miles we learned, we walked slowly, fly by so fast traveling this way. In a truck, we've managed what would have taken us days on foot in an hour and some. When we stop at a gas station in the middle of nowhere, I guess it means Faith needs a break. Molly opens our door to stretch.

An older Buick is parked in front of the store. Otherwise, there are no other vehicles. There is the quiet road and there are trees.

Suddenly, Brynn's voice rings out, cheery and full. "Oooooh, you're finally here!"

Delightful chaos ensues.

Molly jumps up and down in place.

Hank goes running, scoops Brynn up, swings her around. "Brynny! We missed you."

Faith just says, "Surprise!"

When it's my turn to hug Brynn, I mock-whisper, "Hank's been insufferable with you gone."

"Respectfully, you didn't," Hank says.

"I did do, buddy."

Brynn just says, "Tell me how miserable you've been, and I'll tell you how miserable I've been, and we'll all feel better. That's what friendship's all about."

It's the way she says it. Brynn is a sunshine human, but that doesn't mean she's not trying to protect us, that she doesn't get cloudy, that the wind doesn't rage, on occasion.

Aunt Sheila rolls down her window, hands us a tote bag from a weed shop. "Don't forget the snacks."

"Thanks," Brynn says, almost shy.

"It was nothing. I cleaned out the pantry, is all." I don't know Sheila except for what Brynn's told me, but the woman seems uncomfortable. "There's bread and those little mayo packets from the Arby's, and I checked, the tuna is good for another month."

Brynn nods.

"You have your can opener, right?" Sheila asks.

Brynn looks around like she needs someone to save her.

"We don't actually," I say.

"Well . . ." Sheila digs around for a minute. "This is my car can opener. I've found, in life, you never quite know when you need one."

"Thank you," Brynn says again, accepting it.

"I want it back, though. So take care?"

Brynn nods again.

Sheila doesn't wave, but she honks twice, and then drives off. We pile back into the truck. I volunteer to take the truck bed. Molly hops in after me.

I'm working on a new song.

Still haven't finished one about the trail yet. Because there's something missing, yeah. Not the end. The trail doesn't end. What's missing is the bear.

Molly

While we drive a little farther, Tray's working over sections of melody. He doesn't need instruments to do this. It's as if the notes live inside him.

I'm practicing imagination.

Possible futures for one Molly Lee Norris-Norquay, a girl who is excellent in an emergency, who has superior memorization skills, who knows that she'll never be happy stuck in one place, a girl who has a call to adventure woven into the webs of her bone marrow—at least for now—who kissed a sad girl once, a sad boy, too, whose body is wide, fat, capable, who loves hard, loves too much, who is learning to value story as much as science, a girl who is alive, who learns.

I'm new at imagination. It still takes work. But that's how every adventure starts. With stumbling opening notes, with slips and falls. Sometimes, with new scars.

I'm not certain where we're headed. I have an idea. A handful of questions. Brynn texted midweek: School is great! Want to do some fat girl revenge with me one day soonish?

Me: Fat-girl revenge is always in season.

Brynn: Yesssss. Okay. Will get back at you. For now, I
        need to report to English class! *book emoji* *disco
        ball emoji* *tooth emoji*

They've decided, Brynn and my brother, that there isn't a gayer emoji than the disco ball and that every text chat should end with a subtle reminder of the importance of healthy teeth.

It's unhinged and I love it.

When we turn off the secondary highway onto a rough paved road, there's a sign: CAMP HUMMINGBIRD.

So this is fat-girl revenge.

But we don't stop at the gate. We keep driving, another mile, two, then turn onto the property, onto a dirt road. It's mud in spots from recent rain. When we emerge from the trees into a clearing, Faith reverses hard, makes a three-point turn, aiming the truck back the way we came. It's a dead end.

A dumping ground.

The truck doors open.

Faith climbs inside the bed. Matteo and Hank do too, sit on the rails. Brynn settles in, legs hanging over the open tailgate.

We're silent, for a minute, two.

"Anyone going to let the team in on the big old secret?" Hank asks.

Faith puts a finger to her lips. "Shhhh."

"So that's a hard no."

Brynn doesn't turn away from watching the dump. She hardly ever ignores Hank like this, so I refocus. Birds chatter around us up in the trees. It's cool here, in the shade. Someone has dumped broken bunk beds into a pile in the center of the clearing. Green plastic dorm mattresses. Pressure-treated lumber, what's left from an old fence, strewn on top. And everywhere around us, there are food scraps.

Apple cores, rotten produce. Tortillas, the carb-conscious ones that taste like paper, still in the packaging. There are stacks of unopened Oreos, cartons of melted ice cream.

Brynn told me about this, how these were left out. How if you fell into temptation, you'd be charged $500 after every infraction. How there were ways to pay back the debt: additional weekly fasting days, where, after your walk on the trail, you'd clean the toilets and showers, perform other chores. How your parents set how far your balance could go into the negative, the way other privileges could be revoked once you hit that limit.

One child had to do the daily walk without shoes.

I hate this place. Hate it here, already know that places like this are a poison on the land. A poison to communities.

I don't know how long we wait.

The first sign is a rustling in the forest.

The second is deep, low snorting.

When they step into the clearing, we draw pungent wild into our lungs. Hank and Matteo sink down in the truck bed, inch closer to center.

"Finally," Tray says, quiet and reverent.

The black bear is the only one left in Southern California, but it's doing well. Because of these mountains, because of the ranges we had planned to hike, because they are mostly set aside for recreation. In front of us, there are three. One whose coat is classic black, and two who are cinnamon, likely sun-bleached, after for-aging in alpine wildflower meadows.

They paw through the apples, the rotten produce.

My skin prickles. These animals are large, amazing. I've been wanting to see a bear. I walked the San Bernardino Mountains, part of the Sierras, in a world where it should have happened. And it takes driving to this place, where I know there is so much hurt, to a dump in the forest for this to happen.

We watch for a long while, until the bears wander off in the direction they came.

I break the silence. "We're reporting them for illegal dumping, right?"

"Ooooh, yes we are!" Brynn nods. "But this was only our side quest."

We drive back along the rutted dirt road, in no mood for con-versation. Matteo turns the music off. Tray only sighs.

When we reach the *CAMP HUMMINGBIRD* sign, Brynn climbs out of the truck, wearing her backpack. Everyone else stays inside. She invites me along: "Come on, Molly."

I jump over the rail, land in soft dirt.

Brynn squats, opens her pack. It's full up with clothing, her stuffy. She pulls out a bottle of spray paint, then another. "Aunt Sheila gave them to me as a first-day-of-school present. So I could make commemorative art."

I laugh.

Brynn tosses me the pink, claims the orange for herself. Over at the sign, she starts with one word: *FAT.*

Then it's my turn. *GIRLS.*

Hers and then mine.

ARE.

BEAUTIFUL.

We stare at our words. Brynn smiles.

"Wait, wait." Hank jumps from the truck without hesitating, worrying his body will let him fall too far. "May I?"

Brynn nods.

In all orange, Hank writes: *FAT BOYS AND ENBYS ARE TOO!*

Maybe it's never the bear you think you'll see. Maybe we haven't imagined a world where the bear lives as a bear should.

But we're done here.

We drive home with Brynn, because her aunt has given permission for Brynn to spend the night at Faith's place, to miss a few days of school. It's the first time on the whole trip, but we set up a circle of rocks, check the local burn conditions, and we have a campfire. With marshmallows and chocolate and graham crackers.

When we returned to Lone Pine, I made a call.

But reporting the damage isn't enough.

Maybe this is something I can do. Something a girl with my skills is made for. I realize I'm imagining all of a sudden and smile. How practice eventually makes even this easier. I imagine something like conservation biology, a scientist-storyteller who sees how we are all connected, who can trace those lifelines, those heart-lines from living beings to the land, from the land to living beings, who can imagine cities in harmony with the land that holds them.

But for now, in this moment, I'm roasting my third

marshmallow. Searing the crust until it's almost black, offering that gross portion to Tray because it's how he likes his marshmallows, taking the soft insides for myself. I crush it between sweet crackers. Double squares of dark chocolate melted just enough.

Hank and Matteo argue playfully.

Brynn's smiling so wide, telling a story about her new school.

Faith laughs, mouth open, teeth on display.

First, I take a picture of Tray, his fingers sticky, that dimple visible. Then I snap candids of my friends. When they catch me at it, they want more.

"Group shot!"

"Yesssss!"

Hank fusses with his hair, comes to stand on my right. Tray takes the left. Our friends squish in close. We take picture after picture.

I was wrong. There are good nights. Good nights under the stars. Good nights among a constellation of friends.

Sometimes, it's very good to be wrong.

And I know, wherever I end up, whichever future I decide on, that a long time from now, I'll still be telling this story, will still be a freaking minor bear in this world, imagining and walking farther along this trail.

Let's go.

Let's keep on.

A NOTE FROM JEN

I'm what Brynn and other fat activists would call a small fat. As I write this, I am the skinniest I've been in my adult life. No, it would be fairer to say that today I am the skinniest I've been since puberty. I was a chubby child. A girl who grew eventually into her wide swimmer's shoulders. A girl who felt too much, too big, too often, for a very long time.

I've learned to dress the body I have, how to best showcase my shape and curves. Spoiler alert: it's with dresses, skirts, and the occasional loud-patterned jumpsuit. When I was a teenager, you truly had to go to the mall to get clothes, and if you were really lucky, there was maybe one store with a plus-size section. It was probably an Old Navy, with limited-size fast-fashion offerings. These days, a small-fat woman can find a decent number of retailers. There are more and more size-inclusive brands. Sustainable brands too! More fat fashion designers, models, and fashion influencers.

Now there is joy in getting dressed. Now I'm excited about clothing. I've become a later-in-life fashionista. Even swimsuit shopping is, dare I say it, fun? My bikini body, because every body is a bikini body, thanks designers like Gabi Fresh, who make swimsuits for fat girls an absolute treat. And these days, most days, I love my body. Like Brynn and Molly, I am both fat and strong. Fat and gorgeous. For me, *fat* is not a bad word, only a description. Maybe it's a political affiliation.

But that wasn't always true.

No, my statement needs a revision: I didn't always believe these things about myself.

Looking at art from earlier centuries reminds us that beauty, that what was considered an attractive body type, changes based on what society decides is attractive. While things are better for fat people in terms of easier access to necessities like cute clothing, the current ideal, one we can never reach—and should not try to reach simply for the sake of being on trend—remains the one we are judged by.

Diet culture and our obsession with thigh gaps, with a very particular body shape, with showcasing an ideal that wasn't always the ideal woman's body, hurts everyone. And yes, while I've been talking about girls and women here, body ideals and beauty ideals affect men and enbies, do damage to men and enbies too.

It's probably most obvious when we talk about health and BMI (body mass index).

When I bought into this narrative that I needed to be skinny to be healthy, I had a BMI of 38, a low resting heart rate, low blood pressure, could hike mountains, could canoe in the Ontario backcountry for two weeks at a time, taking portages that weren't cleared often, were riddled with downed trees and other obstacles.

Back in those days, I signed up for a diet through an app where the success coach kicked me out of the program, citing disordered eating as the reason. This happened the week after they taught us about intermittent fasting, after I tried it and started to see a change on the scale. They taught me what to do, and then they kicked me out when I did it and it worked.

Oof.

Yes, I made that point, that if it was disordered eating, they taught me how to do it, encouraged me to do it.

And a few weeks later, I quit intermittent fasting because it started to feel disordered for me, for my body, for my life. But so had all the techniques the diet had suggested I try.

While the fat camp that Brynn runs away from is an extreme, places like these exist. While Brynn's parents go to an extreme, many parents who have particular ideas about health and body shape/size and who buy into BMI teach their children to have shame for their bodies and around food. And while Molly's parents have not raised her in a household that has rules regulating food, and she's not been faced with constant judgment about her body in her home, that doesn't mean she hasn't been shaped by the same forces.

Diet culture is literally toxic.

BMI has been discredited, but still gets used.

Being fat is not a problem, yet disordered eating is. If you are someone who lives with disordered eating, there are resources for you. In Canada, NEDIC is an incredible support system. In the US, you can contact the ANAD hotline and other mental health supports like the 988 Lifeline, the Crisis Text Line, and the SAMHSA National Helpline.

Fat activism has a close relationship with disability activism through the body-positivity movement. At the core is this: the world as we have built it, as we have shaped it, is not made for certain bodies. Take airplanes, where I'm writing this, as an example. Air travel is hostile to both disabled and fat people. And some people are disabled and fat. Air travel is exponentially more hostile to them.

The body-positivity movement is not without faults. No movement, no structure, no person is. So perhaps, it's better to say that fat activism and disability activism have a close relationship through the body-neutrality movement. That is, let's not engage in toxic positivity, but instead a neutrality to divergent and diverse bodies. We could use more people who believe in the value of all bodies. We could use more disability justice advocates.

Tray's desire for his summer is to get away from the city and away from people who clobber him with microaggressions and, sometimes, outright anti-Indigenous words and actions. The mountains seem like the right place to do this. After all, there are often fewer people in the mountains.

And for so many of us, wild places are where we feel safe, where we can exist fully as ourselves without input from the rest of the world.

Yet it would be problematic to suggest that the world doesn't follow us to the mountains: that women, girls, BIPOC, trans, nonbinary, queer, and otherly marginalized people don't have to consider more when they go into nature. Safety, yes, from bears and injuries and waterborne parasites. But also, safety from others on the trail.

As Tray points out, quoting John Muir is uncomfortable for some of us. But Tray refuses not to acknowledge that one of the reasons there are so many protected natural spaces open for recreation in Southern California, and across the US, is because of John Muir.

And then the unspoken thing underpinning all of this is that these mountains, the land that we hike on and bike on, the waters we swim in and rivers we canoe, these places are the traditional, unceded lands where Indigenous peoples have lived, and cared for in a reciprocal relationship, since time immemorial. Quoting John Muir should be uncomfortable for more of us.

So what I want to say now, I want to say it to queer and trans and disabled and BIPOC and non-Christian and fat hikers, those of us who go out into nature to test ourselves, yes, but also to rest ourselves. We bring our communities with us when we go to the mountains, to spaces where the trees are loud and the water is loud and the animals and plant life are loud. We do this because that's one of the ways we create safety.

We deserve strong communities.

We deserve communities who support each other across differences, who offer each other mutual aid, yes, but also who recognize that we are stronger fighting together, that we are working toward the same things.

What are you doing to build this future? What are you doing to bring community with you, to care for others, to care for the land when you go to the mountains?

Leave No Trace is only a beginning.

I'll end here, with a reminder that there are fat athletes. If those two words together still cause you to react in negatively charged ways, you have work to do.

A runner doesn't have to run every mile of the marathon.

A dancer can have a belly and hips, thighs that touch, a body that expands into the space it needs while in glorious motion.

To hike a mountain while fat, take one step, then another. On the way down, repeat the process.

It's bear shit to say physical activity, sport, and other adventures on the land are reserved only for certain bodies.

No offense to the bears—obviously.

<3 Jen

JEN'S FAVORITE TRAIL MIX RECIPE

1 CUP OF (CANADIAN) SMARTIES

Some might not consider the core of trail mix to be chocolate, but I do. Balance is key, and you can still find balance when you start with the good stuff. It's part of my philosophy—if you're growing or even if you're grown, a person deserves candy-coated chocolate in their life.

Thanks to Rosemary Brosnan, who like me loves candy, and who pushed me to make this book stronger in so many ways. Thanks to Patricia Nelson, who is incredibly good at her job. After every interaction, I text one of her other clients and say some variation of *I love Patricia* or *Patricia is great at her freaking job!* They always reply: *Yes! We are so freaking lucky!* Maarsi to everyone else who had a hand in getting this story into the world, including Cynthia Leitich Smith, Courtney Stevenson, Suzanne Murphy, Liate Stehlik, Laura Mock, Joel Tippie, Patty Rosati, and Mimi Rankin and the rest of the team working so hard to get my books into schools and libraries, as well as Kathryn Silsand, Jacqueline Hornberger, and Lisa Calcasola.

1½ CUPS NUTS

I'm a big fan of almonds, walnuts, cashews, and pistachios. Hold the Brazil nuts. But hey, you do you. Raw nuts are best. Feel free to toast them at home. You can also add sea salt to your nuts. If you don't add a quarter teaspoon here, add it somewhere else. You need the salt.

I'm also a big fan of the people in my life who have helped me stay balanced while writing *A Constellation of Minor Bears*. Maarsi to Katherine Crocker, who is always one of my first readers and this time around helped me solve a problem by presenting a long-lost aunt who could step in. Katherine said, hey, she could be called Sheila and she could be dating a dermatologist. Big thanks to Edward Underhill, who remains my best petty DM friend; to Jamie Pacton, who is steadfast and always has the greatest perspectives on this business; and to my early readers Maya Prasad, Susan Azim Boyer, and Rachel Menard.

1 CUP SEEDS

You can throw the seeds of your choice—mine include pumpkin, sunflower, and sesame—into the mix loose. But you can also make seed-cluster snackers. I highly recommend this option. Heat oven to 300 degrees Fahrenheit. Mix equal amounts maple syrup and sugar of your choice (2 teaspoons is enough for a small batch). Optional: add half your syrup measurement of vanilla or try other spices. Thin your mix with a touch of hot water. Coat your seeds and bake until browned. Once you can handle the mix, press into clusters. They are then ready to eat.

Thanks to teachers, librarians, booksellers, humans who read a book and then tell everyone about it, anyone who helps get books into the hands of the readers who need them, and everyone who fights against book challenges and banning. Thanks to

WNDB. You've all supported my career in uncountable ways. The seed-cluster snackers are for you!

1 CUP DRIED FRUIT

I'm picky about what fruits I add into trail mix—but unsweetened cranberries and plump golden raisins are my go-tos. If you like something else, do that.

My gratitude in the extreme to everyone who let me borrow their name for this book, including Molly, Hank-the-Tank, Faith, and Brynn, whose namesakes in these pages I hope do your hearts justice. And to your parents, who have been my friends (or my childhood babysitter!!!) and therefore have shaped my life in so many ways.

Thanks to the Novelist Club at Coe for your check-ins and cheerleading while I wrote this book. Seriously, all of you are great. But special thanks to Kayla for letting me borrow her name for a pink-haired baddie lawyer and for the disco ball emoji. Who's next? I need more names and fewer unhinged horse drawings, people.

The biggest thanks to every PCT hiker who has been like, I'm going to meticulously document my experience with a blog. In so many ways, you made this book stronger when you offered to bring me along on your adventure. Thanks also to Joshua M. Powell's *The Pacific Crest Trail: A Visual Compendium* for excellent details, Cheryl Strayed's *Wild* for reminding me a hiking book isn't actually ever about the hiking, and to the many people at Nat Geo who put together the PCT topo maps.

And to fat activists everywhere, to fat people living their lives in both loud and quiet ways, thank you for helping me live my own. Let's keep on.

Thanks to disability activists, and especially to A. H. Reaume, whose activism has taught me so much and made me a better human. Readers, if you want more, start with this essay, which you can find online: "On Reclaiming Brokenness and Refusing the Violence of 'Recovery Narratives.'"

Katherine, you're getting thanked twice, this time, for giving me permission to include your cricket research in this book in small ways. Readers, if you want more, from the source, you'll find "Híyoge owísisi tánga itá (Cricket egg stories)" online.

Thanks to my family for always being the first to preorder my books, so early that they never get in on any of the sales. We are a discount family, so this means a lot to me. Also, we have a new member, so yay, welcoming Naomi to our ranks. You might be the youngest of the cousins, but you'll learn to hold your own.

½ TO 1 CUP POPCORN

Yes, add some of your favorite popcorn to your trail mix. It can be the health-food kind, or it can be air-popped or stove-popped in oil. Here's the fun bit: feel free to dress your popcorn in any way you want. Nooch (nutritional yeast) is yum and hiker friendly with added nutrients! But so is salt and a little cayenne. I can see a pumpkin-spice popcorn or a nutmeg-and-cinnamon-sugar one working too. Have fun!

Books wouldn't exist without readers. So thank you! You're both the reason I do this and the reason this book exists. Much love. <3

A NOTE FROM CYNTHIA LEITICH SMITH,
Author-Curator of Heartdrum

Dear Reader,

I keep thinking about Hank's accident in *A Constellation of Minor Bears*. About painful, overwhelming moments that seem to change everything. There's no warning. You're off guard, relaxed, and maybe even having fun. Something happens in an instant, and suddenly, you're somehow a different *you*, and those you care about are somehow a different *them*.

Or maybe that something—that big moment—comes from within, like Brynn's decision to run away from fat camp—with no solid plan for moving forward or one that's shaky at best.

Those moments land harder, I think, when you're young. You're trying to find your footing in life, and suddenly the Earth herself seems to shift beneath you. You don't know yet how you'll end up on the other side—the healing side—but when you get there, you're hopefully stronger, kinder to others and to yourself. You may not have been ready for what happened, and it may have cost you dearly, but like Molly, Hank, Brynn, and Tray, you'll probably figure out a lot about yourself in the aftermath.

Have you read many books by and about Indigenous people? Hopefully, *A Constellation of Minor Bears* will inspire you to read more. This novel is published by Heartdrum, a Native-focused imprint of HarperCollins, which raises up stories about young Native heroes by Indigenous authors and illustrators. Be sure to seek out other YA novels by Jen Ferguson, if you haven't already read them. Stories like hers are compelling page-turners, to be sure, but they also offer an opportunity, a space, to reflect on big questions and deep feelings.

Mvto,

Cynthia Leitich Smith

In 2014, We Need Diverse Books (WNDB) began as a simple hashtag on Twitter. The social media campaign soon grew into a 501(c)(3) nonprofit with a team that spans the globe. WNDB is supported by a network of writers, illustrators, agents, editors, teachers, librarians, and book lovers, all united under the same goal—to create a world where every child can see themselves in the pages of a book. You can learn more about WNDB programs at www.diversebooks.org.